LESLIE CHARTERIS

The Saint around the World

Series Editor: Ian Dickerson

**MULHOLLAND
BOOKS**

HODDER

First published in Great Britain in 1957 by Hodder & Stoughton

This paperback edition first published in 2014 by Mulholland Books
An imprint of Hodder & Stoughton
An Hachette UK company

1

Copyright © Interfund (London) Ltd 2014
Originally registered in 1957 by Leslie Charteris
Introduction © Adam Rayner 2014

Cover artwork by Andrew Howard
www.andrewhoward.co.uk

A CIP catalogue record for this title is available from the British Library

Paperback ISBN 978 1 444 76646 2
eBook ISBN 978 1 444 76647 9

Typeset by Hewer Text UK Ltd, Edinburgh
Printed and bound by Clays Ltd, St Ives plc

Hodder & Stoughton policy is to use papers that are natural, renewable
and recyclable products and made from wood grown in sustainable
forests. The logging and manufacturing processes are expected to
conform to the environmental regulations of the country of origin.

Hodder & Stoughton Ltd
338 Euston Road
London NW1 3BH

www.hodder.co.uk

CONTENTS

CONTENTS

INTRODUCTION

Proud as I am to have joined that exclusive club of nimble eye-browed thespians who have played the Saint on screen, I can tell you one thing for certain: it is impossible to be Simon Templar.

You try summoning all at once superhuman reserves of charm, wit, grace, athleticism, (cash) and – most importantly – courage. It's quite an undertaking. Even Sir Roger Moore, the original TV Saint, confessed ST's appetite for danger somewhat outstripped his own!

But, of course, it is the impossibility of seeing all these attributes embodied in real life that makes Simon Templar such an enduring character in fiction. It is also what makes him so much fun for an actor to play. To portray Simon Templar is to indulge as a grown-up all your schoolboy fantasies of a 'jet-set' life involving fine suits, fast cars, beautiful women and exotic locations.

The Saint around the World is a classic representation of the 'jet-set' ideal of the 1950s with the Saint near-circumnavigating the globe in six stories. That phrase seems a little dated now but the idea of flitting from one airport to the next, always ready to be swept into a new adventure, remains as glamorous as ever. All of the Saintly qualities mentioned above are on display but so is the man behind the myth; 'The Pluperfect Lady', for example, suggests the tantalising possibility of a woman really getting under the Templar armour . . .

The Saint around the World encapsulates the advantage that the written word will always have over attempts to 'bring it to life' on screen. Years can pass leaving our hero untouched by the ravages of age, the 'perfect' female form can exist many times over, and exotic new locations can be visited on every page without the terrifying budgetary implications this would involve for film and television. And most of all, Simon Templar need not be reduced to mere flesh and blood by an actor like me, he can remain the true ideal: the Saint of our imagination.

Adam Rayner

The Patient Playboy

'I suppose you wouldn't be interested in helping me find my husband,' said the blonde.

'Frankly, I've heard a lot more exciting propositions,' Simon Templar admitted. 'If he doesn't have enough sense to appreciate you, why don't we just let him stay lost, and have a ball?'

'But I really want him back,' she said. 'You see, we've only been married a week, so I haven't had time to get tired of him.'

Simon sipped his Dry Sack.

'All right,' he said. 'Give me a clue. What was it about this bridegroom that impressed you so much, darling?'

'The name,' she said, 'is Lona Dayne.'

'Well, that's unusual, anyway. He must have to listen to a lot of funny cracks about it.'

'Lona Dayne is *my* name, idiot. Not "darling".'

'Oh.'

He regarded her with pleasantly augmented interest. It had been an entirely shallow and stereotyped reaction, he realised, to identify and pigeon-hole her so summarily as 'the blonde'. Certainly she had the hair, of a tint much paler than straw, which his worldly eye inevitably measured against her light brown eyes and traced back from there to the alchemy of some beauty parlour – but wasn't it a mere cliché of fiction that expensively-rinsed blondes were by contrary definition cheap, while the only good ones owed their colouring solely to a lucky combination of chromosomes? The pretty face and approximately 35–23–35 vital statistics which convention also attributes to blondes appeared to be hers without any important debt to artifice. And she could get away with calling him Idiot, when she smiled in that provocatively intimate way while she said it.

'To me, you'll still be darling,' he said. 'At least, until your husband turns up. I suppose his name is Dayne too.'

'Naturally.'

'You can never be sure, these days.'

'Havelock Dayne.'

'It has rather a corny sound, but I guess his parents loved it.'

'I love your dialogue,' she said dispassionately. 'But I wasn't kidding. You *are* the Saint, aren't you?'

Simon sighed. He had heard that question so often, by this time, that he seemed to have used up all the possible smooth, shocking, modest, impudent, evasive, chilling, misleading, or witty answers. Now he could only wish, belatedly, that he had had the forethought to insist on an alias. But while that might have let him enjoy one cocktail party as an anonymous guest, it wouldn't have fitted in with the project that brought him to Bermuda.

It had been a good party, until then. The Saint had thought it a happy coincidence, for him, that a friend from many years back in Hollywood, Dick Van Hessen, was currently managing a miniature movie studio which had been improbably yet astutely set up in Bermuda to take advantage of tax privileges and lower costs to compete for the American television market. At the Van Hessens' hillside house was therefore gathered, almost automatically, a useful cross-section of island personalities: the local bankers and bigwigs, the grim and the gay social sets, the Press and the professions, the merchants and the dilettantes, and a leavening of working actors and visiting firemen on whom all the others could prove how easily they could mix with celebrities. The Saint's cool blue eyes drifted down the long verandah that overlooked Hamilton harbour, but failed to make any pertinent identification among the convivial mob.

'I've met so many people tonight, I couldn't possibly remember half their names,' he confessed disarmingly, and with an unblushing lack of truth. 'Does your husband have anything conspicuous about him – like a green moustache, for instance?'

'You haven't met him tonight. He isn't here.'

'When did you lose him, then?'

'The day before yesterday.'

'And only married five days at the time, according to what you said. It must have been a hell of a wedding. Did you have any inkling that Havelock was such a dizzy type when you agreed to let him love, honour, and pay the bills?'

'He isn't at all. He's lots of fun, of course, but he's terribly ambitious and earnest too. He's a lawyer.'

'I'm looking for a lawyer myself,' said the Saint. 'Only I want one who's already embezzled at least five million dollars. Have you known Havelock long enough to notice him flashing a lot of green stuff around?'

'I'm sorry,' she said stiffly. 'I suppose I was asking for it. I should have known better. But I don't think your dialogue is so excruciatingly funny, after all—'

A quiver of her lips spoiled the trenchant ring that her last sentence was phrased for, and she turned away quickly, but not quickly enough for him to miss the blurring of her eyes. He moved even more swiftly to place himself beside her again where she leaned over the verandah railing with her back turned squarely to the incurious crowd.

'Pardon my two left feet,' he said reasonably. 'I'm afraid the atmosphere of the place got me. I thought you were playing it strictly chin-up and British, so I was going along with the gag. Let's start over, if you're serious.'

She looked at him, blinking hard.

'I am!'

'All right. I know how you're feeling. I wish I could help. But just plain wandering husbands are a bit out of my line. I expect if you asked a few discreet friends and bartenders – or even the police—'

'But I can't. I've had to cover up – tell everyone he's laid up with a terrible cold. You're the first person I've told, and I shouldn't even have done that.'

'Then stop being silly. If he's lost, he's lost, and false pride won't help you find him. Think yourself lucky he isn't really a case up my alley, for which he'd have to be at least kidnapped or even murdered.'

'That,' she said steadily, 'is exactly what I'm afraid of. Or I wouldn't have talked to you.'

Without any change of expression, the Saint's bronzed face seemed to become opaque, like a mask from behind which his eyes probed with a sort of rueful cynicism.

'Now I'll begin to think you're suffering from too much lurid literature.'

'You'd be wrong,' she said flatly. 'Unless I suffered from writing it. Until a week ago, my name was Lona Shaw. Well, that doesn't mean anything to you. But it would if you'd lived in England lately. I've worked for the London *Daily Record* since I was nineteen; and for the last four years I've been their star sob-sister. Do you have any idea how hard-boiled and unhysterical a girl has to be to hold that job on a newspaper like the *Record*?'

Simon nodded. Suddenly, as if a cloud had passed, the mask of his face was translucent again. It was the only outward sign that he had felt and recognised the icy caress of Destiny's fingers along his spine.

'Okay,' he said soberly. 'I'm sold.'

His gaze flickered over the crowded balcony again, warily

conscious of the beginning of one of those unanimous reshufflings that surge intermittently through the human molecules of every cocktail party, and even more sharply perceptive of the covetous glances of certain males within striking distance who had transparently settled on Lona Dayne as the most intriguing target for tonight and were getting set to cut in at the first opening.

Simon huddled strategically closer to her along the rail.

'I gather you came alone,' he said.

'Yes.'

'Me too. No plans for dinner?'

'No. Fay Van Hassen said I could—'

'She won't mind. You just made a date with me, darling.'

He put down his glass, took her by the arm, and steered her firmly and skilfully into an eddy that was flowing towards the exit. The frustrated wolf pack was still standing on its heels as they jostled into the line that was babbling thanks and good-byes.

'Oh, don't go yet,' Fay protested. 'We're going to have some food presently.'

'But Lona's husband might get better tomorrow, and I'd never get her all to myself again,' Simon said with a leer.

'Well, behave yourselves.'

'There should be a taxi waiting below,' Dick Van Hessen said helpfully. 'Send him back from wherever you're going, for the next customers.'

Then they were down the stairs, and the steep narrow driveway, and a taxi was waiting as predicted at the foot of the steep slope where the house perched. Simon put her in and said: 'The Caravelle.'

'I ought to go home, really,' she said, 'and see if there's any message.'

'Which I suppose you've been doing for the last two days. If you're out, he could leave a message, couldn't he?'

'Yes – the caretaker promised he'd be around and listen for the phone.'

'Then you can call in and ask for news later. Meanwhile, you've got at least as much right to be out as he has.'

'But—'

A Bermuda taxi is not a vehicle in which to discuss anything confidential. Being derived from any miniature English car by the sole process of attaching a taximeter to the dashboard, the driver and passengers are huddled together as cosily as olives in a jar. The Saint nudged Lona Dayne gently, and pointed expressively at the back of the driver's head, which he was trying not to bump with his knees.

'What's this about a caretaker?' he said innocuously. 'Aren't you staying at an hotel?'

'We started in an hotel, of course, but we moved into this house just the day before Hav disappeared. You see, we were talking to the caretaker, and he happened to mention that his boss had just written and told him to try to rent it. The owner lives up in Canada and only comes down here in the winter; then Bob – that's the caretaker – goes to Canada and takes care of his house there. Usually the house here just stands empty, but it seems as if the owner suddenly decided he might as well make a few dollars out of it. It's absurdly reasonable, really, and Bob didn't see why he couldn't let us have it just for a month, while he's waiting for someone who wants to take a longer lease. After we saw it, we simply couldn't turn it down – it's on a little island all of its own, the sort of thing you dream of. Only if we'd stayed in the hotel, perhaps we'd have been safer . . . But it's the most romantic spot—'

Simon let her go on chattering trivialities, preferring to have her overdo it rather than go on with the important subject until they were safe from any uninvited audience, or at least until he knew how seriously they should be thinking of safety. He kept her headed off from any reference to her husband until they were settled at a table in a corner of the terrace overhanging the water, and had ordered a chicken in white wine and a bottle of Bollinger to go with it.

'What am I supposed to be celebrating?' she objected half-heartedly.

'I'm prescribing it to give you a lift, which I think you could use.'

He lighted their cigarettes, and settled his elbows squarely on the table, looking at her with sympathetic but disconcertingly penetrating detachment.

'Now,' he said with sudden bluntness. 'What is this all about?'

'Have you heard of Roger Ivalot?'

He winced slightly.

'No,' he said. 'And if I had, I wouldn't believe it.'

'Why?'

'The name sounds even more improbable than your husband's.'

'If you'd been in England lately—'

'I'm sorry. It's already established that I've been spending my time in the wrong places. Just enlighten my ignorance.'

There was, however, some excuse for regarding anyone who had not heard of Roger Ivalot as benighted, as he soon learned.

In a country which is not by tradition or temperament adapted to the breeding of spectacular playboys, Mr Ivalot had succeeded in racking up a number of probable records. One of these could certainly be claimed for the rocket-like trajectory of his ascent from obscurity. Nobody, in fact, seemed to have known of his existence before the day less than two years ago when he had sent engraved invitations to the entire casts of the three most popular musicals then playing in London, bidding them to a champagne supper and dance in the Dorchester's biggest private ballroom, for which he also hired the most popular orchestra available. While some of the stars were snooty or suspicious enough to ignore the offer, almost six hundred guests (including several uninvited escorts) showed up to sample the hospitality; and when a somewhat notorious soubrette, professing indignation because no one had been asked to take a champagne bath, peeled off her clothes and had herself showered from bottles held by a flock of eager volunteers, nothing less than the simultaneous outbreak of World War III could have prevented Mr Ivalot becoming a celebrity overnight.

'I just wanted to meet a lot of people who liked to have fun,' he said to the newspapers, which (of course with the exception of *The Times*) could hardly fail to note such goings on, 'and throwing a big party seemed the quickest way to do it.'

Perhaps because he happened at a time when England, reacting from the longest hangover of post-war austerity that any European country had had to endure, and flexing the muscles of a new self-confidence, was ripe for any hero who struck a dizzy enough contrast with the drab years behind, Mr Ivalot was just what the circulation managers ordered. Although he threw no more parties of such indiscriminate grandiosity as the one which launched him into London's café society, from then on he never lacked a convivial entourage, about three-quarters of it feminine, for his almost nightly forays into the gayest cabarets and bottle clubs; and in an otherwise dull season the more uninhibited journals were delighted to adopt him as a gratifying reliable source of copy.

The news value of his extravagances was enhanced by an occasional quixotic touch. The celebration of Guy Fawkes Day in London that year was materially enlivened by Roger Ivalot who drove through the East End in a large truck loaded to the toppling point with fireworks, which he distributed to incredulous urchins on a succession of street corners. Nothing like the resultant bedlam of fire and explosion had been seen in that area since the last visit of the Luftwaffe. And at Christmas he rode through the slums again, this time on a stage-coach which he had resurrected from somewhere, accompanied by three music-hall beauties, all of them in Dickensian costumes, tossing bags of candy from a seemingly inexhaustible supply to all the children who turned out to stare.

'All it took was money,' he told the reporters. 'And I've a lot of that.'

He liked making corny jokes of that kind about his improbable cognomen. 'I've a lot of living to do yet,' was another. But the nickname that stuck, with his enthusiastic endorsement, was 'Jolly Roger'. His acceptance was made official by the huge skull-and-crossbones flag which draped his box at the Arts Ball on New Year's Eve, where he and his whole party appeared in some version of a pirate costume, even though some of the female members had startlingly little material to work with between their top boots and cocked hats. He even tried to adopt the same pattern for his racing colours, to put on a horse he bought which was entered in the Grand National; but here the stewards of the Jockey Club drew the line. Within six months of his début, he had become practically an institution; and when he announced that he was leaving to have a fling in Paris and continue from there on a trip around the world, a noticeable gloom overspread the bistros.

'But I'll be back again in the autumn,' he told his friends consolingly.

He had always paid cash for everything, even for his biggest parties, so that there had never been an occasion for anyone to inquire into his credit or bank references; but he claimed to be the British Empire's first uranium millionaire.

According to him, he had foreseen the coming boom before the dust had settled on Hiroshima, and had invested in a skilfully selected list of mining enterprises in Africa and Australia. While he was shrewdly secretive about the precise location of his holdings, the soundness of his judgment appeared to be adequately evidenced by the amount of money he had to spend.

It was in answer to the obvious question of how even a uranium millionaire's income could survive modern taxation with so little visible injury, that he had explained that he made his legal home in Bermuda, where there was no income tax.

True to his promise, he had returned in November, and the pattern of his first season had been more or less repeated, with the difference that this time he was already a well-known character with a large if not exactly *élite* circle of friends. Before the advent of another spring, only the most strong-minded comedians could get through a monologue of any length without hanging some gag on Jolly Roger Ivalot.

This year, however, Mr Ivalot's departure was not signalised by a mammoth thirty-six-hour farewell party, as it had been the previous time. In fact, it was first confirmed, after several days of unwonted quiescence, by a solicitor who had been trying to serve him with a summons to appear and defend himself in court. Mr Ivalot, it transpired, had got wind of this project and had strategically taken himself out of jurisdiction, without saying good-bye to anyone.

'And how many people were discovered holding the bag?' Simon asked, with anticipative relish.

'Only one that we know of,' Lona Dayne said. 'He'd just had one of the usual slip-ups with his Jolly Rogering. One of his girls was going to have a baby – twins, as a matter of fact.'

'Ah,' said the Saint. 'A bag holding people.'

She let that wilt in an interregnum of withering silence.

'He didn't owe anybody – I told you he always paid cash,'

she said after the pause. 'He hadn't sold any shares or promoted anything. His furnished flat was paid up to the end of the month. He'd just packed up and gone.'

The expectant mother, a nominal actress whose gifts sounded more thoracic than thespian, alleged that Mr Ivalot had been promising to marry her for more than a year. But although she had found herself pregnant almost immediately after his return, he had persistently evaded or postponed setting a wedding date; and when he finally proposed a cash settlement of some five thousand pounds as an alternative, it began to dawn upon the poor girl that his love might not be as passionate and deathless as he had proclaimed. By then she was on the verge of her fifth month, and an X-ray had shown that she was preparing to endow the world with not one but two little Ivalots. This was the last straw that drove her to issue an ultimatum to the effect that unless Mr Ivalot came through with a wedding ring within a week she would continue their romance through a lawyer. It was not, she explained later to the former Lona Shaw, who interviewed her, that she thought that money could heal a broken heart, but that she felt it her maternal duty to see that her imminent offspring were not left to face a lifetime of illegitimacy with a lousy £2,500 capital apiece, instead of their rightful inheritance of millions.

This fair and sporting warning was her gravest mistake, for Mr Ivalot had promptly elected to vanish rather than contest the suit.

A lawyer with a fat contingency fee in prospect was not to be so easily discouraged. He promptly forwarded the papers to an attorney in Bermuda, with the request that they be served on Mr Ivalot there. And that was when the blow fell that punctured a fabulous legend and at the same time paradoxically inflated an otherwise routine scandal into the sensation of the year. For according to the advice that came back to London, nobody in Bermuda – no attorney, bank, real estate agency, newspaper, or any individual who had been questioned – had ever heard of Mr Roger Ivalot, nor was he listed in any official registry or directory.

'In fact, he never had been here,' said the Saint.

'That's what I couldn't quite swallow,' Lona Dayne said. 'I think it out this way. The Bermuda thing came out when somebody asked him about taxes. It seemed to me that that question might really have taken him by surprise. He had to have an answer quickly, and a good one, without having too much time to think about it or what it might lead to. But what he suddenly realised was that it might occur to the authorities to start investigating anyone who was throwing money around as lavishly as he was, in the hope of catching a tax dodger, and from what's come out since he obviously couldn't risk being investigated. He had to head that inquiry off right away. But how likely would he be to come up with Bermuda unless he knew a lot about it? I kept on thinking about that.'

Simon nodded appreciatively.

'That's pretty sharp thinking. Most people wouldn't have known about that tax angle. But if he'd run into someone who really lived here—'

'There wasn't too much risk of that. You wouldn't find many people with a home in Bermuda visiting England in the winter. But he might very easily have run into someone who'd visited here, so he had to be ready to talk about the place like a native. Which still made it look as if he must have spent a lot of time here, at least.'

The mystery of Mr Ivalot had all the earmarks of a monumental swindle, but it became even more baffling as weeks went by without anyone turning up who claimed to have been swindled. That is, with the exception of the pregnant starlet, whose loss was debatable; and her plight and the cruelly clouded future of her two still unborn little bastards became a matter of popular concern and the grist of many columns of tear-squeezing prose for Lona Shaw.

'And you came here to go on milking it?' Simon asked.

'Well, not quite. You see, I met Havvie' – the Saint managed to suppress a shudder – 'when he was in England last year on his holiday, and he'd been after me with letters and telephone calls to marry him ever since, and we really did get on awfully well together, so eventually I said yes. Then I had to get leave from the *Record*, and I've always been a thrifty type, so I sold them the idea that I ought to stay on salary if I came here and went on trying to dig up something about Ivalot. Then I only had to tell Havvie that I'd set my heart on a honeymoon in Bermuda, and everything was fine.'

'You've given me a new concept of romance,' murmured the Saint.

Her recital of the saga of Jolly Roger Ivalot, somewhat less succinct than it has been recapitulated here, had taken them all the way through dinner and dessert, and now they were sitting over Benedictine and coffee. Once again he lighted cigarettes for them.

'What was your plan of campaign when you got here?'

'We gave out a story to the local papers that the *Record* had unearthed a terrific clue which was expected to flush Ivalot from his cover within two or three days. I suppose that was before you got here, or you'd have read it.'

'I guess it was. But if I'd read it, I'd have thought it was rather an old wheeze.'

'It might still have scared Ivalot, if he *was* here,' she said. 'I hoped it might tempt him to try to make a deal, or—'

'Or something more violent?'

'That's what Havvie was afraid of.'

'He should have been. The rivers and ponds are full of amateurs who've had that kind of brilliant idea – anchored in concrete blocks.'

'That's why he's in trouble now,' she said bitterly. 'He's taking my place.'

'How?'

'He wouldn't let me take the risk. He insisted that if there were going to be any games like that, he was going to play the reporter and draw the fire. He said that nobody here would know Havelock Dayne as an attorney from Philadelphia, and nobody would associate Mrs Dayne with Lona Shaw, and if there was going to be any rough stuff he could take care of himself better than I could, and if there was any real detecting to do I might find out a lot more if nobody knew I was more than an ordinary dizzy bride. He was terribly intense about it, and in some ways he made a bit of sense too, and I didn't want to start off our married life with a quarrel, so I let him have his way. And that's why this has happened to him.'

'I still don't know just what has happened,' said the Saint.

She took a gulp from her glass.

'The day before yesterday, I went into Hamilton after lunch, to do some shopping. Havvie decided he'd rather stay home and fish. When I got back, about five, he'd left a note. Here it is.'

She produced it from her purse. It was crumpled and smeared from many readings.

Fantastic break on Jolly Roger. This is It! Must get after it at once or he'll get away. Don't worry even if I don't get home tonight. Love and XX.

H.

'You're sure he wrote this?' Simon asked automatically.

'Unless it's an absolutely perfect forgery. And it would've had to be done by someone who knew that he always signed his letters to me with just an H.'

Simon handed the note back, and for perhaps the first

time that evening his face was completely grave, without even
a give-away trace of mockery in his eyes.

'And since then you haven't heard another word?'

'Nothing.' The task and distraction of drawing the
complete background for him had sustained her so far, but
now he could see her straining again to keep emotion from
getting the upper hand. 'That is, unless ... I've *got* to call
home now.'

'Go ahead.'

He finished his liqueur, his coffee, and his cigarette, with
epicurean attention to each, holding his mind in complete
detachment until she came back; and presently she was at the
table again, but not sitting down, her face pale in the subdued
lamplight and her hands twisting one over the other.

'We've got to go to the house at once,' she said, in a low
shaky voice. 'Or I must. There's been a message. Not Havvie.
Someone who said he'll call again, until he gets me. And he
said I mustn't talk to anyone, if I want my husband back.'

2

The island lay less than a hundred yards off shore, out in the Sound. Simon judged that they were somewhere in the middle of the deep horseshoe curve that is the approximate profile of the south-western end of Bermuda, where the segmented chain of land curls all the way back over itself like a scorpion's tail. From the tiny landing-stage just below the road, where a taxi had dropped them off, he could clearly see the outlines of the white rain-catcher roof of the house that crowned a hillock which might have been an acre overall. Overhead electric wires bridged the distance to the island by means of two intermediate poles standing in the water, and below the place where the wires took off from the little landing-stage was an ordinary bell-push which Lona Dayne pressed with her finger. Almost at once a floodlight went on over a dock on the island opposite them, and a man came down and got into one of the skiffs that was tied up there and began to row over to them.

'Usually we'd leave the dinghy we came ashore in tied up here,' she said. 'But since I've been alone, Bob insists on ferrying me back and forth. I'm sure he doesn't believe I can row a boat.'

'How much does he know about all this?' Simon asked.

'About as much as I've told you. Except that he still thinks my husband is really the reporter, like everyone else here. But obviously I couldn't tell him the story I've been telling everyone else, about Havvie being in bed with a cold.'

'Why – is he still caretaking, even though you've rented the house?'

'There are servants' quarters where he sleeps, and he still does the gardening. He sort of goes with the place.'

'And you mean to say he hasn't spread this juicy bit of gossip all over Bermuda?'

'Wait till you meet him!'

That was only a matter of moments. The man shipped his oars as the skiff glided in, and stood up to catch and hold on to a ring bolt set in the concrete of the landing-stage.

'Has there been another call?' Lona Dayne demanded frantically, while he was still steadying the boat alongside.

'No, ma'am.'

'Did you tell me *everything* they said, on the phone?'

The caretaker looked up at the Saint, through plain gold-rimmed spectacles which combined with a bony severity of jaw and the total hairlessness of his shiny black cranium to give him the air of some kind of African archdeacon.

'That was the message, ma'am,' he answered. 'Not to talk to *anyone*.'

'Simon, this is Bob Inchpenny,' Lona said. 'Bob, this is Mr Templar. I'd already told Mr Templar everything, before you gave me that message.'

'Oh yes, ma'am.'

The caretaker regarded Simon with even more critical reserve; and the Saint realised how ridiculous the suggestion that this man might be a wellspring of idle gossip must have sounded to anyone who knew him. Simon had seldom encountered a Negro who bore himself with such an austere and almost overpowering dignity.

They got into the dinghy, and the caretaker picked up the oars and began to row stolidly back to the island.

'What did he sound like, this person who telephoned?' Lona asked.

'Sort of muffled, like he was disguising his voice.'

'Couldn't you guess anything about him?' Simon persisted.
'For instance, what nationality would you say he was?'

The coloured man pondered this for several strokes, with
portentous concentration.

'I'd say he might be an American, sir.'

The Saint turned to Lona.

'You must have heard almost everything about Jolly Roger.
Did you ever hear what he sounded like?'

'Not exactly. It must have been pretty ordinary English. If
he'd sounded like an American, I'm sure it would've been
mentioned.'

Simon was still thinking that over when they reached the
island dock. He stepped out and gave her a hand, and let her
lead him up the alternations of steps and meandering path
that wound up the slope to the house.

The living-room that she took him into was very large, but
so cunningly broken up that it seemed to consist entirely of
inviting corners. The formal centre was an enormous fire-
place flanked by a pair of huge but cosy couches; on one side
of them was a spacious alcove that contained a sideboard and
a modest dining-table, and on the other side a bay that was
almost completely walled with bookshelves encircling a built-
in desk, while yet a third wing suggested relaxed entertainment with a door-sized bar niche and the cabinets and
speaker fronts of a hi-fi sound system and the slotted shelves
of an impressive library of records. And between all those
mural features there was still room for several stretches of
full-length drapes, now drawn out in neatly extended folds
but promising windows for unlimited sunlight and air in the
daytime. It was a room which, in far more than adequate
justification of its name, asked to be lived in, offering every
adjunct to a kind of timeless tranquillity that could make
calendars superfluous.

'Now do you get an idea why we couldn't resist it?' Lona Dayne said.

He nodded, conscious of the associations that must have heightened the strain that she was fighting.

'You'll both be enjoying it again before long,' he said quietly, 'if I'm still any good at these games.'

She turned and walked briskly over to the bar.

'How about a whisky and soda?'

'Thanks. But make mine with water.'

'Going back to your last question,' she said, making herself busy with her back turned, and speaking in a resolutely clear and businesslike voice, 'I'm certain now that Ivalot always passed as British. You see, one of the things that's made him so hopelessly hard to trace is that there's so little real information about him. In the hotels where he stayed, for instance, the only record was the name, Roger Ivalot – address, Bermuda. Only a British subject could have registered like that. If he'd been taken for a foreigner, he'd've had to fill out a form with a lot more questions than that, and give a passport number as well. And then we'd either have had more facts to go on, or the police would've been leading the hunt for him, for making false declarations.'

'Whereas right now there's no official interest?'

'I've told you, there's nothing against him except a paternity suit, and that sort of thing doesn't concern Scotland Yard.'

With a discreet knock, the caretaker entered.

'Will it be all right if I wait in my quarters, ma'am,' he asked respectfully, 'until you want me to row Mr Templar ashore?'

Lona Dayne turned with the Saint's drink in her hand, nonplussed for an instant, and then Simon took it and said calmly: 'That won't be necessary. I'd much rather take you ashore, Lona, to an hotel, where I think you'd be safer than out here.'

'But this is almost like a castle with a moat around it!'

'And anybody who can row, or even swim, can cross a moat. Unless it's guarded. So if you're determined to stay here, which you probably are, to be around for any more messages that come in, I'm going to stay and join the garrison.'

She hesitated barely an instant.

'That would be quite wonderful,' she said frankly, and he admired her for not making any half-hearted protests. 'Bob, would you make sure that everything's shipshape in the spare room before you go to bed? And thank you for waiting up.'

'Yes, ma'am.'

The caretaker withdrew, looking more than ever like an Ethiopian pontiff with a troublesome congregation.

'I'm afraid this shocks him even more than your husband's disappearing act,' Simon remarked.

'I can't help that. I'll be perfectly honest now and admit that I've been scared for myself too. But I'd have tried not to tell you if you hadn't mentioned it first.' She picked up her drink and brought it over to join him. 'It's true, isn't it – a man in Ivalot's position might do anything?'

The Saint selected a corner of one of the big settees and let himself down into it.

'That depends on how desperate he is – which means, what he has to feel desperate about. You say nobody's filed any criminal charge against him. So that would mean that he chose to pull up stakes and vanish completely, leaving all the fleshpots that he seems to have thought were fun, just to duck a common paternity suit. But half of those suits are plain ordinary blackmail, anyway – which Jolly Roger seems to have suspected, since he offered a fairly handsome settle-ment. From the rest of your account, he doesn't sound like a guy who'd be unduly concerned about his reputation, at any rate with the blue-nosed set. So if the little mother's price was too high, why didn't he just get himself a tough lawyer and fight it?'

'You tell me,' she said. 'I've been going around it all by myself until my head's swimming.'

'Well, I'd say it suggests that he had something pretty big to hide. I don't see him being so scared of the lawsuit; but the lawyers would certainly start investigating his means before they got into court, in order to prove how much he could afford to pay, and I'm inclined to think that's what scared him. Did anyone ever check on these uranium mines he was supposed to have an interest in?'

'Yes, we did. We contacted every Australian and South African mining company that has anything to do with uranium. None of them had ever heard of him, and his name wasn't on any of their lists of shareholders. But of course, his shares wouldn't necessarily have to be in his own name.'

'No. But it's usually only millionaires and big operators who're concerned about keeping their holdings hidden. According to Ivalot's story, as you told it, he wasn't in either category when he bet his shirt on the atomic future. So why would he have bought stocks then under a phony name?'

'Perhaps even in those days he didn't want to be investigated.'

'Perhaps. But another thing. He must have done something to earn a living and save up a stake before he invested in uranium. While you were doing your research on him, didn't you ever turn up anything on that background?'

'I tried to, naturally. But I didn't find out anything. If anyone asked him, he must have managed to dodge the question.'

'So what this all boils down to,' said the Saint, 'is that we don't have one single solid fact about him before he exploded on London like a bomb, and everything you've told me except what he actually did in London before witnesses is probably pure fiction.'

'Except that he did have a lot of money.'

'He spent a good deal of money. But not millions. We don't know how much he had left when he checked out.'

'And he *is* in Bermuda.'

'Apparently. Which only leads to another question: why? When things got too hot in London, he took a powder. Nothing happened to the gal who was giving him trouble. But here, it's your husband who disappears. Why?'

She put her clenched fists to her temples.

'What are you driving at?' she pleaded. 'You're only making it seem more hopeless!'

'I have to do this, Lona,' he said steadily. 'It's the dull part of playing detective. First I have to prune off everything that we don't actually know at all. It isn't till we've trimmed off all the camouflage and confusion that we'll get a good look at what's really left. And raising more questions sometimes leads to more answers. For instance, that last one. The two most likely reasons why our boy hasn't left Bermuda are either (*a*) that he feels better able to cope with things here, or (*b*) that it's harder for him to leave. I wouldn't call those sensational clues, but they might come in handy before we're through.'

She recovered herself again, with a toss of her blonde head something like a dog shaking off water.

'I'm sorry,' she said, smiling very hard. 'I must remember, I told you I was tough. What next?'

'Something very important. Do you have a picture of this character?'

'No. That's what makes it even more impossible.'

'A playboy like that never got his picture taken?'

'Photographers don't go popping flash-bulbs all over the place in England like they do in America, or at least in American films. They'd have to ask his permission, and if he didn't want any pictures he could get out of it.'

Simon scowled thoughtfully.

'And yet he didn't care how many people saw him making an exhibition of himself – he did everything to attract attention. Damn it, it doesn't make sense . . . Wait a minute, though. Maybe it does. It means he wasn't afraid of anyone in England recognising him; but a news photo might go anywhere in the world.'

'Another clue?'

'Could be. But you must have a description of him.' She screwed up her eyes a little, concentrating.

'Ordinary height – about five feet ten. Medium build, but quite muscular. The girl with the twins said he was in very fine shape for his age – and please don't say whatever that vulgar expression is getting ready for, Simon, I think I've already heard every possible joke on that subject. He told her he was fifty-three. But a lot of people thought he looked older, because he was half bald, and the fringe of hair that he had left was very grey, and so was his beard—'

'Oh, no,' groaned the Saint. 'Not a beaver, too?'

'Not a royal growth. The kind that just carries the sideburns on down around the jawbone until they meet and make a tuft on the chin.'

'Which can be grown in two weeks and change the outline of a face completely. And I was just going to ask you what type of face he had.'

'And I was going to tell you it was round. But I see what you mean. Everyone says he was always smiling – the Jolly Roger business, of course – and that would help his face to look round, too.'

'Mouth?'

'Biggish – the smile would help that, I know, don't tell me. And of course he had a moustache.'

'Of course. He would. Teeth?'

'Good.'

'Nose?'

She moved her hands helplessly.

'Did you ever try to make the average person describe a nose? It wasn't a great beak and it wasn't an Irish pug and it wasn't broken. It was just a nose.'

'Eyes?'

'Brown. Two.'

Simon Templar unrolled and came up on his feet in an ultimate surge of exasperation.

'God burn and blast it,' he erupted, 'do you realise that that adds up to practically nothing at all? A middling-sized guy with strictly conventional features – the greatest physical assets any crook could start with. Everything else could be grown or glued on and shaped and/or dyed or worn as an expression, on this foundation you still haven't described. We don't even have a clear picture of his age, except that I'll bet that it's less than fifty-three. If you want to do a good job of faking, it's a lot easier to pretend to be older than younger – as I shouldn't have to tell a woman. But as for the spinach on this act . . .'

He groped around for an illustration, and his gaze lit on a framed photograph on the mantelpiece. He targeted it with a dynamically out-thrust forefinger.

'Why,' he said, 'I could pin the same shrubbery on that guy, and he'd fit your description.'

'That guy,' she said, out of an icy stillness, 'happens to be my husband.'

The Saint stood transfixed, his eyes almost glazed with the fascination of the frabjous idea that his runaway train of thought had gone hurtling into. But she never noticed that teetering instant of thunderstruck rigidity, for within the same full second the telephone began to ring.

She started towards it with a tensely even step, but reached it in a rush.

Simon was beside her as she picked it up. With an arm lightly around her, he pressed his ear to the other side of the receiver.

'Hullo,' she said.

He was inappropriately aware of her hair brushing his cheek and her faint perfume in his nostrils, while he listened to the voice which he could hear thinly but quite clearly through the plastic. It had a forced and unmistakably artificial timbre, with a strong nasal twang.

'Mrs Dayne,' it said, 'I'll let you talk to your husband as soon as Mr Templar has left Bermuda. But if he isn't on a plane tomorrow, you can consider yourself a widow.'

There was a soft click, and that was all.

3

The Saint awoke early in the morning, for there had been no further reason to stay up late the night before.

He had made the only possible offer directly their eyes met after she hung up the dead telephone: 'I'll leave tomorrow, of course.'

Her face was a tortured battleground of uncertainty.

'Thank you for making it easy for me,' she said. 'Even if you were the best hope I had . . . But you do understand, don't you?'

'I do indeed. I know why the parents of kidnapped kids pay ransom. You couldn't force me to go; but I can't take advantage of that. However' – his smile was a thing of coldly dazzling deadliness – 'I'll still be working until the last plane leaves.'

He had found out that she had some sleeping pills, and had persuaded her to take one.

'We're talked out tonight,' he said. 'At least you can be fairly sure that your husband's alive, and that you'll hear from him tomorrow. This is your chance to get some rest. Let me do the worrying.'

He had not worried at all, for that was a sterile indulgence of which he was constitutionally incapable. But he had been happy to find that the guest-room which had been prepared for him was directly opposite the master bedroom: she had, gratefully accepted the suggestion that both doors should be left ajar, and thereafter he had slept with the tranquil self-confidence of a cat. But nothing had disturbed the night; and when he opened his eyes and saw daylight, many things had sorted themselves out in his mind, and he knew that for that period there had been no real danger.

He found his way out of the house and down to the water in the dressing gown she had lent him – it was so obviously part of a bridegroom's going-away outfit that the loan seemed like an embarrassing kind of compliment, but he had to take it. It was easy to slip into the almost lukewarm water in a tiny cove on the seaward side of the island without benefit of swimming-trunks. He churned back and forth for a while, drifted along the shore to watch the questings of a school of yellow-striped fish, and finally hoisted himself out on to a rock where the sun quickly dried him. In front of him was only the blue Sound, embraced by the main chain of islands and dotted with smaller satellite islands; local folklore claims that the Bermudas are made up of 365 islands, one for every day in the year, but the actual number is much less than half that, and a large number of those have a somewhat slender claim to be counted, being mere outcroppings of coral which have barely managed to raise their heads above high water. Small sail-boats, launches, and a couple of the busy ferries that bustle endlessly to and fro to link a dozen landings spaced around the harbour and the Sound, made the view look absurdly like an animated travel-folder picture: no one is ever quite prepared for the fact that Bermuda, more than almost any other highly advertised place, looks so instantly and exactly like its postcards. But after his first appreciative survey, the Saint turned his back on the panorama and concentrated on the humped contours of the island that he was on, trying speculatively to fit them with another geological item which he recalled from a guide-book he had been reading.

After a few minutes he put on the borrowed robe again and walked back up over the close-cropped grass. Near a corner of the formal garden that surrounded the house he came upon the coloured caretaker planting an oleander hedge, making a neat row of eighteen-inch cuttings bent over in interlocking arcs with both ends set in the ground, but characteristically looking more like a grave-digger than a gardener.

'Good morning, sir,' he said, with studiously impersonal politeness.

'Good morning.'

Simon paused to light a cigarette. His gaze swept around the panorama again, and from that vantage point he could see more than two-thirds of the private island.

'There's something I've been meaning to ask,' he said. 'Exactly how did Mr Dayne leave here when he disappeared? Did he get a phone call first? Or did someone come to see him? Did he say anything when he left?'

'I'm afraid I have no idea, sir. I'd gone into Somerset to do some shopping, and when I came back Mr Dayne was gone.'

'Well, when you came back, was another of the boats from here over at the landing, besides the one you'd taken?'

'No, sir. Just the one I'd used.'

'Then someone must have come and picked him up in a boat.'

'That must be right, sir.'

The Saint rubbed his chin for a moment.

'By the way,' he said, 'I noticed a small Chris-Craft tied up at the dock last night. Is that working?'

'Yes, sir.'

'I think we might use it to run into Hamilton this morning.'

'Yes, sir, of course – to get your ticket.'

Simon's eyes flickered fractionally.

'How did you know I was going anywhere?'

'Mrs Dayne just told me what happened last night, sir.

She's in the kitchen, fixing breakfast. I'm sorry, sir,' the care-taker said stiffly.

'So am I,' said the Saint briefly, and went on into the house.

He put his head in the kitchen door and asked: 'How soon are you serving?'

'In about five minutes, or whenever you're ready,' she answered, and added: 'You'll find an electric razor in our bathroom.'

'Thanks.'

In well under ten minutes he had shaved, rinsed himself under a shower, dressed, and was sitting down to a platter of perfectly cooked eggs and bacon.

'I see you were brought up right,' he said. 'Frying an egg sounds like the easiest job in the world, but I'm always amazed how seldom it's done properly, without making bubbles in the white and a leathery brown crust underneath. Even in France, the land of the great chefs, nobody has the faintest notion of how to fry an egg.'

'You don't have to cover up,' she said steadily. 'I know how the idea of running away must be hurting you. So I've decided that if you think it's the wrong thing to do, you mustn't do it – even if I beg you to.'

'I have to make a plane reservation anyhow,' he said. 'Has it dawned on you that you're being watched? I'd never met you till yesterday evening; and yet I was the main thing our pal had on his mind when he phoned you last night.'

Her eyes widened a little.

'You mean Ivalot himself could have been at the Van Hessens' – or at the restaurant where we had dinner—'

'Not necessarily. He may have an accomplice, or even a gang – we don't know. But he's pretty sure to find out whether I've booked myself out of here as ordered. Then if his phone call meant anything at all, he'll be practically forced to wait and see whether I do leave. And maybe I'll wait and see, too.'

He stared out of the window of the dining alcove with such a preoccupied air that she would have sworn that his thoughts were on anything but the view which it framed, so that it surprised her when he said presently: 'This is an even dreamier spot in the daytime. I wonder why the owner doesn't live here all year round.'

'Perhaps his home in Canada is even nicer.'

'D'you know anything about him?'

'Only that his name is Stanley Parker. And I believe he's quite elderly. Why do you ask?'

'I'm practising – I've got a lot of questions to ask in a hurry today. As soon as we're finished, I'm going to Hamilton and start in earnest. I guess you'd better come with me so I won't have to worry about you. We'll take the speedboat, because it's quicker than a taxi, and it'll make it tougher for anyone who's thinking of tailing us.'

He had already observed with approval that, doubtless because of her professional background, she breakfasted with hair and clothes and make-up in shape to face the world as soon as she stood up from the table, and she joined him at the dock with a minimum of delay after their second cups of coffee. The caretaker had the Chris-Craft waiting alongside and was wiping off the seats.

'Do you know the way, sir, or do you wish me to take you?' he inquired disinterestedly.

'I can find it, thanks,' said the Saint. 'And you'd better be here in case there are any more messages.'

He pushed the clutch forward and opened the throttle until the light hull was planing. For less than a mile he drove the boat north-east across the Sound, and then he began to veer more to the east, towards Burgess Point and the coastline of Warwick Parish. Lona Dayne twitched his shirt-sleeve and pointed.

'Stay as you were, to the left of that island. It's the shortest way through to Hamilton.'

'I've got a call to make on the way,' he explained.

He swung still farther to starboard, to miss another larger island that emerged ahead. As they ran along its shore the façade of a Florida Keys fishing village came into view, with the functionally arched roof of an enormous hangar rising above the picturesquely weatherbeaten fronts. Simon cut the engine and laid the speedboat skilfully in beside a pier that projected from the strikingly un-Bermudian waterfront.

'This is Darrell's Island, where our host of last night operates,' he said. 'I just want to ask him something – and we haven't got time to show you how they make TV pictures. I'll be right back.'

He left her sitting in the boat and disappeared through an opening in the scenery. Having been given the tour once before, on his arrival, he found his way with the faultless recall of a homing pigeon through the partitioned alleys which had miraculously created a modern television picture studio within the shell of an abandoned airport that dated back to those pessimistic days when only seaplanes and flying boats were thought suitable for air travel over water; and Dick Van Hassen looked up defensively as he crashed into the office, and then recognised him with a grin.

'Well! What can we do for you today?'

'You're busy and I'm in a hurry,' said the Saint, 'so I'll leapfrog the trimmings. All I want is a good lawyer.'

'*What?* Did she hook you already?'

'Let's try to build it into a half-hour show – some other time.'

'The one I like best is a fellow named Fred Thearnley,' Van Hessen said. 'He's done a few things for me, and he's a lot more on the ball than some of 'em.'

'Would you phone him and use your influence to see if he can squeeze a few minutes for me about as soon as I can get there?'

'Sure.'

Simon returned to Lona with an appointment for eleven o'clock. He started up the boat again, and sent it skimming through the channel to the left of Hinson's Island, and then threading between other smaller islands towards the north shore of the gradually narrowing bay, now sheltered between the hills of Pembroke and Paget on either side with the white-sugar roofs and pink-icing walls of fairy-tale candy houses studding their green slopes. He slowed up past the Princess Hotel, a birthday cake moulded in the same style, and stopped and tied up at the Yacht Club dock farther on. He looked at his watch.

'We've got plenty of time to do my airline errand first,' he said.

They cut through by the Bank of Bermuda and walked eastwards past the open wharf where the cruise boats berth in the very heart of the city, and up Front Street to the BOAC office. Their last plane left for New York at 4 p.m., and he was able to get a seat on it.

The lawyer's office turned out to be back in the direction they had come from, a few doors from Trimingham's, which is the biggest department store that the highly conservative proportions of Hamilton have to offer. Simon escorted Lona to its entrance.

'You'll be as safe here as you could be anywhere; and with all this merchandise to look at, unless you're a female impersonator you won't even miss me. Just stay away from the doors, and I'll find you in about half an hour,' he said, and left her.

Mr Thearnley was a large man put together of ellipsoid shapes, with a florid complexion, very bright baggy eyes, sparse sandy hair, and a moustache of such luxuriant dimensions that it would have provided a more than adequate graft to replace what was lacking from the top of his head. The upper part of him was very correctly dressed in a black alpaca coat, white shirt with starched collar, and dark pinstriped tie; but when he rose from behind his desk to shake hands he revealed that, in conformity with local custom, his lower section was clad only in knee-length shorts and long socks. The effect was inevitably reminiscent of the time-honoured farce routine in which the comedian bursts into public view fully dressed except for having forgotten to put on his trousers; but Mr Thearnley was just as unaware of anything hilarious about it.

'Well, Mr Templar,' he said affably, 'what can I do for you?'

'Answer some silly questions,' said the Saint, and sat down. 'I'm sure you haven't a lot of time to waste, so I'll fire them as fast as I can, and I hope you won't think I'm too blunt . . . One: do you know another attorney in this town by the name of—?'

He gave the name of the attorney to whom the solicitors for Mr Ivalot's concubine had referred their case, which he had found out from Lona Dayne on the way over from Darrell's Island.

'Only for about thirty years,' Mr Thearnley said with a smile.

'Would you vouch for him without any qualification?'

'Now I'm beginning to think you were serious about asking silly questions.'

'I'll be more specific. If he were asked to serve papers on somebody in Bermuda who accidentally happened to be a friend of his, would anything induce him to report that he couldn't find any trace of this defendant?'

Mr Thearnley's eyes had visibly congealed.

'If the person concerned were a friend of his, he would simply decline the case and give his reason. He would not tell a lie. He is the most ethical man I have the good fortune to know.'

'I'm sorry,' said the Saint. 'I don't know him, and I had to ask that to confirm that a certain person is definitely untraceable here by any ordinary means ... Let me try something less delicate: How would anyone here go about getting a passport?'

'A British subject?'

'Yes, of course.'

'He fills out an application, and submits it with a couple of photographs—'

'And a birth certificate?'

'No, that isn't required. But the form has to be attested by someone who's known him for a certain number of years. Not just anyone; it has to be someone with a recognised professional standing. A bank manager, a doctor, or a minister, are the usual ones. Or a lawyer.'

Simon lighted a cigarette. It was an effort to subdue a flood-tide of excitement that rose higher as one joint after another of the framework that he had put together in his mind was tested and the whole structure still remained solid.

'The last one may be the hardest,' he said. 'There's a Canadian, by the name of Stanley Parker, who owns a house on a small island, way out towards the other end of Southampton. Do you happen to know anyone who knows him?'

'This is quite a small place,' Thearnley said. 'As a matter of fact, I know a little about him myself.'

'How old would you say he was?'

'That's hard to guess. He's certainly quite senile.'

The Saint raised his eyebrows.

'As bad as that?'

'Well, he gives that impression. It may be partly because he's had a stroke and can't even speak. As it happens, the agent who made the sale is a client of mine. I don't know how Parker heard about it, but he wrote from Canada and said he'd take it and he'd be here with the cash as soon as the deed could be drawn up. The asking price was a bit steep, as usual, because people always expect to do some bargaining, but Parker didn't haggle at all.'

'How long ago was this?'

'About six years ago. I prepared the conveyance myself, and that's how I met him, when he came in to sign it. He just grunted and nodded to whatever was said to him, didn't even read the papers, and scratched his name on the dotted line. Then he handed over a huge envelope full of twenty-dollar bills and waited for us to count them. The agent and myself had to count almost two thousand each. We gave him a receipt, and the keys, and he grunted again and tottered out. My friend's conscience gave him a bit of trouble after he'd seen the man, because he hadn't really expected to get the full price, and he wondered if he could be accused of taking advantage of an imbecile. I had to tell him that we had no evidence that Parker was *non compos mentis*, and that a man who carried about twenty thousand pounds in an old envelope might be so rich that he just couldn't be bothered to argue about the price of anything.'

'Have you ever seen him since?'

'I ran into him once in my dentist's waiting-room when I was coming out, and once at the airport when I was meeting a plane. I think he must have played hermit out on his island most of the time.'

The Saint stood up.

'I'm very much obliged to you,' he said. 'I may be leaving here rather soon, so would you be shocked if I offered to pay cash for this consultation?'

'Tell Dick I'll stick it on his next bill.' The lawyer also rose, again oblivious of what his naked knees did to his dignity. He seemed to be wavering between two tormenting inward doubts, one as to whether he might have indiscreetly answered too much, the other as to how discreetly he could indulge some curiosity of his own. He said, taking a plunge: 'Or we'll call it all square if you'll tell me what this is all about.'

'If everything works out, and I'm still here tomorrow, I'll come back and tell you – that's a promise.'

'You know,' Thearnley went on, 'from the trend of some of your inquiries, I'm rather surprised at one question you haven't asked.'

'What was that?'

'About Mr Parker's background.'

'What was it?'

'My friend the estate agent tried to find out something about him, naturally, but all he could find out was that Mr Parker had once been a lawyer, too.'

'These woods seem to be full of them,' said the Saint gravely, and made an exit before Mr Thearnley could decide how to respond to that.

Lona Dayne was dispiritedly trying on shoes when Simon tracked her down in the store, and he had never seen a woman so relieved to be rescued from a bewildered salesman.

'I can't get used to being dragged around like a doll,' she said edgily, as he marched her back towards the boat. 'Where are you taking me now?'

'Back to the island. But I have to make a slight detour, by way of Cambridge Beaches, which is the place where I was staying before I met you.'

Even at that moment, he couldn't help being amused by the suddenness with which her pique became crestfallen.

'I forgot,' she said in an empty voice. 'You've got to pack, haven't you.'

'I want to pick up a gun,' said the Saint. 'We're going to meet Jolly Roger.'

4

Lona Dayne maintained a taut and stubborn silence all the way out to the secluded cottage colony at Mangrove Bay, waited in the boat while he went ashore, and succeeded in prolonging that super-human self-discipline until they had passed under Watford Bridge again on the way back.

Then at last she said resentfully: 'Why do you have to be so mysterious? I think you're deliberately trying to force me into the part of a stupid *ingénue*.'

'Darling,' he said, 'haven't you ever read any whodunits? Don't you know that the detective always acts very mysterious and keeps the big surprise up his sleeve till the last few pages?'

'This isn't a whodunit.'

'Oh, yes, it is. And I'm not a very experienced detective. So I've had to take advantage of my privilege because I haven't had the nerve to come right out with my theory – in case it turned out to be really as crazy as it sounds, and I ended not only with egg on my face but with ham too.'

'Don't get coy with me,' she said. 'I'm Lona Shaw – remember?'

Simon smiled with his lips closed, his blue eyes narrowed against the brilliant blue of the sea and sky as he turned the speedboat southward and tried to get an exact bearing on the island they had to return to.

'You wouldn't dare to send your editor a story based on my kind of deductions,' he said. 'Nearly all my thinking seems to be negative – a process of clearing away the undergrowth so you can find out where the solid ground is. I've seldom heard a story that was so fogged up with false clues. For instance, the accent of the guy who talked to you on the phone last night.'

'It sounded very American to me.'

'And to me. In fact, exaggeratedly American. But what we have to remember is that an accent can be faked. Roger Ivalot sounded English. So an American accent cropping up here sounds like an attempt to confuse things – perhaps to suggest that he has accomplices which he hasn't got at all. But a man who would play those tricks of dialect might very well have done it before. Therefore Ivalot's English was probably the first fake. A man who'd lived here for several years should be able to do a very passable imitation – even if he was raised in America.'

'Or Canada.'

'I'm glad you brought that up,' he said. 'Did you ever notice how in the stories you quoted, Jolly Roger had his uranium interests in South Africa and Australia – but not a word was said about Canada, where some of the biggest uranium strikes of all have been made? That was an omission that stood out like a flat chest at a beauty contest – if I may scramble a metaphor in mid-stream. Almost from the moment I heard it, I would have liked to bet that Canada was the one place that our boy would turn out to have his deepest roots in.'

'You're still keeping the riddles going,' she said sulkily. 'That's all very plausible and clever, but you must have a lot more up your sleeve.'

'But the next step takes me out on a limb. I also say that our boy is a lawyer.'

The frown darkened on her brow.

'Last night you were starting to say something—'

'This script is full of lawyers,' he interrupted quickly. 'That's another confusing feature of it. But it set me thinking about human characteristics. Lawyers are cautious. Lawyers make a technique of procrastination. What does any smart lawyer do when he knows he's got a very shaky case? He uses every dodge and device in the book to keep getting it postponed and continued and adjourned – because until it actually comes to a court and a verdict, he still hasn't lost it. Your husband disappeared because our boy thought he had to do something fast and drastic; but after that, he didn't know how to go on with it. That's why nothing else happened for two days. Perhaps he hadn't finally worked anything out until last night, when you got the first message. But then I upset him again by showing up in the act. So when he talked to you later, it was to tell you to get me out of here. Another delay. That's why I was so sure we were safe last night and today. He's still stalling for time.'

'So are you,' she said angrily. 'Will you tell me just one thing straight?'

He grinned, throttling back as they circled around to the lee side of the private island, and switched off the engine to coast to a perfect dead-stick landing at the dock.

'In a few minutes,' he said. 'I have to make a phone call first.'

She walked speechlessly beside him up to the house. But now she realised that he was enjoying himself, and she would not give him the satisfaction of making her protest again.

While he was dialling a number, he said: 'To give you something to go on with – does anything ring a bell with you about a man who's excessively self-conscious about names?'

Without a word, she turned and went over to the bar cupboard.

He said to the telephone: 'Mr Van Hessen, please. This is Mr Templar.'

He put his hand over the mouthpiece and said: 'Another thing. Weren't you surprised that a character like our boy, who was so anxious that you shouldn't talk to anyone, would leave such a melodramatic warning with anyone who answered the phone, like your caretaker?'

The only reply was a heavily restrained clinking of glassware.

He said to the phone: 'Oh, Dick. Glad I caught you. Have you got to know anyone in the police higher up than a traffic cop? . . . Good. And do you have one of the Company boats there? . . . Better still. Will you please call this Inspector, and persuade him to let you pick him up and bring him out to Parker's island right away – you know, where the Daynes are staying. I mean as quickly as you can get here. I can't call him myself, because if I gave my name he'd think someone was pulling his leg . . . No, I don't want to say any more on the phone, but this is the most serious thing I ever asked you . . . Okay, feller. Thanks.'

He hung up.

Lona Dayne was standing beside him with a glass in her hand.

'A nice drop of sherry before lunch?' she suggested sweetly.

He took it.

'Is it poisoned?'

'If it was, no jury would convict me.'

He moved to the end of one of the davenports, studied it for a couple of seconds in relation to the doors into the room, and slid a blue-black automatic out of his hip pocket and behind a cushion.

'Tell me one thing,' he said. 'If I'm quoting you correctly, you were talking to this caretaker, and his boss had just told him to try and rent the place. But how did you happen to meet him and be talking to him in the first place?'

She raised a glass of her own to her lips, holding it with a tense care that just failed to be completely casual.

'I've been waiting for that,' she said. 'This house must have something to do with it, of course.'

'How did you meet Bob?'

'He came to see us at the hotel, the same day our story came out in the papers. He said that he once worked for a Mr Rogers here, who threw a lot of wild parties, which he couldn't forget – you've seen what a strait-laced type he is. With that coincidence of names, he wondered if it could be the man we were looking for. But his description didn't fit anywhere – his Mr Rogers was very tall and thin with a big hooked nose. Then it was after we'd ruled that out that he went on talking about this house and the island . . . Please,' she said, with her voice suddenly rising a sharp third, 'don't say how half-witted you're thinking we must have been—'

He was at the telephone again, and did not even seem to have heard her.

'Did you ever see this trick?' he inquired.

He took off the handset, and dialled four numbers, and put the handset back again. Immediately, the telephone began to ring. He let it ring a few times, and then picked up the handset again.

'If you know the right combination, you can make any telephone ring like an incoming call,' he said. 'But do you know where all the extensions are in this house? It could be done from any of them.'

He hung the instrument up and turned away.

'Once upon a time,' he said, 'there was an attorney in Toronto named Robert Parker Illet. He was born and educated in England, but taken to Canada after his parents died in a flu epidemic and raised there by a maternal uncle. Seven years ago he was hardly middle-aged, but he'd built an inspiring reputation. It was so good, in fact, that he had a wide-open chance to embezzle five million dollars, with no more trouble than writing a few cheques. I told you I was looking for him when we first met, but I don't think you took me seriously.'

She stared at him with her chin dropping and her mouth and eyes equally open, temporarily stunned out of any vestige of poise.

'Plenty of lawyers have had chances like that,' he went on, 'but this one grabbed it. He packed the loot in a couple of suit-cases, in cash and bearer bonds, and vanished into the blue. When I heard about the case a few months ago, I decided to go after him like I'd go on a treasure hunt. First, because he'd been gone so long without being caught, I figured he must have gone farther than the United States. But where could he go without a passport? Spies have forged passports; big-time international crooks can get 'em; but a previously respectable attorney wouldn't have any idea where to buy one. That narrowed it down to Central America and the West Indies. I found out that he didn't speak any Spanish, and I decided that that might have made him leerier of the Latin countries. Most people – even policemen – automatically think of the banana republics as the perfect place for a crook to hide, but I can tell you that there's nothing so conspicuous down there as an obvious gringo. However, that still left plenty of British islands. But then I found out that Illet had spent a couple of vacations here, and it was the only one he seemed to have visited. I bet on another hunch that this man might be most likely to head for a place that he knew a little about, where he could melt as quickly as possible into the local scene, rather than a place that'd be totally strange to him; and I decided to start sniffing around here first.'

'But if he'd been here even as a tourist, there'd be people who might remember him!'

'Not in the identity he was going to create. He had another

lawyer's trait: patience. With five million bucks stowed away, he didn't have to rush out and start splurging. Even if he laid low for ten years, it'd be like earning half a million a year, tax free, which was a lot better than he could've done legitimately. My guess is that he originally planned to hibernate at least until the statute of limitations ran out, when he'd be absolutely in the clear. In a nice house like this, with his books and his records, it shouldn't have been too hard to take. Of course he couldn't have much social life, but some men don't mind that. I expect he went to church regularly, though. An innocent unsuspecting minister would be the easiest person for him to cultivate who'd be qualified to endorse a passport application after knowing him for several years – and he had to get a passport eventually, to go to places like London and Paris where he could make the playboy splash that he'd always secretly dreamed of.'

Simon had moved over to the corner of the chesterfield again. He put his half-empty glass down in precarious balance on the back, and lighted a cigarette.

'Unfortunately,' he said, 'our boy's good resolutions weren't quite equal to the strain. He stood it for several years; but counting over all that spinach that he couldn't spend, and thinking about the rip-roaring times he could have with it, his patience finally ran out before the statute of limitations would have let him thumb his nose at the law. He had to break down and treat himself to one preliminary fling, and in the role and disguise of Roger Ivalot he thought he could get away with it. He did, too. But then, like dopes who experiment with dope, he found it was habit-forming. Six months later he had to go back for more. And before that encore was over, he found himself threatened with a lawsuit which he knew damn well could make all his castles in the air end up like iron balloons. That was the reason he couldn't stay and fight it. And you know now why he couldn't take it on the lam in the same way from Bermuda; this is where he has his only other identity, and he's stuck with it. You can't create those things overnight.'

'But if he'd got a passport here in the name of Ivalot,' she objected, 'we'd have found a record of him in no time.'

'So he didn't,' said the Saint. 'He didn't become Ivalot until after he'd landed in England – after a couple of weeks which he'd spent in any small flat growing those fast chin-whiskers and the other fuzz you've described, which in turn would have been after an overnight stop in a back-street hotel which he left very early before anybody was up in the morning, so they wouldn't notice how different he looked after he made his first personality change.'

'Then how did he leave here?'

'Under the name he was known here by. Didn't I ask you to notice his complex about names? "Ivalot" was outrageous, but he took the bull by the horns and disarmed everybody by making jokes about it. To his corny sense of humour, his other name must have been just as funny. For a man who was going to ease into a fortune the slow patient way, what could be more apt than the old-English-sounding name of Inchpenny?'

The door from the dining area to the kitchen swung gently open, making a very muted creak; but Simon Templar did not jump. He turned his head almost lazily, and smiled cordially at the man standing there. He heard Lona Dayne gasp at the sight of the gun in the caretaker's hand, but the Saint declined to bat even the proverbial eyelash.

'I was wondering how much longer this would take you, Bob,' he murmured. 'But there – that would be the legal training again. You wouldn't tip your hand till the very last moment, when you knew I had every loose end tied together and you were an utterly dead duck.'

'You really do mix your metaphors horribly,' Illet said

primly. 'But I must admit your thinking was quite brilliant. And so was Mrs Dayne's, up to a point.'

Simon glanced sympathetically at the blonde, but she was still striving heroically to recover from her last relapse.

'This is Mr Robert Parker Illet, the legal weasel I was talking about,' he explained kindly. 'The Stanley Parker who bought this place, I imagine, is the ancient uncle who brought him up – now in his second childhood, and a convenient stooge for an operation like buying this house. But it was our boy who had all the fun out of it: as the caretaker, he could have the same use of it without anyone bothering him. You were looking for him as Jolly Roger Ivalot, the playboy of Piccadilly. You were never even close to recognising him as Bob Inchpenny, the coloured caretaker and apparent candidate for churchwarden.'

Illet came slowly across the room, holding his gun very competently.

'You were rather lucky yourself,' he said. 'If you hadn't met Mrs Dayne, I don't think you'd have recognised me.'

Simon observed him with critical detachment.

'It's one of the best jobs of blackface I ever saw,' he conceded. 'You were smart to shave your head all over – nobody would notice whether your hair was kinky or not, and you didn't risk showing a margin on your skin make-up. You were lucky to have brown eyes and rather thick lips to begin with – but who ever looks at a Negro and wonders if he could be a white man in disguise? You only made one conventional mistake. For some strange reason, four out of five crooks who take an alias don't seem to be able to shake off the habit of their original initials. That's where you started to click with me the minute I met you.'

'It's a pity you're so clever,' Illet said, coming closer. 'I'm going to search you now, and I hope you won't do anything silly, but I'll warn you that I was a commando in the last war.'

Simon drew at his cigarette, deeply enough to inhale enough fumes for a smoke-ring, but keeping his elbows away from his body and his hands ingratiatingly above his shoulders, while Illet felt his pockets and around his waist and under his arms.

'Havelock Dayne never left this island, did he?' said the Saint. 'A lot of this rock is hollow – I was remembering a couple of spots where they take tourists, Leamington Cave and Crystal Cave, over near the Castle Harbour. I think one thing that may have helped sell you on this place is that there's a lovely little private cave right under our feet.'

'There's a door to it in the basement,' Illet said, stepping back. 'Mr Dayne is there now.'

'Alive?' Simon inquired, rather carefully.

'Certainly. You remarked very observantly that I'm cautious. It was as easy to chain him up there alive as to kill him. And if anything had gone wrong, the penalty for kidnapping here is much lighter than for murder. I hope I can keep you and Mrs Dayne alive, too – until I'm quite sure that everyone's given you up and it's safe to kill you.'

The Saint shrugged.

'Well, that's almost friendly,' he drawled. 'We'd better get going, because that policeman you heard me send for should be here very soon. May I finish my drink? And did they teach you this in the commandos—'

He reached for the glass he had put down, but in the same movement he bumped clumsily against the couch with his knee. The glass tilted and began to fall. His hand followed it frantically, but somehow veered off and dived behind the cushion. It came out again instantly with his automatic in it, and without even a fragmentary pause he shot Mr Ivalot-Inchpenny-Illet – having taken everything into consideration, only through the right forearm.

5

There was no difficulty about finding the entrance to the cave – it was a locked door in the cellar which the 'caretaker' had once told Lona Dayne led only to a store-room in which Mr Parker kept a lot of old trunks full of personal papers. Nor was there any additional problem about finding Havelock Dayne, by way of a crooked tunnel that sloped down into a limestone cavern of quite spacious dimensions considering the size of the island that covered it. It must have been discovered long ago in the course of excavating for a rainwater cistern; but however Illet had come to hear of it, he had evidently envisaged an emergency use for it, in his prudent way, for the iron ring set in concrete to which the missing bridegroom was attached by a long chain was no antique but had certainly not been installed within the past week.

Mr Dayne was dirty and unshaven, but looked as if he would be fairly personable when he was cleaned up. He revealed no physical damage, but he had been badly frightened, and was correspondingly indignant when he realised that there was nothing more to be frightened about. He seemed to be a very serious-minded young man, who did not regard being chained in a cave for three days and nights as an amusing adventure.

'This settles it – you're resigning from that goddam newspaper right away,' was one of the first things he said.

'We'll talk about that as soon as I've cabled this one last story,' said his bride, with what a more experienced spouse would have identified at once as ominous serenity.

Simon Templar was less interested in various other things that they had to say to each other than he was in a couple of large mildewed valises which he located in another corner of the cave. They were not locked, and when he opened the lids he knew that he had never seen so much cash all in one place at one time.

'Here are those personal papers you were told about,' he murmured. 'If this episode had gone exactly the way I was dreaming when I took up the trail, and I weren't involved now with you respectable citizens, I suppose I'd have left Jolly Roger trussed up upstairs just as he is now, but with only my Saint drawing chalked on his bald head for a souvenir; and I'd still be gone with the boodle before the cops got here – if I'd ever even sent for them. And now all I can do is hope for a lousy few hundred thousand dollars' reward.'

'If you helped yourself to a few handfuls in advance,' Lona said, 'we'd never tell anyone. Would we, Havvie?'

An infinitesimal, scarcely perceptible spasm passed over the Saint's face, as at the twinge of an old wound.

'I wonder if Mrs Havelock Ellis called her husband that,' he said in suddenly appalled conjecture; but neither of them was even listening to him again.

The Talented Husband

I

The young man at London Airport was very impersonal, very polite. He looked up from the passport and said: 'Oh, yes. Mr Templar. Would you step this way, please, sir?'

Simon Templar followed him obligingly from the reception room in which the other passengers from the plane were being processed. The most respectable citizen receiving an invitation like that, no matter how courteously phrased, could have experienced a sensation of vacuum in the stomach; but to Simon such attention at any port of entry had become almost as routine as a request for his vaccination certificate. For the days when harassed police officers and apprehensive malefactors, not to mention several million happily fascinated readers of headlines, had known him only by the name of The Saint were so far behind as to be almost in the province of archaeologists. And of all the countries on earth which had enjoyed the ambiguous benediction of his presence, England, which had been privileged to be the first to feel the full impact of his outlawry, would probably be the last to forget him.

The Saint was very pleasantly unperturbed by the prospect. In fact, he had been looking forward to it for a long time. And as he strolled into the small office to which he was escorted, and the young man went out again and quietly closed the door, he knew that all his optimism had been justified and that this visit would at least begin as beautifully as he had dared to hope.

He gazed across at the cherubic round face of the man who sat there behind the desk disrobing a stick of chewing gum, and his eyes danced like laughing steel.

'Claud Eustace Teal,' he breathed ecstatically. 'My own dream dog. I mean bloodhound. Have you wondered too if we should ever meet again?'

'Good morning, Saint,' Chief Inspector Teal said primly. 'What brings you back here?'

'Haven't you heard? I'm playing two weeks at the Palladium.'

Mr Teal fought for the somnolent authority in his stare. He had fought for it stubbornly ever since he had started waiting for the plane to land, as he had not had to do for many relatively peaceful years. Even five years of war, which had included the fondest ministrations of the Luftwaffe, now seemed in retrospect like a mere ripple in the long interlude of tranquillity with which he had been favoured since he last had to cope with the Saint.

Now that vacation in Nirvana might have lasted no longer than since yesterday. He saw the Saint exactly as he had remembered him in nightmares, outrageously looking not a day older, the tall lean figure just as sinewy and debonair, poised with the same insolently vivid grace, the tanned pirate's face just as keen and reckless; and it was as if the years between had passed over like a flight of birds.

'I'm not doing this because I want to,' Teal said heavily. 'The sooner we get the formalities done, the sooner you can be on your way. When someone like you comes back here, we have to ask why.'

'All right, Claud. I really came back on account of you.'

'I said—'

'But I did. Honestly.'

'Why me?'

'I heard you were going to retire.'

Mr Teal's molars settled into his spearmint like anchors into a bed of sustaining guck. He said, with magnificent stolidity: 'How did you manage to hear that?'

'There was a piece in *Time*, recently, about Scotland Yard. Among some thumbnail sketches of the incumbent hierarchy of beefy brains, your name was mentioned as one of the old-timers shortly to be moved over to the pension list. It's true, isn't it?'

'Yes.'

'They gave you a fine record. All your most celebrated successes. The only big thing they didn't mention, for some reason, was how you never succeeded in catching me. But I suppose you gave them the information.' Simon surveyed him with affectionate appraisal. 'You certainly look wonderful, for an old man, Claud. I'd certainly have recognised you anywhere. The hair a little thinner, perhaps. The jowls a little fuller. The stomach—'

'Just for once,' Teal said grimly. 'Let's leave my stomach out of this.'

'By all means,' said the Saint generously. 'And it'll leave a lot of room. After all, how much more convex can a thing be than convex?'

Like a man struggling to hold down a paroxysm of seasickness, Chief Inspector Teal felt all the frustrated bitterness of the old days welling up in him again, all the hideous futility of a score of humiliations brought on by his dutiful efforts to put that impudent Robin Hood behind the bars where every law said that he belonged; and enriching it was the gall of a hundred interviews such as this, in each one of which he had not only been thwarted but made farcically ridiculous. He never could understand how it happened, it was as if the Saint could actually put some kind of Indian sign on him, but it was a black magic that never failed. Normally a man of no small presence and dignity, impressive to his subordinates and respected even by the underworld, Mr Teal could be reduced by a few minutes of the Saint's peculiar brand of baiting to the borders of screaming imbecility.

But now he would not, he must not, let it happen again . . .

'Yes, I'm retiring,' he said doggedly. 'Next week. And since you've been away this long, you could have stayed away just a few days longer.'

'But I had to be in on your last performance, Claud. And as soon as you heard I was on this passenger list, bless your old fallen arches, you hurried out here to welcome me and—'

'And tell you, whatever you're thinking of doing here, if you know what's good for you, you'll put it off for at least a week!'

The speech, which had a certain breathlessness built right into it, ended on something like a yelp. Teal had not meant it to. He had meant to speak firmly and masterfully; but somehow it had not come out like that.

'You yelped,' said the Saint.

'I did not!' Teal stopped, and cleared his throat with a violence that almost choked him. 'I'm just warning you to behave yourself, and we'll let bygones be bygones. Is that clear?'

'Of course,' said the Saint earnestly. 'In fact, just to prove how forgiving I am, I'm only here to make sure that your career ends in a blaze of glory. I'm going to make sure that you solve your last case – even if I have to do it for you.'

'I don't need your help.'

'Why, is it going that well?'

'Quite satisfactorily, thank you.'

'You've got the goods on him already?'

'It isn't my business to get the goods on anyone,' Teal said ponderously. 'Just the evidence, if there has been a crime.'

'But you're reasonably sure the guy is guilty?'

'I think so. But proving it is another matter. These

Bluebeards are pretty tricky to . . . But what the devil,' Teal blared suddenly, 'do you know about the case?'

'Nothing,' said the Saint blandly. 'Except what you're telling me.'

The detective glared at him suspiciously.

'I don't believe you.'

'You pain me, Claud. Do you think I'm a liar?'

'I've known it for twenty years,' Teal said hotly. 'And let me tell you something else. You're not coming back and getting away with any more of your private acts of what you call justice. If anything happens to Clarron, I'll know damn well who—'

'Clarron?'

'Or Smith, or Jones, or Tom, or Dick, or Harry!' shouted Teal, and knew just how lame a recovery it was.

Simon lighted a cigarette.

'Clarron,' he murmured. 'Well, well. Where is he living right now?'

'I suppose you want me to believe you don't know that too.'

'Once again,' said the Saint reproachfully, 'a more sensitive soul might take offence at your delicate insinuations that I fib.'

Mr Teal made a last frantic clutch at a self-possession which had already assumed some of the qualities of a buttered eel.

'Just let me tell you,' he said in a laboured voice, 'that if I catch you going anywhere near Maidenhead—'

'Maidenhead?' mused the Saint. 'A charming spot. I've been wanting to see it again for years. And somebody told me only the other day that an old pal of mine is now running the famous pub there on the river. As a matter of fact, that's one of the first places I was planning to visit. I might even drive straight out there, and skip London entirely.'

'If you do,' yammered Teal apoplectically, 'I'll—'

His voice strangled incoherently as the Saint's mocking brows lifted over clear cerulean eyes.

'What will you do, Claud? It's still a free country, isn't it? Maidenhead hasn't been made a Forbidden City. Hundreds of tourists go there without being arrested. I don't see why you should pick on me . . . I don't even see why you should keep me here any longer, if you feel so unfriendly. So may I get my bag from the Customs and breeze along?' The Saint hitched himself lazily off the corner of the desk where he had rested one hip for a while. 'But if you do think of some crime to charge me with, I hope you'll run down and make the pinch yourself. It'll give the natives a laugh. You'll find me at Skindle's.'

2

'You must forgive the wop kind of welcome,' Giulio Trapani said, releasing Simon from an uninhibited bear-hug. 'But it is so good to see you again!'

'It's good to see you,' said the Saint. 'And as a contrast with the Scotland Yard treatment I got at the airport, I wouldn't care if you kissed me.'

He sat up at the bar, and Trapani went behind it and brushed the bartender aside.

'I mix it myself,' he said ebulliently. 'Whatever you'd like.'

'At this hour, just a pint from the barrel – warm, flat, nourishing, and British. I was thinking about it all the way over on the plane. It may be an acquired taste, but it's still the only beer in the world that tastes like a meal.'

'It still isn't the same as before the War,' Trapani said, setting a tankard before him. 'But this is the best you can get.'

'Nothing is ever the same, after enough years,' said the Saint.

He drank deeply and contentedly. The brew still tasted good, without its forebears near enough for easy comparison.

'You've made a change too,' he said. 'This is a lot more pub than the old Bell at Hurley.'

'Skindle's, Mr Templar, is an hotel.'

'A good hotel should also be a good pub.'

'I try to make it a good pub too – with trimmings.'

Simon nodded, and glanced out for a moment over the river. It was still early in the season, but it was one of those warm sunny days of almost unbelievable balminess which the climate of Britain can produce as capriciously as it will inevitably snatch them back under a mantle of rain, cold, or fog; and on that pleasant reach of the Thames the skiffs and punts were moving up and down, drifting with their own portable radio or gramophone music or propelled by vigorous and slightly exhibitionistic young males, with girls in bathing-suits or print dresses reclining on gay cushions as luxuriously as any Cleopatra on the Nile, exactly as they had done when he was last there; and he thought that some things like that might survive all changes.

A girl came in from the riverside, in shorts, giving away legs that men would have spent money to see across a row of footlights, with dark rumpled hair and the face of a thoughtful pixie; and the Saint turned away again with some reluctance.

'And you,' Trapani was saying eagerly. 'How is everything? You didn't really have any trouble, of course?'

'Not really.'

'And you're going to relax here and have a good time. I'm so glad that you heard about me and came here. Is there anything you want, anything I can do? You only have to ask me.'

Simon put down his tankard and looked up from it speculatively.

'Well, Giulio, since you mention it – would you happen to know anyone living around here by the name of Clarron?'

'Why, yes, Mr Reginald Clarron. I think his house is on the river, quite near here. I don't know him personally, but I've heard of him.'

Trapani flashed a quick look around the bar. It might have been nothing but the automatic vigilance of a professional host, but Simon noticed it. There were not many customers just then – the girl with the legs who had just come in, who was being served a Martini, two young men in flannels who were drinking Pimm's Cups, a thin elderly man in a dark suit with the anxious air of a travelling salesman, and a stout middle-aged woman in a respectable high-necked long-sleeved black dress, with a cupola of carroty hair capped with a pie-dish straw hat trimmed with some kind of artificial fruit salad, who was sipping a glass of port in the corner. She looked, Simon thought, like the prototype of every comic housekeeper he had ever seen in vaudeville.

'What sort of a guy is he?' Simon asked.

'A very distinguished-looking gentleman. Very charming, I've heard. But he doesn't go out much. His wife is an invalid. She had a terrible accident a few months ago. But if you know them, I expect you heard about it.'

'Just how did it happen?' Simon evaded innocently.

'They were out shooting together. He put down his gun to help her over a fence, and it went off and shot her. His own gun. They saved her life, but her spine was permanently injured. Of course, he can never forget it. He spends all his time with her.' Trapani had lowered his voice discreetly, and his glance flicked away again for a moment. He leaned over and explained in an undertone: 'That woman in the corner is their housekeeper.'

Her ears must have been abnormally sharp, or perhaps it was not too hard to interpret the furtive glance and the lowered voice, but the woman allowed no doubt that she had taken in the whole conversation.

'Indade I am,' she called out in a rich cheerful brogue. 'And a sweeter master an' mistress I niver worked for. Jist as devoted as if they were on their honeymoon, an' her so patient an' forgiving, an' himself eatin' his heart out, poor man, with an awful thing like that on his conscience. Begorra, if anyone says a word aginst him, they'll be answerin' for it to me.'

'I've never heard one, Mrs Jafferty,' Trapani assured her hastily.

'Sure an' it'd bring tears to the eyes of a potato to see them together, with himself waitin' on her hand an' foot, readin' to her or playin' cards with her or whativer she has a mind for, an' bringin' flowers from the garden ivery day.'

She squeezed herself cumbrously out from behind the little table, picked up a market bag that bulged as bountifully as her figure, and waddled across towards the Saint.

'An' why would you be askin' about them, sorr – if I may be so bold?'

'A friend of mine said I should look them up, if I happened to be around here,' Simon answered.

He had to think quickly, for this was a little sooner than he had expected to need a ready answer. And her eyes were very sharp and inquisitive.

'I'm on me way home now, sorr, with a bite for their dinner. If you'd be tellin' me the name, I could tell them what to look forward to.'

'This was a friend of Mr Clarron's former wife. He mightn't even remember her. A Mrs Brown.'

'From America, maybe? Mr Clarron's late wife was an American lady, they tell me.'

'Yes,' said the Saint gratefully. 'From New York.'

'And your name, sorr, in case you should be callin'?'

'This is Mr Templar, Mrs Jafferty,' Trapani said.

Simon gazed at him gloomily.

'I'll tell him you were askin',' Mrs Jafferty said. 'And good day to ye, gentlemen.'

She hitched up her bag of groceries and bustled busily out.

'I'm sorry,' Trapani said. 'Did I do wrong? You hadn't told me you wanted to be incognito.'

'Forget it,' said the Saint. 'I hadn't had a chance to. It's not your fault.'

He emptied his mug and put it down, and Trapani picked it up.

'Another? Or do you feel like some lunch?'

'Mr Templar is having lunch with me,' said the girl with the legs.

Simon Templar blinked. He turned, with a cigarette between his lips and his lighter halted in mid-air. Finally, he managed to light it.

'If you say so,' he murmured. 'And if Giulio will excuse me.'

'I excuse you and congratulate you,' Trapani beamed.

The girl drained her cocktail and came over, putting out her hand as the Saint stood up.

'I'm Adrienne Halberd,' she said.

'I'd never have recognised you.'

She laughed.

'That may take some explaining. But do you mind if I rush you off? I'm expecting a phone call at home, and I've got to get back for it.'

'I'll see you later,' Simon told Trapani.

She was on her way to the other door, and he followed her.

'I walked over,' she said as they came out in front of the hotel. 'But I expect you've got a car.'

'That rented job over there.'

They got in; and she said, pointing: 'That way, to the right, and I'll tell you where to turn.'

Simon spun the wheel and relaxed, letting cigarette smoke float from mildly amused lips.

'And now that we're alone,' he said calmly, 'may I ask any questions? Or do we go on playing blindfold chess?'

'All of a sudden? You didn't argue when I practically kidnapped you.'

'I never argue with legs like yours, darling. But sometimes I ask questions.'

'You *are* the Saint, aren't you?'

'True. But my mind-reading gifts have been slightly exaggerated.'

'You were asking about Reggie Clarron.'

'Which should prove that I didn't know much about him.'

'You knew he'd been married before.'

'An inspired guess. A fat friend of mine happened to tag the name "Bluebeard" on him, rather carelessly, just a few hours ago. Bluebeards, if you remember, don't get much of a rating with only one wife. It was worth taking a chance on.'

'All right,' she said. 'I took a chance on you. He's only had two so far, I think; but you might help to nail him before he finally manages to kill the third. Not to mention saving the prospective fourth.'

The Saint raised his eyebrows.

'He has one picked out already?'

'Me,' said the girl.

3

The dining alcove was one corner of the living-room of her cottage, sharing the row of gaily curtained windows that looked out over the green lawn that sloped down to the river bank. They sat there over some excellent cold roast beef and salad and mustard pickles, and the Saint sipped a tall glass of Guinness.

'He isn't a mystery man at all,' Adrienne Halberd said. 'That's what makes it so difficult.'

'One of those open-book boys?' said the Saint.

'Absolutely. He went to a good school, where he didn't get into any particular trouble. Then he became an actor. He never made any hit, but he managed to make a living. He didn't care much what he did, as long as it was something theatrical. He got married the first time when he was twenty-five. He and his wife were both in the chorus of some revue. Later on they joined up with one of those troupes that used to play on the piers at the seaside in the summer. He was about thirty when she got drowned in a boating accident.'

'Why did he wait that long?'

'It wasn't so long after she'd inherited some money from an uncle in Australia; and right on top of that they'd taken out mutual insurance policies.'

'So then he became a capitalist.'

'He still wasn't so awfully rich, but he moved up a notch. He helped to produce some shows in London, which were mostly flops. But he always got other people to invest with him, so his own money lasted longer than you'd think. He was getting a bit short, though, when he married his second wife.'

'The American?'

'Yes. That was after the War, when the tourists started coming over again. He married her, and they went to America together – after taking out insurance policies for each other. Six months later she was electrocuted. She was lying in the bath listening to a small radio, apparently, and it fell in.'

'Just doing his bit to improve Britain's dollar balance,' Simon remarked.

'Then it was the same story all over again – a night club, plays, a film company that never produced anything, and some other business schemes. Never anything crooked that you could put your finger on, except that his partners somehow always lost more money than he did. And about a year ago he married the present Mrs Clarron.'

'He sounds like a real cagey operator. At least, until that shooting accident misfired – if we should use the expression.'

She nodded.

'That was when the Southshire Insurance Company got very interested, as I told you. Being stuck three times in a row was a bit too much. Of course it *could* all be coincidence, but it had to be looked into.'

Simon regarded her appreciatively.

'They're not so stupid. I'd have taken a long time to spot you as a detective.'

'It's a new discovery,' she said spiritedly. 'They found out that investigators could do a lot more if they didn't look like investigators, and somebody told them that a woman with brains isn't obliged to look like a hippopotamus.'

He grinned.

'I must tell Teal that the same could apply to policemen,'

he said. 'What does he think about you butting in – or doesn't he know?'

'Oh, he knows all right, and he disapproves strongly. But there's nothing he can do about it. I told him that the insurance company stood to lose ten thousand pounds if Clarron managed to get away with killing another wife, and they couldn't afford to bet that much on Scotland Yard being smart enough to stop him.'

Simon chuckled aloud.

'I'm beginning to think of you as a soul-mate. But you still haven't told me how you visualise me in this set-up.'

'In rather the same way,' she said seriously. 'I know it'll sound ridiculous, but I've always been your wildest fan. I started reading about you in my teens, and idolising you in a silly way. I can't have altogether grown out of it. When I heard you asking about Clarron in Skindle's, and heard your name, it just hit me like a mad flash of inspiration. I'd give anything to get even with Teal for the patronising way he's talked to me, and I knew you'd sympathise with that, and besides, this case would be a great big feather in my cap. That is – if we could get together . . .'

The Saint finished his plate and leaned back. The tranquil glow that he felt was fuelled by more subtle calories than a good meal satisfyingly washed down. For his luck, it seemed, was as unchangingly blessed as ever. He had been in England only a few hours, and already the old merry-go-round was rolling at full throttle in his honour. A problem, a pretty girl, and Chief Inspector Teal to bedevil. What more had he ever asked? It was as if he had never been away.

'You just got yourself soul-hitched, darling,' he said. 'Now what's the music you think we might make together?'

'I've told you everything I know, for a start. But what do *you* know?'

'Not another thing. The worthy watchdogs of the Yard

undoubtedly spotted my name in a routine check for incoming undesirables, and Teal came huffing out to the airport to warn me to keep my nose clean. I knew that Teal had to be working on some case, even if he is retiring; and whatever it was, I figured I could do a memorable job of lousing it up for him.'

'You mean you didn't know about Clarron before?'

'Teal took it for granted that I did, and let out the name. Then I needled him some more, and he mentioned Maidenhead. That was plenty for me to start on.'

She stared at him with sober brown eyes, and bit her lip.

'That's rather disappointing.'

'I've done plenty with less, in my time,' he said cheerfully. 'But you're still holding something back. What was that about you being the next victim?'

'Oh. Yes. You see, I've got to know him quite well. He thinks I'm a young widow with money.'

'And that you might be available if only he were free?'

'That's right. That's why I talked the insurance company into letting me rent this cottage, to make it easy. It's right next door to his house.'

The Saint raised his eyebrows over the cigarette he was lighting.

He got up and stood at the window. Looking out at an angle, he still could not see the other house; and he recalled that when they arrived at the cottage he had not clearly seen an adjoining house, since the front of the cottage was well screened with trees; but at the back only a low hedge separated the lawns that went down to the river.

'I've done more than that,' Adrienne said. 'Once I got him over here, and pretended to be a bit tight, and more than hinted that when my imaginary husband was ill with pneumonia I'd helped to make sure that he didn't get over it.'

'The soul-mate approach again?'

'It was a trick I read about in a mystery story. But it didn't work on him. He's too – what did you call it? – cagey, even to fall for that.'

A man had come into sight on the next lawn, at first inspecting a stretch of hedge with the diagnostic eye of an amateur gardener, then turning and looking back over it towards the cottage. Then he walked down a little farther and came through an opening in it.

'We'd better hurry up and think of a new approach that includes me,' said the Saint. 'Lover Boy is coming to call.'

Mr Reginald Clarron's failure to achieve any notable success on the stage was only due, he would always be convinced, to the cloddish stupidity of the public. About his own outstanding talents he had no doubt whatsoever. Where lesser thespians played their parts for a couple of hours behind the footlights, he could sustain his for twenty-four hours a day, with no help from a script, and sell them to an audience that did not have to be pre-conditioned by the atmosphere of a theatre. He prided himself on having every flicker of expression and every inflection of voice under conscious control at every moment. It would be trite to observe that he would have made a formidable poker player; he already was.

He had a passably good-looking face without a single distinctive feature, but like a good showman he applied distinction to it with the full cut of his artistically long but carefully brushed grey hair and a pair of glasses with extra heavy black frames, so that a recognisable caricature might have been made of those two items along with no face shown at all. His figure, at least as far as it was ever displayed to the public, was most commendable for a man of fifty-five; and only a certain fleshiness around the chin betrayed a tendency to *embonpoint* which skilful tailoring was able to conceal elsewhere.

He had not batted an eyelid when he heard the name Templar, although instinct told him that there was only likely to be one Templar who might be making inquiries about him.

He still could not imagine how that Templar could have become interested in him, but he had read enough to believe that the Saint's nose for undetected crime verged on the supernatural. Nevertheless, he was not going to let himself be stampeded by the uncomfortable fact, which he believed was the main reason why less astute malfeasors had been the Saint's easy prey.

'I can't imagine what the man can be up to,' he told his wife boldly, for he was clever enough never to create complications for himself with lies or evasions that were not strictly necessary. 'I'm quite sure that poor Frances never mentioned a friend called Mrs Brown. The very name is an obvious subterfuge.'

'I do hope he isn't after my jewels,' Mrs Clarron said.

She touched the sapphire pendant that showed in the open neck of her bed-jacket, with fingers glittering with diamond and ruby rings. Except for being propped up on pillows, she looked as if she had been decorated for a grand entrance at a first night at the opera.

Mr Clarron pursed his lips.

'I don't want to alarm you, my love, but that's quite a possibility. I still wish you'd let me put them in a safe deposit for you. To keep fifty thousand pounds' worth of jewels in the house, these days, is simply asking for trouble.'

'Please don't start that all over again, dear,' she pleaded wanly. 'They're insured, aren't they? And since I can never go out and show them off again, wearing them for you is the only pleasure I've got left. I know you can't understand how a woman feels, but it does make me happy. And they *are* mine, after all.'

Mr Clarron stoically refrained from arguing. He had already devoted some of his best performances to that theme, without making any impression on her whimsical obduracy.

It had been somewhat of a shock to him when, shortly

after their marriage, he had discovered that the millionaire's baubles which she displayed so opulently were not complemented by any proportionate resources in the bank. Her late husband, who had catered to her obsession by showering precious stones on her like a sultan, had apparently mortgaged his business assets so improvidently to do it that after his death they had barely realised enough to pay the inheritance taxes. Not that her value in gems alone was anything to be sneezed at, but it was less than Mr Clarron had been counting on. And her fanatical refusal to let the jewels out of her own custody for a moment had made it plain that nothing but a third widowhood would show him an appreciable profit.

However, a recent brainstorm had shown him how her jewellery could be made to return a double dividend, and he was quite glad that the original accident he had planned for her had failed and left him the chance to improve on it.

'Very well, my dear,' he said. 'But if he should call here and I happen to be out, you must refuse to talk to him on any pretext.'

'I wouldn't dream of it. I'd be completely terrified. And I think you should warn the police about him at once.'

'Of course, I should have done that already,' he said.

Looking up from the garden at Adrienne Halberd's cottage, he was troubled by another consideration. He was forewarned that she had been in the bar at Skindle's when the Saint was asking about him, but he had no way of knowing what might have developed between them later. With unlimited confidence, he decided to take that bull also by the horns.

It was a blow under the belt when the girl admitted him at the back door and he instantly saw the lean bronzed man lounging on the couch under the window as if he owned it.

'I beg your pardon,' he said. 'I had no idea you had company.'

'Don't be silly, Reggie,' she insisted breezily. 'Come on in. We were just talking about you, anyway. This is Mr Templar. I picked him up at Skindle's. I heard him asking about you there, so we got talking.'

Mr Clarron's acting ability and stage presence still somehow stood by him.

'Mrs Jafferty told me,' he said, with absolute naturalness. 'But frankly, I just can't place that Mrs Brown you spoke of.'

'I'm not surprised,' said the Saint. 'I didn't mean to spring it on you quite so bluntly, but Mrs Brown was her sister. Mr Brown is better known to the FBI as Bingo Brown, the racket boss of Baltimore.'

'The Saint knows all the gangsters, of course,' Adrienne contributed blithely. 'He started telling me such fabulous stories about them, I just had to bring him home to hear more.'

'Indeed?' Mr Clarron's voice was impeccably distant. 'But in this case I'm sure he's mistaken. My late wife had no sister.'

'I didn't expect you'd have heard of her,' said the Saint. 'When she took up with Bingo, her family disowned her and agreed never to mention her name. But she was still very fond of your late wife, and ever since that odd accident she's been pestering Bingo to find out if you were a right guy. So when I happened to run into him just before I was leaving, he asked me to look you up. Of course it's absurd but—'

'I think you have put it in a nutshell, Mr Templar,' Clarron said icily. 'But if you want me to discuss this preposterous fabrication, I must do it another time.' He turned to the girl. 'I only dropped over, my dear, to ask if you would be home this evening. I have to run up to London on business, and won't get back until late; and it's Mrs Jafferty's night off. I know everything is all right, but I'd just feel happier to know that my wife could call you in an emergency.'

'Of course,' Adrienne said awkwardly.

'Thank you, my dear.'

Mr Clarron bowed to the Saint with courtly frigidity, and walked out without faltering.

He was immune to panic – the career of a successful Blue-beard calls for cold-blooded qualities that would scarcely be comprehensible to more temperamental murderers. But in much the same way as he had heard of the Saint, and perhaps less critically, he was well imbued with legends of the implac-able code of America's gangdom.

He still had not lost his head. He could conceive that the fantastic thing that the Saint had suggested might be true, without actually having to concede that it was. But that only meant that he must delay no longer about setting in motion a plan that he had already worked out to the ultimate detail – had, in fact, already prepared all the mechanical ground-work for.

If anything, the Saint's inexplicable and unforeseeable intrusion might even be woven in to its advantage, by such an uncommon genius as his.

He had realised this with an almost divine supra-conscious-ness while Adrienne Halberd was still introducing the Saint, and had spoken the essential words without even thinking about them, impelled by nothing but his own infallible instinct.

Mr Reginald Clarron walked back up the lawn to his own house without the slightest misgiving, concerned solely with the rather tiresome minutiae of killing his third wife that night.

5

Although the longest run of any play which Mr Clarron had helped to produce had been four weeks, he could legitimately claim to be a West End producer, and as such he received a continual stream of plays for consideration. The cream of the crop, of course, went first to other producers with a more encouraging record of hits; but Mr Clarron read all that came to him, always on the look-out for anything good enough for a promotion from which he at least would benefit, and always dreaming that some day something would fall into his hands of which he would be the first to see the potentialities, which would rocket him to wealth and prestige overnight.

From the manuscripts on his desk he selected the one which had lately impressed him the most, and telephoned the author who lived in London.

'I really think we might do something with your play, my boy,' he said. 'I'd like to discuss just a few minor revisions with you. I don't get to town very often, but I have to run up this afternoon. Could you manage to have dinner with me? ... Fine! Let's make it rather early – I don't want to be away from home too long.'

Then he called his dentist, complained of a maddening toothache, and persuaded the man to squeeze him in for a few minutes at the end of the day.

Thus he consolidated his reason for leaving his wife alone on what had already been announced as Mrs Jafferty's evening off. If the dentist could find nothing wrong with his teeth, the pain could always be attributed to neuralgia.

To his wife he said: 'Since I have to make the trip, confound it, I really ought to see the fellow who wrote that play we read last week. I was just talking to him on the phone, and he told me that one of Rank's men is very excited about it. I'd hate to let it get away, with the picture rights half sold already.'

'Of course, dear,' she said. 'I'll be perfectly all right, if you'll fix my table for me like you've done before.'

'No one ever had such a wonderful wife and deserved it less,' he said, with considerable truth.

The table was a piece of hospital furniture, built like a travelling bridge and high enough to span the bed. A system of ropes and pulleys which he had rigged up enabled her to pull it up to her or push it away as she wished.

From the kitchen he brought up linen and silver, china and glass, bread and butter, sugar and cream, a bowl of strawberries, a decanter of wine, an electric coffee-pot, and an electric chafing dish of Irish stew which she would only have to plug in and heat when she was ready.

Into the stew he had thoroughly stirred a certain tasteless drug which is much too easily obtainable to be freely mentioned in this connection, which in sufficient quantity induces profound sleep in about half an hour and death shortly afterwards. Taking no chances on a capricious appetite, Mr Clarron had used enough to put away four people.

'It smells heavenly,' he said, lifting the lid and sniffing. 'But I kept some back for my lunch tomorrow, so you needn't try to save any for me.'

He made sure that the television set was in the right position for her to watch from the bed – it had a remote control that she could operate from the night-stand – made sure that all was in order with the devices that would make it unnecessary for her to be taken to the bathroom, saw that her books and magazines were within easy reach, checked the table again, fluffed up her pillows, and said: 'Is there anything else you might possibly need, my love?'

'Nothing,' she said. 'Just hurry back and spoil me some more.'

Mr Clarron kissed her tenderly on the forehead. He felt pretty good himself. He was giving her the most humane death he could think of, even more peaceful than the lightning extinction of her predecessor. He was glad that he was not callous enough to hurt women. Only his first wife could really have suffered at all in her passing; but he had been quite an amateur then.

He was in the best of spirits when the young playwright met him at his club.

'The Irish stew is very good tonight, sir,' said the dining-room steward.

It seemed almost like an omen.

'My favourite dinner, and I thought I was going to miss it. Not that it could be half as good as Mrs Jafferty's – our housekeeper,' Mr Clarron explained to his guest. 'She makes the best you ever tasted. Of course, she would. Irish as Paddy's pig, but a marvellous old biddy. They don't make 'em like that any more these days.'

'How long have you had this treasure?' asked the young man perfunctorily.

'Only three weeks – and believe me, my boy, I sleep with my fingers crossed. We've had a bad time with servants. My wife being an invalid makes it specially difficult, it's bound to make extra work. But Mrs Jafferty never complains. And to think that I came near not hiring her at all.'

'Really?' said his guest politely.

'I got her through an agency, you see, but she didn't have any references. I mean, nothing that I could actually verify. She'd been in her last job for more than twenty years, but then the people had gone off to live in New Zealand and she didn't want to leave England. She had a glowing letter of recommendation, but of course those can be faked. And even the place where she'd been staying since then, she'd only had a room there for a few days, and she'd been out all the time looking for jobs, so they knew nothing about her. I have to be extra careful, you know, because my wife insists on keeping all her jewels in the house.'

'A bit risky, isn't it?' said the other, stifling a yawn.

'It wasn't an easy decision to make. But we were getting quite desperate, and if she was as good as the letter said I was afraid of losing her to somebody else while I was waiting for a reply from her last employers in New Zealand. So I decided to take the gamble. And I must say she seems to be honest to the last halfpenny. I let her do all the shopping, and our bills are the smallest they've ever been . . . By George, though,' Mr Clarron said with a sudden frown, 'a suspicious character did turn up in Maidenhead today, asking where I lived. Wouldn't it be frightful if they were . . . ? Oh, but that's too far-fetched. But I wish I hadn't thought of it just now.'

'Talking of suspicious characters,' said the playwright, straw-clutching feverishly, 'what did you think of the old man who comes to the door at the beginning of my second act? I've wondered if it would be more effective to keep him off the stage a bit longer, to build up the suspense.'

Mr Clarron nodded attentively, and thereafter confined himself admirably to the subject of their meeting. He had sounded most convincing, he thought, in his rehearsal.

He enjoyed his Irish stew. At any moment, he estimated, his wife would be eating hers.

6

'I don't like it,' Adrienne Halberd said abruptly.

'Now that you've told me about those jewels of Mrs Clarron's, I like it a bit less myself,' Simon admitted. 'It just might occur to Lover Boy now to improvise a burglary in which she gets bumped off, and try to make it look like my work.'

Her pixie face was almost sullen with concentration.

'I expect you could take care of yourself. I'm talking about that story you cooked up, about some gangster called Bingo Brown being married to his last wife's black sheep sister, and you being a friend of theirs.'

'It was the best I could do in the few seconds we had.'

'But don't you see, it might panic him into doing something drastic in a hurry, in the hope of getting away with his loot before you do something to him.'

'That was roughly what I had in mind.'

'But that would be *helping* to get another wife murdered!'

'When you hinted to him that you'd at least half killed a husband,' Simon said, 'mightn't that just as well have encouraged him to widow himself, knowing you wouldn't hold it against him?'

'All I hoped was that it might make him *talk* about it. And then, with a tape recorder—'

'Oh, I know. Just like in a detective story. But maybe he's read stories too. It might just as well have only encouraged him to get the job over without talking.'

She stared at him resentfully.

'Well, if you're so smart, how else can you get evidence against his kind of murderer?'

'It isn't easy, darling. You can only stick close to him and hope that you're close enough when he tries it again.'

'But you can't use a human being like – like a sort of live bait!'

'Mrs Clarron isn't in much more danger, by and large, than she's been all along. Maybe Reggie is a bit more anxious to get it over; but on the other hand there are now two of us keeping an eye on her. We saw Reggie drive away. I've been sitting by this open window ever since, and I have ears like a watchdog. When Reggie or anyone else comes near that house, I'll know it.'

'But you can't stay here all night.'

'I can think of worse fates.'

'You might think of some better dialogue.'

'I'm here now,' he said practically. 'And I'll stay for dinner, if I'm invited.'

She stood up and paced restlessly.

'Oh, you can stay. I think you'd better. I've got some chops in the Frig.'

'And some more beer?'

'You've just drunk the last I had.'

He got up and stretched himself.

'It sounds like a thirsty vigil. While you're toiling over a hot stove, suppose I run out and buy some more. I'm about out of cigarettes too, anyway.'

She hesitated an instant.

'No, I'll go,' she said. 'I'd rather you stayed here. If anything violent did start to happen next door, I think you'd be more use than I would. But only for brawn, I mean!'

He thought that over for as brief a moment, his quizzical eyes on her; and then he shrugged.

'Okay, Brains,' he said good-humouredly. 'Would you like to take my car?'

'I've got my own, thanks. I'll throw on a skirt and be back in a minute.'

It was, of course, easily fifteen minutes before she drove into the tiny garage again, and already she had seen that the Saint's hired car was no longer outside the cottage.

Even so, she tried frantically to believe for a fraction longer that he might only have moved his car up the road to a less conspicuous place, to make a returning Clarron believe that he had left. She ran into the cottage calling his name, but the empty rooms had no answer.

There was a note stuck on the refrigerator door.

Decided I might only mess things up for you after all, so I pushed off. Thanks, apologies, and good luck.

The signature was a little stick figure with a rakishly-tilted halo.

She ran out into the dusk, almost calling his name again. But the only response, she knew, would have been the faint sounds she heard of a radio or television programme playing in the house next door. She looked back and up from farther down her lawn, and saw the light shining blankly and steadily against the ceiling of an upstairs bedroom window. She rushed back into her cottage and flung herself at the telephone.

7

Mr Reginald Clarron got off the train at Maidenhead at
10.12 p.m., exchanged greetings and a few trivial words
about his trip with the station master, climbed into the car he
had parked at the station, and drove home at his normal
sedate speed.

He noticed that the strange car which must have been the
Saint's was no longer outside the cottage next door, and
thought that his auspices might be even better than he had
hoped.

As he unlocked his front door – he was glad he would be
spared the necessity of faking a burglarious entrance, with all
its possible pitfalls, for of course he had let it be known that
Mrs Jafferty had a key – he heard the inexorable voice of a
BBC announcer holding forth from the receiver upstairs.

Exactly as he would have done on any similar normal
evening, Mr Clarron took pains to hang up his hat in the hall,
stick his superfluous umbrella in the stand under it, pull off
his gloves and lay them in the calling-card tray. He would not
be so foolish as to omit one iota of his habitual routine. He
even went into the kitchen, drew himself a glass of water, and
drank it, as he always did before he went to bed.

Then he tiptoed up the stairs and softly opened the door
of his wife's bedroom.

The television set was still on, and so was the bedside light,
but his wife seemed to be asleep. She lay on her stomach with
her face buried in the pillows.

'My love,' Mr Clarron said loudly.

She did not stir.

The table was pushed down towards the foot of the bed. A glance verified that she had eaten and drunk the wine, although the bowl of strawberries had scarcely been touched and the coffee-cup was two-thirds full. Using his handkerchief, he lifted the lid of the chafing dish and saw that it had almost been emptied. He put the lid back and returned to the head of the bed.

'My dearest,' he said, and pulled on her shoulder as if to turn her over.

Her weight resisted him with a curious heaviness; and when he let go she fell back limply, without a sound.

Mr Clarron suddenly became a whirlwind of activity, for at this point any lapse of more than a few seconds might have to be accounted for.

He hustled out of the room, across the landing, and into his own bedroom. In the top drawer of his dressing-table lay a clean pair of white cotton gloves. As he picked them up and rapidly pulled them on, there was disclosed underneath them a light claw-ended crowbar of the type used for opening small crates – which Mrs Jafferty had purchased a week ago at the local ironmonger's in the course of her household errands. Mr Clarron hurried back with it to his wife's bedside.

Her jewels were kept in the top drawer of the bedside table, where she could easily reach them. As a concession to his concern for their safety she had had a combination lock put on it and made a coy secret of the combination, even though he had tried to point out that the drawer was still no stronger than the wood it was made of. He proved this in a matter of seconds with a couple of quick leverings with his crowbar, splintering the front of the drawer out with a pleasantly surprising minimum of noise.

He pulled out her jewel case, opened it on top of the night stand, and rapidly transferred its contents to his pockets. He let the crowbar lie on the floor where it had fallen. He leaned over his wife, unfastened the clasp at the back of her neck, and pulled the necklace and its sapphire pendant from under her. He picked up her hand to twist the rings off her fingers . . .

He did not know precisely what stopped him, whether it was a movement glimpsed out of the corner of his eye or the faint squeak and stir of air that went with it. But he turned his head, and with that became frozen.

The door of a massive old wardrobe across the room was swinging stealthily open.

The door itself cut off the light of the bedside lamp from what was inside. But the shadowed opening was still not too dark for him to see, and recognise, the bulgingly bovine shape of Mrs Jafferty, the unmistakable mound of her atrociously carrot-tinted hair.

Mr Clarron's intestines seemed to turn into coils of quivering lead, and his lungs sagged through his diaphragm and took all his breath with them. A draught from the North Pole squirmed over his skin and brought out beads of clammy sweat where it touched.

'Faith an' begorra,' said the broadest brogue outside Killarney, 'if it isn't himself robbin' the trinkets from his poor darlin' wife, and her not yet cold from his poison an' all!'

There was a breaking point even to Mr Clarron's adamantine self-control. He turned and ran out of the room, screaming.

He had no idea where he was going or what he was going to do. He stumbled down the stairs, in a pure frenzy of planless flight, flight for its own primitive sake, spurred by the unreasoning need to get away anywhere from the impossible incomprehensible thing that he had seen. Out of the house, anywhere, where he could have one moment's reprieve to encompass the exploding debris of disaster, to try and grab the pieces together and re-shape them into some form that would magically ward off utter catastrophe . . .

He threw open the front door and plunged solidly into the comfortably cushioned façade of Chief Inspector Claud Eustace Teal.

Mr Teal said '*Oof!*' – caught him as he bounced off, and set him upright in the hall.

'What's the matter, Mr Clarron?' Teal asked drowsily.

As his torpid bulk evacuated the doorway, it revealed two uniformed men on the step outside.

'My wife,' Clarron babbled. 'Dead in her bed! Drawer broken open – her jewels gone! And Mrs Jafferty—'

He broke off there. The first words had come out, incoherently enough, but unhesitatingly, with a kind of reflex assurance made glib by the number of times he had mentally rehearsed just such a speech. But after he had blurted out Mrs Jafferty's name he did not know how to go on. He had never visualised having to say anything about her in her presence.

Mr Teal, however, did not seem to notice the aposiopesis. He was staring over Mr Clarron's shoulder, and upwards, with his baby-blue eyes dilating in a most peculiar manner.

'Bejabers,' trumpeted a voice of distilled shamrock, 'and if it isn't me ould friend the fat boy of Scotland Yard, himself, arrivin' late for the wake as usual.'

Mr Clarron turned, drawn by an awful but irresistible magnetism.

Billowing down the stairs came an exuberant female figure crowned with a bird's-nest of hideous ginger hair.

'She must have done it,' Clarron chattered hysterically. 'I should never have taken her without references. She was hiding up there—'

'Sure, and is that any way for a gentleman to be talkin',

tryin' to put the blame on an honest workin' woman? And himself all the time schemin' to murdher his own wife, the poor soul, an' run off with his fancy lady next door, who I see sneakin' in here already to be with him before the body is cold!'

Teal glanced back for a moment, at Adrienne Halberd who was sidling in behind the two constables; and turned back to the staircase with a tingle of purple creeping into his rubicund complexion.

'Take off that ridiculous get-up, Saint,' he roared, 'and let's hear what you think you're up to!'

'Well, if you insist,' said the Saint meekly. 'But I was just starting to get the feel of the part.'

He unbuttoned the old-fashioned black dress, peeled it off, and draped it over the stair rail. Underneath it he wore a kind of upholstered combination garment extending down to his knees and padded in all the necessary places to produce Mrs Jafferty's voluptuous contours. He took that off and hung it similarly over the rail, where it slid down to join the dress. Completing his descent of the stairs, he removed the orange-coloured wig and set it carefully on the banister knob at the bottom.

'It's Templar!' croaked Mr Clarron. And for one delirious instant he felt inspired, invulnerable. 'He did it in that disguise! He was with Mrs Halberd this afternoon when I said I was going to London. She's probably his accomplice—'

'*Miss* Halberd,' Teal said precisely, 'is a police officer, acting under my orders.'

'As it eventually dawned on me,' said the Saint. 'And there never was a Mrs Jafferty, except when Reginald dressed-up in that outfit. Instead of trying to dream up the perfect alibi, which has tripped up a lot of bright lads, he dreamed up the perfect scapegoat. And before he has any more attacks of genius, and before I budge from here, I wish someone would go through his pockets, where they'll find Mrs Clarron's jewels. And if he has anything to say after that, ask him why he's wearing those white cotton gloves.'

8

'What do you mean, it eventually dawned on you that I was with the police?' Adrienne Halberd demanded sulkily.

Simon lighted a cigarette.

'The way you picked me up at Skindle's was rather determined,' he said. 'But I could swallow that temporarily. When you told me you were investigating for an insurance company I could take that for a while too. There are such things as female private eyes, even if they aren't very often eyefuls. And when you said you'd been a distant adorer of mine since you were in pigtails, it was piling it up a bit tall, but I could still open my mouth that wide. Weird as it may seem, I have met such crazy gals. But with all that build-up, you'd set yourself a lot to live up to. And soon after you found out that I hadn't any information to add to what you'd told me, or any definite plan to let you in on, you changed quite startlingly. Gone was the worshipping bug-eyed fan. You became impatient, critical – even caustic. You couldn't see any merit at all in the idea that I ad-libbed on two seconds' notice when Reggie started to amble over. And it wasn't such a bad one, either. But it made you almost rude.'

'If I remember,' she said, 'you weren't such a paragon—'

'But I wasn't trying to sell anything, darling. You had been. And the transformation was just too sudden. A real fan would have thought anything I suggested was marvellous, no matter how screwy or dangerous it sounded. And then I realised something else. This was Claud Eustace's last big case, and he'd warned me to keep out of it, but I told him I intended to stick my nose in anyway. Yet I came straight to Maidenhead, and none of the local constabulary was around to meet me and back up Teal's orders. More surprising still, there wasn't even a vestige of a cop anywhere around here, keeping tabs on Reggie or trying to save Mrs Clarron from being bumped off. So at last I connected. The cop had to be you. Teal had plenty of time to phone you while I was driving down from London Airport, tell you I was headed for Skindle's, tell you to pick me up there, rope me, keep me handy. The explanation you had to hatch up between you wasn't so hard to invent; but I could almost hear the wheels whirring in Teal's fat head, and see his buttons popping with pride at his own brilliance.'

Chief Inspector Teal thumbed open a tiny envelope of spearmint and mailed the contents in his mouth.

'All right,' he said trenchantly. 'But what happened after Miss Halberd left you at her cottage?'

'After she left me to phone you for more advice,' said the Saint smoothly, 'I went over those random hunches again and convinced myself. Then I knew I wouldn't have much more time to work on my own, and I really was seriously worried about what my appearance and my story might rush Reggie into doing. And I decided I just had to see if I couldn't find a clue in his house – which you couldn't have tried without a search-warrant. You know my methods, Claud. Impulsive. So I picked up the phone and called Mrs Clarron, and said I was the local police.'

'Falsely representing yourself to be a police officer,' barked Teal.

'For which I might easily get fined a few pounds,' said the Saint sadly. 'I said that Mr Clarron had asked us to keep an eye on her on account of a suspicious character in the neighbourhood; and it was really a break when she wasn't a bit surprised. Reggie had warned her about the Saint. So I asked if we might send a man over to make sure that everything was all right. She said yes, but she couldn't let him in. I said that was all right, Mr Clarron had left us a key. I moved my car up the road, walked back, and jiggered the lock, which is a very easy one.'

'He broke in,' jabbered Mr Clarron forlornly. 'He admits it!'

It was not a very effective effort, considering the heap of jewels from his pockets which one of the constables was laboriously inventorying while the other counted them on to an outspread handkerchief; and Teal glanced at him almost pityingly.

'I told her I wanted to check all the windows,' Simon went on, 'which gave me an excuse to roam through the house. I didn't have to roam far. In Reggie's bedroom, the first thing that caught my eye was a typical old theatrical trunk. I opened the lid; and right on top was this wig, and underneath it those dowager-size falsies.'

He paused for a dramatic moment which he could not deny himself, releasing a leisured streamer of smoke.

'It was all clear in a bolt of lightning. There was no mistaking that hair – I'd seen Mrs Jafferty at the pub, as Adrienne can tell you. And she'd told me that he was an actor, and once played with a sort of minstrel troupe. And I could see Reggie's face as I'd met him this afternoon, and of course it was Mrs Jafferty's, with the powder and rouge and lipstick off and those horn-rimmed glasses added. And I remembered that in those old music-hall skits with a comic charwoman, which Mrs Jafferty had reminded me of nothing else but, the part was nearly always played by a man.'

'Go on.'

'What a wonderful gag, Claud! He passes himself off as his own housekeeper, and creates an identity that a dozen tradesmen and villagers will vouch for – only telling his wife that he can't find anyone and he's doing all the housework himself. Being confined to her bed, she never saw him go out or come in in that costume; and they never had visitors. So when she's found dead, and her jewels are stolen, and Mrs Jafferty has disappeared, it's so obvious that he doesn't need much of an alibi. The beetle brains of the C.I.D. are so busy combing the country for Mrs Jafferty that they'd never think of anything else.'

'But what did you *do*?' Teal almost howled.

'I didn't stop there. In the top drawer of his dresser I found those gloves he had on, and a small crowbar which is now on the floor of his wife's bedroom where he used it to jimmy her jewel drawer. No doubt someone would swear Mrs Jafferty bought it. I went to the maid's room. There were a few clothes and personal articles which a woman like that would have – he was that thorough. And I also found this, which you can bet Mrs Jafferty bought from the local chemist.'

He produced a small dark bottle from his pocket and handed it over.

'Believe me, Claud, that was a jolt. I'd hoped to goose him into something rash, but it was meant to be something that I could move in fast and prevent – like perhaps a clonk on the head with that crowbar. And now I was certain that this was the night, with him going to London and Mrs Jafferty supposedly out. But poison . . .'

Adrienne Halberd was reading the label on the bottle over Teal's shoulder, and her face had gone white.

'She had a lovely plate of Irish stew,' said the Saint remorselessly. 'I said, just to clinch it: "I bet your cook is an Irish woman." "Oh, no," she said, "we haven't been able to get a cook for weeks. My husband has to do everything, but he does it so well—" '

A sort of inarticulate sob came from the talented husband;

and Mr Teal somewhat belatedly remembered an official obligation.

'Mr Clarron,' he said formally, 'it's my duty to warn you that anything you say will be taken down and may be used in evidence. Now, did you wish to make any statement?'

'I did it,' Clarron said hopelessly. 'Everything. Just as he said.'

Teal nodded to the constable with the note-book.

'And the one before?'

'Yes. I knocked the radio into her bath.'

'What about the first one – the one who was drowned?'

'I killed her too,' Clarron said with his head in his hands. 'I upset the boat and held her under.'

Suddenly the girl thrust herself between them.

'You idiots, all of you!' she cried insubordinately. 'We might still save this one. We should be getting a doctor—'

'Don't waste his time,' said the Saint. 'I tried to break it all to Mrs Clarron, but it was tough going. As you can imagine. She got quite hysterical at one stage; but luckily there was quite a hysterical play on television at the same time, so nobody outside would have noticed much. But at least she lost all her appetite. I took advantage of that to arrange the table as if she'd been eating, and put most of the stew, the wine, and the coffee in other containers, which you can take for analysis if you need it. I got her half convinced, but I knew she was in no condition to play dead when Reggie came in, even if I could have talked her into trying; and she had to do that if he was to book himself all the way to the gallows. So when I heard his key in the lock, I just gave her a little judo tap on the neck.' Simon smiled apologetically. 'She should wake up any minute now, and all she'll need is an aspirin and a good dinner.'

As if on cue, a dull moan reached them from the floor above; and Adrienne ran up the stairs.

9

It was somewhat later when Teal, Simon, and the girl wound up back at the cottage next door.

The uniformed men had taken Mr Clarron away, and a nurse had arrived to take charge of his wife. Mrs Clarron had refused to let a doctor be called in with sedatives, but she was quietly and methodically getting drunk, which would eventually have a similar effect. The Saint couldn't blame her.

'That's the one ugly thing left,' he said. 'She's still got to live with the results of Reginald's first attempt. And I'll always wonder if it wouldn't have been kinder to let her eat that stew.'

'Perhaps you won't have to,' Adrienne said. 'She told me that the specialists had been talking about another operation that might fix her up.'

The Saint's eyes lightened.

'Then maybe it's not so indecent to celebrate after all. And some celebration certainly seems called for. I suppose you did bring some beer when you thought I'd be waiting when you came back, and Claud and I should drink a parting toast.'

'You're forgetting,' Teal said stodgily. 'I don't drink. Fat men didn't ought to drink.'

Adrienne made him a cup of tea.

'The one thing that puzzles me,' Simon said, 'is why you took so long to show up at Clarron's, Claud, after I disappeared from here. Or, put it another way, how you were on his doorstep at the ideal moment.'

'After you left London Airport,' Teal said reluctantly, 'I came down to the Maidenhead police station and waited for Miss Halberd to get in touch with me. When she reported that Clarron had gone to London, I had a man watch the railway station to let us know when he came back. Then she phoned and told me you'd left, and I hoped you meant it. I came over and joined her here. We were informed as soon as Clarron got off the train, and we started watching his house. I was afraid he might try something desperate soon, after the scare you'd given him, and I could only hope we'd be able to prevent it. As soon as he started screaming, we rushed over.'

'But you hadn't spotted that Mrs Jafferty was purely fictitious.'

'Not yet.'

'And if I hadn't been there, you still wouldn't have been in time to save Mrs Clarron's life.'

'We might have been able to get her to a hospital in time.'

'You wouldn't. But even if you had, you'd only have been looking for Mrs Jafferty. And even if you'd discovered that she was a phony, you could only have convicted Reginald of attempted murder. It took the fright I threw into him to make him confess everything.'

'That's probably true,' Teal said grudgingly. 'But it still doesn't excuse your interfering and taking the law into your own hands.' His voice rose a little. 'And one of these days—'

'Now you're forgetting,' Simon reminded him gently. 'There aren't going to be any more of these days for you. You're retiring, and you'll only read about me in the papers.'

Chief Inspector Teal swallowed.

He looked ahead into a vague Elysian vista in which there were no problems, no apprehensions – and no taunting privateer with unquenchable devilment in his eyes and an impudent forefinger pointing like a rapier at his stomach. It would be very restful; and there would be something lacking.

'That's right,' said Mr Teal. 'I was forgetting.'

He hauled himself sluggishly to his feet, and put out his hand; and for almost the first time in all those years Simon saw something very like a smile on his round pink apoplectic face.

'I'm rather glad it ends up this way,' Teal said. He glanced self-consciously around him. 'But I've still got work to do tonight. And I think Miss Halberd has some apologising to do which she might rather do in private. The rent's paid on this cottage to the end of the month,' he added inconsequently. 'So if you'll excuse me—'

'Damn it, Claud Eustace,' said the Saint, 'I'm going to miss you too.'

The Reluctant Nudist

INTRODUCTION BY LESLIE CHARTERIS*

The narrative calendar now jumps some twenty-three years to a summer in the south of France, when I learned that the Ile du Levant, just a few miles across from the resort where I was staying, was inhabited by nudists – or, as they prefer to be called, naturists. But more than that, and especially intriguing, was the fact that it was not a 'colony' or a club, but simply a public place where nudity was officially tolerated by local ordinance. You didn't have to be introduced or join anything, you just paid your fare and went over on the regular ferry, you didn't even have to take any clothes off if you didn't want to, but you would have no legal complaint if you were shocked by anything you saw.

The friend who has appeared in many Saint stories under the name of Monty Hayward was vacationing at the same hotel, and he had never seen anything like that, but he professed to be sturdily unshockable and highly curious, so we went over together to have a look.

Again it was a rare and illuminating experience, and a useful addition to our anecdotage; although before we had been on the beach very long we were as naked as the most devoted (as proved by their area of suntan) habitués. The habitués, obviously, had developed an imperviousness to the stares of the voyeurs, who were undoubtedly numerous; but

* From 'Instead of the Saint – V', *The Saint Mystery Magazine* (USA), April 1965

just because of this we both felt a sort of moral compulsion to disassociate ourselves at least in costume from the more conspicuous peeping Toms.

I did not then and have not since become a convert to the faith of Nudism. What this confession leads up to is only that out of the exploratory trip with Monty emerged, eventually, a Saint story titled 'The Reluctant Nudist', which was first published in the *Saint* magazine and subsequently in the collection *The Saint around the World*.

As I have often asserted, I have written very few stories which were not documented by my own personal researches, in pursuit of which authenticity I have never spared myself any peril or hardship . . .

I

'When do you start taking your clothes off?' Simon Templar asked, with a faint hint of malice. George McGeorge wriggled unhappily inside his pastel-blue silk shirt and sharply-creased slacks. Between the crown of his stylish Panama and the soles of his immaculate suède shoes, he was almost conspicuously a young man to whom the ministrations of tailor and haberdasher were more than ordinarily important. His rather vapidly good-looking face took on a tinge of pink under its urban pallor.

'Not before everyone else does, anyway,' he said.

'Never mind about anyone else,' Simon persisted. 'I think it would give Uncle Waldo a big glow to see that you were entering into the spirit of the thing right from the start.'

'In that case, he'd be still more bucked if I could introduce you in your birthday suit too, and tell him that I'd even made another convert on the way over.'

'That wasn't in the deal, George. I offered to come with you as moral support and as an interested observer – not as a sort of trophy. And because it sounded like one of the few places left in the world where I could feel reasonably sure of not getting mixed up in some sort of crime. I'm banking on the idea that nudists couldn't carry around much stuff worth stealing, and that murder is a lot more difficult where it would be such a problem to conceal a weapon.'

'The closer I get to it,' Mr McGeorge said darkly, 'the more I wish one of 'em would strangle Uncle Waldo.'

The Saint grinned, and gazed with tranquil anticipation at the islands spread before the bows of the little ferry. There were three of them to be seen, the fourth member of the group being just below the western horizon; reading from right to left he could identify, from an earlier glance at a map, the small hump of Bagaud, the much larger bulk of Port-Cros, and finally, the longest and most easterly, the Ile du Levant, which was their destination. Lying in a corner of the Mediterranean which is still virtually *terra incognita* to the American tourist army, whose Riviera extends no farther west than the outskirts of Cannes, they are known to prosy official cartographers as the Iles d'Hyères, but to the more flowery-minded authors of travel brochures as the Golden Isles; while one of them, to a still more specialised public, stands for the closest approximation to the Garden of Eden to be found within the borders of civilisation.

For this island of about six miles in length and roughly a mile and a quarter in average width, which is separated by only nine miles of water from the unglamorised but busy little Provençal resort of Le Lavandou, is the beneficiary of an official dispensation which remains unique among the local ordinances of Europe.

'You see,' Mr McGeorge had explained it, 'over there it's perfectly legal for anyone – I mean women as well as men – to go around in a sort of triangular fig-leaf effect, and nothing else.'

This happened at the bar of the Club at Cavalière, the most exclusive hostelry on that stretch of the coast, where they had drifted into one of those usually sterile bar-stool conversations to which this was to prove a notable exception.

'Oh,' said the Saint. 'A kind of semi-nudist colony.'

'Not even semi,' the other said. 'That's only in the village. When they go swimming, they're allowed to take *everything* off. And the point is, it isn't a colony or a club. It isn't private property, and you don't have to belong to anything or join anything. Anybody can go there. And you don't even have to take off your hat if you don't want to. It's just that there's no law against taking off practically everything if you like – and from the pictures I've seen, most of them seem to like.'

'Zat is right.' Raymond Vidal, proprietor and host of the Club, who had been listening, chimed in with genially expansive corroboration. 'It was about nineteen 'undred twenty, zat two docteurs from Paris, name Durville, very serious men, wish to bring people to be cured by ze sun, and zey start to make ze village which zey call Héliopolis. And so zat za patient can get ze most sun wiz ze least clozing, zey arrange a *tolérance* from ze Commune of Hyères so zat no one 'as to wear more zan ze *slip minimum*. But it is all quite open. It is very beautiful, very natural. You should go zaire and see it.'

'I have to go there,' said Mr McGeorge, with no echo of enthusiasm, 'to see my uncle.'

He looked like a young man who should have an uncle – preferably one with a considerable fortune, a strong sense of family responsibility, and no wife or offspring of his own. Without some such source of bounty, one would only have felt sorry about his prospects in a callously competitive world. He was the first specimen that Simon had encountered in many years of a type that he had thought was virtually extinct – the spoiled butterfly of good family, a good education which had left no mark on anything but his accent, of ingenuous snobbery, impeccable manners, cultivated indolence, a gift for fairly amusing and decorative frivolity, and absolutely no conception of a world which did not revolve around the smartest clubs, the most fashionable resorts, and the most glittering parties. How he had ever managed to navigate himself that far from the languid eddies of the Croisette and the Cap d'Antibes was already a mystery;

and that such a creature could have a personal link, however tenuous, with a place like the Ile du Levant, was an anomaly that no inveterate student of oddities could casually pass by.

The Saint signed to the bartender for some more Peter Dawson.

'Tell me about this uncle,' he begged, with fascinated sympathy.

'He lives there,' said McGeorge, in the same tone in which he might have admitted that his uncle was addicted to cheating at cards.

Mr Waldo Oddington, Simon learned, patiently probing for information as he would have extracted morsels of succulence from the shell of a cracked crab, was the brother of McGeorge's mother, and by this time McGeorge's only surviving kin. Brother and sister had been deeply attached to each other, in spite of Mr Oddington's lifelong record of eccentricities, and one of the late Mrs McGeorge's last injunctions to her son had been that he should never forget that blood was thicker than water, and that in his veins the Oddington strain of fluid was a full fifty per cent represented. George McGeorge had dutifully tried to live up to this, encouraging his uncle to regard him almost as the son which Mr Oddington, a bachelor, had never begotten for himself; although one gathered that this had been no easy task for a young man of Mr McGeorge's highly developed respect for certain conventions.

'He's spent his life getting one bee after another in his bonnet. About the first time I can remember him visiting us, when I was a kid, he insisted on having the bed taken out of his room and sleeping on the floor. Said it was the only way to have a healthy backbone. He thought it was disgraceful that Mother was letting me sleep on a mattress and ruin my spine. Another time he had a theory that expectant mothers would have a much easier time if they went around for the last few months on all fours. He got in a bit of trouble when he started telling this to perfectly strange women that he saw in the street. He's had a fling at vegetarianism, theosophy, yoga, folk-dancing, and trying to live in a tree. Of course, he started going to nudist camps years ago. Then he finally heard about this Ile du Levant. Naturally he had to go and see it; and he's been living there ever since. At last he's found the one place where he can lead what he calls a normal civilised life and never needs to put any clothes on even to go out and buy a stamp. That would be fine as far as I'm concerned, if only he hadn't asked me to visit him.'

'Do you have to go?'

'I've put it off as long as I can, but I can't make it so obvious that I'd hurt the old codger's feelings.'

Simon could well understand that the feelings of a certain ass of old codger are customarily treated with the utmost consideration. Not letting it sound too obvious, he remarked: 'At least it sounds like a nice inexpensive fad. Or wouldn't that make any difference?'

'Well, he doesn't have to worry too much about money.' McGeorge seemed a little embarrassed and anxious to change that subject. 'But lately his letters have been full of some French girl who appears to be living with him, and I've wondered if she's thinking of hitching on to a good thing.'

'It couldn't be love, could it?'

'It could be, I suppose. But he's over sixty and she's only twenty-five.'

'I wouldn't think a guy like that could be sold on anything so conventional as marriage.'

'I know! Free Love was another thing that he used to be steamed up about. But you never can tell,' Mr McGeorge said pessimistically. 'Anyhow, that's another reason why I thought I'd better go and looks things over.'

Simon needed no diagrams to visualise the threat that a

belated romance could pose to a man in the position to which George McGeorge seemed so perfectly adapted, and he rather admired the other's brazen candour.

It was the first time that the Saint, whose years of adventure had taken him to some of the most outlandish reaches of the globe and whose fund of uncommon lore was sometimes astounding in its range, had ever heard of the Ile du Levant and its peculiar tradition; but even for him there could still be something new under the sun, and it was just as likely to be something so close to familiar settings that he might never have noticed it if he had not stubbed his toe on it. Now that he had stumbled on it, a closer look became almost mandatory. The idea of visiting such an informally accessible Eden intrigued him, not pruriently, but with a most human curiosity. The privilege of simultaneously watching the reactions to it of such a person as George McGeorge was an added spice, while the possibility of also observing the by-play between Mr McGeorge and his Uncle Waldo made it completely irresistible.

Simon Templar gazed dreamily out at the island, still visible beyond the terrace where they sat, and said: 'I wouldn't miss that island if I had to swim there. Maybe we could go over together.'

Which was how they came to be sitting side by side on a bench on the good ship *Flèche d'Or*, watching the rugged slopes of the island loom rapidly nearer over the intense blue water.

The little ferry, which still had the sturdy lines of a converted fishing-boat, was dressed with gay strings of flags from the masthead to the bow and stern, which gave it a very gallant and festive air. In the pilot house, the captain, who called himself on his own handbills Loulou the Corsair, was eating breakfast with his crew of two men and a boy, all of them stripped to the waist, barefooted, and with brightly coloured bandannas knotted around their heads. This meal, Simon had noted with some awe, consisted of a long loaf of bread, a wedge of blue cheese, a cylinder of salami, and a large slab of raw beef, from all of which they alternately hacked off generous hunks with their clasp-knives, nibbling whole cloves of garlic between mouthfuls and washing them down with swigs from a bottle of white wine – a heroic performance which would have been a grave shock to those who have been brought up to believe that the French working man embarks on a full morning's toil with no more sustenance than a croissant and a cup of coffee. The entire combination, with the sunlight sparkling on harmless little waves, gave the voyage a play-acting zest that could not possibly attend a ferry trip anywhere else in the world.

The other passengers, some thirty of them on that early run, could mostly be separated without much difficulty into two broad groups. One, which could be distinguished by generally paler skins, a subtle tendency towards superfluities of apparel or ornament, and a state of ill-concealed trepidation or excitement, consisted of the inevitable sightseers and perhaps a few tentative recruits. The others, usually marked by a deep tan, a simpler carelessness of costume, and a more earnest or relaxed demeanour, could be picked out with relative certainty as habitués or at least full-fledged initiates. The Saint, with his bronzed skin, in the cotton shirt and old shorts and espadrilles which he had sensibly chosen to wear, could easily have passed for one of the latter. McGeorge, on the other hand, was easily the most conspicuous example of the first category. Anyone seeing them together would have assumed at once that it was the Saint who had business on the island, and that McGeorge was the one who had decided on the spur of the moment to come along for the ride – and was now vainly regretting the impulse. It was a switch that Simon found highly diverting.

None of the passengers had yet disrobed to any unorthodox extent, but McGeorge did not seem to derive much solace from the delay. His eyes had become fixed on a flattish promontory of rock that stood out a little towards them from the body of the island. On it, tiny figures could be seen lying or strolling and sometimes plunging into the water like seals.

'Would you,' McGeorge asked huskily, at last, 'say that they had anything on?'

Simon kept his eyes focused as the point drew steadily nearer.

'No,' he said at last. 'I wouldn't.'

'Oh, Lord,' said McGeorge, as if right up until that moment he had been clutching a wisp of hope that all the reports about the Ile du Levant might still somehow prove to be a myth.

The ferry headed into the narrow gap between Levant and Port-Cros, and began to swing in towards the eastern island. Loulou personally took the wheel again and tooted a cheerful annunciatory blast on the ship's horn, while his fellow Corsairs dispersed efficiently fore and aft to make ready the mooring lines.

From the water, dusky green slopes of brush and stunted pine rose steeply to a rounded summit some four hundred feet above. All over the hillside, the tile roofs and tinted walls of villas and more considerable buildings broke through the scrub at decent intervals, while near the peak, somewhat unexpectedly, stood out the unmistakable lines of a modern chapel. The ferry kept turning still more sharply in towards a little cove that opened suddenly ahead of it, with the rusty hull of an old ship sunk across part of the entrance for a breakwater, and the reassuringly normal-looking windows and terrace of a typical small restaurant overlooking it from a ledge just a short climb above the jetty. To the right of the port as they approached it, the lower slopes were dotted with white and orange glimpses of scores of little tents, and on the rocks below the outlines of basking campers could be made out in just enough detail to establish that they were letting no artificial obstructions come between them and the health-giving rays of the sun.

'Does your uncle live in one of those?' Simon asked, indicating the canvas settlement.

'I'm sure he'd prefer to,' said McGeorge glumly. 'But he moved all his belongings here, most of them being books, so he had to break down and put a roof over them.'

To make his aspect even more incongruous, he was clutching a large and sinister-looking weapon which resembled a cross between an ancient arquebus and something out of a science-fiction armoury. From one end of it protruded the sharp end of a wickedly-barbed spear, which the rest of the contraption was apparently designed to propel.

'What *can* you take for a present to a simple-life maniac?' he had explained plaintively, when he showed up with it at their embarkation. 'It seems that about their only entertainment here is swimming around in diving-masks and shooting at wretched little fish. So I went to a tackle shop and asked them what was the latest tool for it, and they sold me this beastly thing.'

A sizeable and lively congregation stood waiting on the quay. Some of them who were more or less conventionally clothed, but sun-scorched, could be identified by their baggage as visitors who were waiting to end their stay with the return trip of the ferry. The rest were obviously residents or at least seasoned sojourners who had come to meet newly arriving friends, to collect packages from the mainland, or simply to inspect the latest specimens from the outside world. A few of those wore bikinis that would have satisfied the modest requirements of any ordinary French beach; but as the distance lessened from yards to feet and eventually to inches, it became eye-fillingly manifest that the majority were fully content with the minuscule G-string confection prescribed for wear within the city limits.

'This is just like landing on one of those South Sea islands you used to read about,' Simon remarked, surveying the reception committee with interest. 'Only these natives are a hell of a lot better-looking.'

It was indeed hard to realise that they had voyaged less than an hour from Le Lavandou, and already Loulou's assistant Corsairs had jumped ashore and were pushing through the array of bare breasts and buttocks to make fast their lines with all the indifference of long familiarity. Mr McGeorge stood gripped in a kind of paralysis in which only his eyes moved, and they swivelled frantically as if torn between the compulsion to see everything and a terror of being caught staring at anything. But at last they found something that they seemed to feel they could safely rest on.

'There's Uncle Waldo,' he croaked.

Simon followed him on to the dock without the slighest foreboding of what that innocent visit was to lead to.

2

Mr Waldo Oddington was a rather tall wiry man whose age was not too evident even to the extremely complete scrutiny which his nominal garment permitted. His hair, which was scanty, was an indefinite grey; and although his nut-brown body might have been rated on the scrawny side by some æsthetic standards, its muscles looked hard and his abdomen was as flat as a board. He wrung his nephew's hand with a vigour that made Mr McGeorge wince.

'Good to see you, my dear boy! And it's about time. I thought you'd never run out of excuses.' His very bright hazel eyes examined McGeorge more closely. 'What's the matter with you? Have you just been sick?'

'No, we had a perfectly smooth crossing.'

'Then why are you so pale?'

'London, you know,' said McGeorge vaguely. 'And New York before that.'

'Terrible places,' pronounced Mr Oddington. 'Millions of imbeciles making themselves neurotic with the noise and bustle, and poisoning themselves with all the fumes they breathe. Why do you think their insanity rate and their lung cancer rate keep rising in almost parallel lines on a graph?'

Not having any ready answer to this, McGeorge somewhat desperately proffered the spear-gun he had been holding.

'I brought this along for you, Uncle,' he said. 'I hope you like it.'

'Now that's what I call using your head.' Mr Oddington hefted the weapon and beamed over it like a ten-year-old who has just been presented with the newest model Space Patrol disintegrator. 'I really appreciate it, dear boy. We'll try it out this afternoon . . . But I know you've been dying to meet Nadine.'

He pushed forward a fair-haired golden-skinned girl who had been standing near him. She smiled, making dimples in a mischievous, pretty face.

'How do you do,' she said, with only a little accent.

Mr McGeorge did not look as if he had been dying to meet her, but as if he might well die from doing it. His *savoir faire*, which probably no normal contretemps could have ruffled, was plainly unequal to the requirements of being presented to a shapely young woman who seemed quite unconscious of wearing nothing above the waist. A crimson flush swept over his face, and he groped blindly for her out-stretched hand with his eyes fixed glazedly on a point just over the top of her head.

As hastily as possible, he turned to grab the Saint's arm, as if it had frantically occurred to him that Simon might escape.

'I'd like you to meet a friend of mine – Mr Templar. I brought him with me. I hope you don't mind.'

'Delighted!' Mr Oddington surveyed the Saint's lean broad-shouldered lines with undisguised approval. 'You look very fit, sir. I'm sure we'll have a lot in common. And you must meet Mademoiselle Zeult.'

Simon shook hands with the girl, without especially restricting himself on where he looked. It seemed to him that she was no more displeased than any fully clothed woman would have been who sensed that her figure was being admired.

'Well, we don't have to stand around here,' Mr Oddington said briskly. 'I expect you're dying to get out of those clothes.'

'Oh, no,' said McGeorge faintly. 'I mean, we're in no hurry. I mean, if there's anything else you want to do—'

'We have to pick up a few groceries in the village; but that's on our way. And, of course, you'll want to buy your slips.'

'Our what?'

'These things.' Mr Oddington indicated his own peculiarly tailored kind of sporran.

'We don't really need those, do we?' McGeorge said.

'I'm afraid you do. It's strictly against the law to go around the village stark naked. Damned nonsense, I think; but there it is.'

'I mean, I've already got trousers, and Templar's got shorts—'

'You don't want to be taken for tourists and have everyone *staring* at you, do you?' asked Mr Oddington incredulously.

He shepherded them away up a narrow deeply-rutted road along which some of the crowd were already dispersing, while others were stringing out along a footpath that led along the shore in the direction of the clustered tents. The road curved up the hill without any serious attempt at easing its slant. A battered truck laden with miscellaneous cargo and with a half-dozen grinning riders perched on top slowly overtook them, and they had to step off the edge of the lane to let it by. It groaned past them in four-wheel drive, leaving a fine haze of dust in its wake.

'Our only piece of mechanical transportation,' Mr Oddington said. 'It hauls heavy stuff up from the ferry – and people who are too lazy to walk.'

'How far do we have to go?' McGeorge asked.

'It's only half a mile from the port to the village centre, and my place is just a little farther up.'

Mr Oddington's stringy legs maintained a remarkably youthful pace, and his bare feet did not even seem to notice the stony roughness of the slope on which McGeorge frequently stumbled in his elegant shoes. But when McGeorge fell behind, Nadine Zeult moved in front of him, looking from that angle as if she were wearing nothing whatever except a piece of string. The Saint saw McGeorge shudder and turn on a panicky burst of speed that took him safely ahead of the sight; and Simon found himself walking beside the girl.

'How long have you been here?' he asked, to make conversation.

'Since May, this year. Is it your first time here?'

'Yes.'

'I came first in August last year, only because a boy I was with wanted to see it, and I have been here ever since. Perhaps you will be the same.'

'It's a little early to think about that,' Simon murmured.

'I think you will enjoy it.' She looked at McGeorge's back, to which the shirt was already clinging sweatily. 'But I do not think Mr Oddington's nephew will. Do you know him well?'

'As a matter of fact, I hardly know him at all.'

'They are not a bit alike. I can tell. Already I'm wondering why Mr Oddington is so fond of him,' she said with astonishing frankness.

Before Simon could decide on a suitable answer, Mr Oddington announced: 'Here we are. This is Héliopolis!'

A stranger might not have recognised it at once as the village centre if he had not been told. Since leaving the shadow of the restaurant that overlooked the harbour, they had passed signs indicating other restaurants and hotels, and a shop, on other equally rough roads that branched off to their left to follow the contours of the hill and which doubtless served the villas which had been more visible from the sea. Now there was only a very slightly increased concentration of commercial activity; a few yards above another restaurant and bar which they had just passed there was a grocery store on the right, and opposite that a stall festooned with an indeterminate variety of merchandise ranging from pottery to postcards, while facing them was a hotel rather poetically named the Pomme d'Adam, with another shop a little above it on the hill to the right and another hotel farther along in the same direction. The fact that all these enterprises were loosely grouped around a fairly large bare open space where three roads met still fell rather short of making it a kind of sun city's Times Square.

Mr Oddington led the way into the grocery store, where he and Nadine chatted and chaffered with sociable lengthiness over the purchase of a disproportionately small quantity of victuals. The proprietor and his wife, Simon noticed, were completely and conventionally clad, but entirely uninterested in the condition of their customers. When the goods had been collected in a string bag, and the total added up on the margin of an old newspaper, Mr Oddington opened a horizontal zipper near the upper margin of his *cache-sexe*. George McGeorge, who now had a rosy flush from no other cause than the exertion of the recent climb, at this point reversed his system of colour changes and turned pale. Mr Oddington, unaware of having provoked any consternation, extracted from the unzippered pocket a tightly folded wad of paper money, counted out enough to cover his bill, replaced the remainder together with his change, and calmly zipped the pocket up again.

'After all, George,' Simon observed reasonably, 'even in this Garden of Eden they use money, and where else *could* he have a pocket?'

Mr Oddington picked up the string bag and herded his party across the street. He waved an expansive hand towards a string of fragments of fancifully printed cotton hanging over the proscenium of the stall, which at first glance would have been taken for a row of ornamental pennants.

'Now,' he said, with a twinkle that was faintly suggestive of a challenge, 'you can choose your minimums.'

The young woman behind the counter leaned forward to spread out a wider choice of patterns. She was herself modelling one of her own skeletal creations – apparently the working and trading personnel of the village were freely divided between those who took the maximum advantage of their legal liberty and those who preferred to ignore it. McGeorge grabbed blindly for the nearest piece of cloth; and the girl pointed out to him, giggling, that he had picked out a female model. With the air of a Greek philosopher accepting a cup of hemlock, he took the first alternative she offered and turned rapidly away.

'You pay,' he said to the Saint. 'I'll settle up with you later.'

Simon did not mind being stuck with the trivial cost, as he expected to be, with the almost certain compensation of seeing McGeorge forced to wear the article. He selected for himself a scrap of cotton print with an interesting motif of bees and flowers and the built-in zippered pocket whose utility he had seen demonstrated, and resolved that for McGeorge's benefit he would wear it as if he had been doing it all his life.

Mr Oddington glanced around to reassemble his flock, and Simon discovered that Nadine was no longer with them. He saw her in a moment, across the street, talking to a young man of about her own age who kept looking across at them. The young man had rather long well-oiled black hair and the build of a Greek statue; from the way he posed, and the rather spoiled set of his handsome face, one got an instant impression that he had familiarised himself with all his own natural assets in a great many mirrors.

'Nadine,' Mr Oddington called, somewhat peremptorily.

The girl smiled and waved back.

'Go on – I'll catch up with you.'

Mr Oddington frowned, but led the way up the hill to the left. They climbed for a few more minutes, then turned down a still narrower side road.

'If you're so fond of swimming, Uncle Waldo,' McGeorge said, with a slight edge in his voice, 'why don't you live near the water?'

'Much better view up here,' Mr Oddington said cheerfully. 'And it's wonderful exercise walking back and forth.'

He suddenly ducked down a winding path through a thicket of oleanders, and in another moment they were at the back door of a house. He opened it without recourse to a key, and they entered a little vestibule with an open kitchen on one side. Mr Oddington stopped there to put down his string bag of provisions and transfer some of them to the refrigerator.

'I see you don't object to some modern conveniences,' Simon remarked.

'Why should I?' said Mr Oddington. 'Science offers good things and bad things impartially. The test of intelligence is to take the good things and not feel that that obligates you to accept everything. Some people here have their own electric plants, but I get along nicely with bottled gas. It does nearly all the same things, except running a water-pump. There's a rain-water storage tank under the house: it fills up in the winter, and it's big enough to last me all summer.' He pointed to a large lever on an exposed pipe in one corner. 'We use that to fill a gravity cistern under the roof. It's better than an electric pump. It never gets out of order, and it's good for the biceps.'

He took them through an archway on the other side of the vestibule into the living-room. It had a bare tile floor, book-shelves lining two walls, a desk with a typewriter, and a few cane chairs. Opposite the archway, big french windows stood open on to a terrace beyond which there was indeed a fabulous view over the sapphire sea, with a corner of Port-Cros at one side and the coast of the mainland in the distance.

Mr Oddington steered them off to the right into a short passage-way, where he exhibited a tiled bathroom on one side and two small bedrooms on the other, both of them with french windows on to the same terrace that ran along the whole front of the villa. The bedrooms contained a spartan minimum of furniture, but they did have beds.

'Don't you sleep on the floor any longer, Uncle?' McGeorge inquired.

'Nadine pointed out to me that even birds build nests and line them with feathers,' Mr Oddington said. 'I have been giving her argument a fair trial, and so far I have felt no ill effects.'

They went on out to the terrace and gazed at the panorama.

'How did you meet this girl?' McGeorge asked.

'Well,' Mr Oddington said, almost as if their relationship had been reversed, 'I hate having to clean house, and also I needed someone to help me with the typing of my book—'

'What book?'

'I am writing a book about everything I have discovered which will enable anyone to live to be hale and hearty at a hundred. Of course, I won't be able to publish it with real authoritativeness until I'm a hundred myself, but that gives me another thirty-six years to get all my facts and principles systematised.'

'I see. But how did you find Nadine?'

'I stuck an advertisement on the bulletin board at the *Mairie*, and she happened to see it. She was only over for the day, but the place had got her – it does that to some people, you know, like love at first sight, when they realise that there's something here that they've always unconsciously wanted. But to stay here for more than a short holiday, she had to be able to earn a living. It was Fate, of course – a perfect example of it. She came to see me, and I liked her at once.'

'But you told me yourself that it was more than a business arrangement.'

'Later on, yes. She's a very attractive girl, as you've seen for yourself by this time, and the idea that a man of over sixty is practically decrepit has only been built up by burlesque comedians on the strength of the type of specimens they see in their audience. I think we shall have a very happy marriage.'

The Saint, who had been leaning on the balustrade and trying to look as though he were politely ignoring the conversation, turned in time to see McGeorge flinch as if he had taken a tap in the solar plexus.

'You haven't done this already?'

'No, but we were only waiting till you could be here. After all, you're the only family I have.'

'It's as serious as that, is it?'

'You know my views about motherhood for women. I certainly mustn't deprive Nadine of such a vital function. And to complete my studies of every phase of the natural life, I should have the experience of being a father.'

'All right,' McGeorge said, in a slightly strangled voice. 'But you used to say that marriage was a barbaric formula – I can quote you – designed originally to perpetuate the servitude of women, and developed by modern courts to achieve the enslavement of man.'

'My dear boy, that is still true,' replied Mr Oddington blandly. 'However, since we still live in a semi-barbaric society, we sometimes have to bow to its tabus. Nadine has reminded me that a child of unmarried parents, I refuse to call it illegitimate, is subject to an endless series of petty embarrassments which it would only be selfish to inflict on it when they can be averted merely by submitting to a few minutes of mumbo-jumbo and signing a piece of paper.'

Whether McGeorge would have found a ready answer to that remained unsettled, for he still seemed to be recovering from a state of shock when Nadine Zeult herself came out from the living-room to join them.

'You are all so serious,' she said, taking them in with her impish amber eyes. 'That is what always happens when men are left alone.'

'You were the one who left us,' Mr Oddington said, his mouth tightening irritably as at an unfortunately revived recollection.

The girl laughed, and went over to cuddle his arm and kiss him on the cheek.

'You are pretending to be jealous, Waldo,' she said blithely, 'and it makes you adorable. Now I am here, what do you want us to do?'

Mr Oddington graciously allowed himself to recover his good humour while portentously studying a sundial set in a stone table permanently built into the terrace.

'We've used up so much of the morning that it's hardly worth going to the beach now,' he said. 'Let's have an early lunch and go for a swim afterwards.'

'I will bring you a drink while I fix it.'

The girl left, and came back in a few minutes with a bottle of St.-Raphaël and three glasses with ice in them. She disappeared again, humming light-heartedly, and Mr Oddington uncorked the bottle.

'How about an *apéritif?*'

'You're full of surprises, Uncle Waldo,' said McGeorge, who had recovered some of his self-possession at last. 'I didn't think you approved of that sort of thing.'

'I have not changed my principles, but I am capable of expanding them,' Mr Oddington said severely. 'It took me a long time to realise that wine and such beverages were strictly vegetarian products and therefore did not conflict with my views on diet; I admit it, and I am not ashamed to have discarded a baseless prejudice. But I still do not drink the blood of animals or decoctions of dead bodies.'

Simon tentatively eased a package of Pall Malls from his pocket.

'Would you mind,' he ventured, 'if I smoked a strictly vegetable cigarette?'

Mr Oddington chuckled with great good humour.

'Nobody maintains that all vegetables are good. Some are even poisonous – such as tobacco. I'm quite sure you know that. But the first law of this island is tolerance, and if you wish to gamble with your own health I can be sorry but I have no right to object.'

The Saint offered his pack to McGeorge, who took one defiantly, and lighted one for himself with an unfamiliar feeling that Mr Oddington had somehow come out disconcertingly ahead on points.

Lunch was a much better meal than he had expected. There was a minestrone so thick with vegetables and so heavily crusted with grated cheese that it was almost as satisfying as a meat stew, and a pilaff of rice and peanuts and mushrooms with a smothering of fried onions that was surprisingly tasty. With a bottle of Ste-Roseline *rosé* to wash it down, and a fresh peach to finish it off, it was not too inadequate for a hot day.

'I shall now take a siesta for exactly half an hour,' announced Mr Oddington, when they had all helped with the dishes. 'One day some pompous nincompoop of a physician will get himself a great reputation by officially prescribing what the Mediterranean people have always done by instinct.'

Simon found himself in the other bedroom, taking off his shirt, while George McGeorge sat and watched him morosely.

'Well, Templar, what do you think?'

'Me?' said the Saint. 'I love your Uncle Waldo. He's

probably one of the few completely happy people in this complicated world. He's found his Bali H'ai.'

'And the girl to go with it,' McGeorge said. 'I heard her telling you on the way up, about how she came here the first time with a boy friend. And you saw the gigolo type she was talking to in the village, and the way Uncle Waldo felt about it. How much would you like to bet that that isn't the same boy friend? And that they haven't had everything figured out all along?'

Simon pursed his lips.

'Yes, I had thought about that. I can see why it would bother you.'

'Don't think I'm just going to sit still and let it happen,' McGeorge said.

His habitually weary and rather querulous voice had such a coldblooded intensity that the Saint realised for the first time, with an odd thrill of indefinable apprehension, how seriously he might have mis-estimated that effete and stuffy young man.

The walk to the beach at Rioufrède was mostly downhill, across the central intersection of Héliopolis and down a road that started at right angles to the one they had trudged up from the port, so that Mr Oddington's energetic pace was easy even for McGeorge's unconditioned legs to keep up with. Mr Oddington, whose siesta seemed to give him the fire to start an afternoon as if it were a whole new day, drew their attention to the rusty barbed wire on one side of the road and an occasional faded sign posted behind it, and held forth trenchantly about the recent invasion by the French Navy and its attempt to take over the whole island as a base for guided-missile experiments, and the stubborn struggle of the residents to retain their foothold.

'Bureaucracy's the same everywhere. As if they didn't have half the Sahara desert doing no good to anyone, this was the only place they could pick on to play with their stupid toys. They couldn't set up shop in a place like Timbuktu, which nobody would have missed. It was more fun to destroy a place that stood for just a little more freedom from regulations than anywhere else. But they got a surprise when they found that they'd stirred up a hornets' nest!'

From the pugnacious thrust of jaw that went with that, Simon added to his observations the awareness that Mr Oddington was capable of fully as much stubborn aggressiveness as his nephew had unexpectedly revealed, and the newborn conviction grew on him that the inevitable conflict might not be pretty at all. But it was not easy to pursue that thought with the sun baking scent from the pines and the mellow air more consciously experienced by his skin than he would have thought possible. He was wearing his 'minimum' with all the aplomb he could muster, as he had promised himself, but the white stencil left by his regular swimming-trunks was something that no mere resolve could obliterate.

'Don't feel like a freak,' Mr Oddington said sturdily. 'Every one of us has been through the same stage. But did you ever have a more comfortable walk?'

'It's certainly the perfect costume for a hot day,' Simon admitted. 'But what's it like here in the winter?'

'Hardly anyone stays, but I like it. We have heat in the house, and it never gets so cold outside that you can't keep warm if you walk fast enough.'

Presently they turned off the road, down a well-worn foot-path to the right. The path started mildly, grew rapidly steeper, and finally became precipitous. When it was little more than a goat-track slanting down the side of a cliff, the stunted bushes thinned out to unmask the first sudden view of the cove it was leading down into. It was a deep little bay enclosed between two steep slopes of rock, hardly big enough to contain a football field, and reaching back to a broad cres-cent of pebbly beach. There were half a dozen heads bobbing in the water and three or four dozen people lying or sitting or walking about on the beach; and the actuality of their free-dom from inhibition, which could be basically established at the first glance, was a momentary jolt even to the Saint. He thought it was merciful for McGeorge that the condition of the path made it extremely hazardous for the eyes to wander for most of the remainder of the descent.

But that took no longer than a few flights of stairs, and then they were down on the beach themselves, with the astonishing display of epidermis all around them. Apparently this cove was a little too far for the ambition of the majority of merely curious sightseers, who probably felt that they had worked hard enough for a sensation by the time they had struggled up to the village centre, or else the route was not too well publicised, for the Saint fascinatedly counted exactly one scattered handful, two men and three women, who were even technically over-dressed for a game of Adam and Eve.

'Well, now we can make ourselves comfortable,' said Mr Oddington.

And, untying the string, he stepped gratefully out of his irksome habiliment.

'Aren't you coming for a swim, George?' he demanded. 'You look dopey. It'll wake you up.'

'It still isn't quite a full hour since we finished lunch,' said McGeorge, clutching even at that swiftly vanishing straw.

'Nonsense,' scoffed Mr Oddington. 'An old superstition. Look at seals. They swim *while* they're eating.'

McGeorge somehow managed to refrain from mentioning that he was not a seal.

'I – I'm not so used to the sun as the rest of you,' he pleaded. 'I don't think I should have too much all at once. Besides' – he grabbed at another inspiration – 'we've still got lots of things to talk about.'

'We'll have the whole evening for that, my boy.'

'The last ferry leaves at five, doesn't it?'

'But you weren't thinking of going back today, were you?'

'Obviously. You know we didn't bring any luggage.'

'I thought you might have a toothbrush in your pocket. You'd know I could lend you a razor. You knew that we didn't wear clothes here. What on earth would you put in your luggage?' asked Mr Oddington, in devastating perplexity.

The Saint had been gazing around, inventorying details of the general scene with unabashed interest and studiously keeping aloof from the argument. At that moment his eyes came to rest on the statuesque figure of a man standing on a ledge of rock about thirty feet up the trail down which they had recently scrambled, staring steadily down at them. Simon recognised him at once as the self-satisfied Adonis whom Nadine had been talking to in the village. It seemed unnecessarily imaginative to assume that the man had followed them there, but the Saint automatically re-scanned the walk through his mind like a film and confirmed that he had not had any occasion to look back. However, it would probably have been equally easy for anyone who knew Mr Oddington's habits to foresee where he would go in the afternoon.

'I feel like talking now, Uncle Waldo,' McGeorge said stubbornly.

He put on the shirt which he had brought with him and sat down firmly, with his knees drawn up, huddling the shirt around him like a small tent.

Mr Oddington glanced wistfully at the new spear-gun which he had brought along with him. His jaw tightened; and then, surprisingly, he also sat down.

'All right, George, if that's how you feel. We'll talk a bit.'

Simon could not tell who else had seen the man on the rocks above.

Nadine Zeult touched his arm.

'Will you come for a swim with me?' she suggested tactfully.

A little triangle of cloth fluttered down on to the beach as she ran into the water.

The Saint ran in after her. Much as he would have given to find an excuse to stay and listen, there was nothing else he could do about it. He stumbled into a plunging dive and swam violently for about twenty yards without lifting his head, until the effort had neutralised the first cool contrast of the water. Then he turned over and pushed his hair back, treading water, and found the girl not far away.

'It's good, isn't it?' she said.

'Very good,' he smiled.

He had an idea she was referring to something more than just the ordinary goodness of a temperate sea, but his reply was safe and would have been the same anyway. Somehow it was always a new surprise, because the opportunities were so rare, to rediscover the fantastic difference between swimming in the raw and swimming in anything else at all. Perhaps it was not only the unfamiliarity of total physical liberation, but a throwback of memory to old swimming-holes and boyhood truancies and golden days of innocence that could never come again.

She swam idly along for a while, drifting towards one side of the bay, and the Saint paddled lazily beside her because it was the most natural thing to do. Presently they were close to a smooth step of rock, and the girl climbed out on to it and sat there, shaking the water out of her yellow hair, like a sea-nymph. After a moment, the Saint pulled himself up beside her.

'Tell me now what you think,' she said.

'I'm enjoying myself,' he told her.

'You should stay a long time.'

'That's another matter. This is quite an experience, sort of out of this world – and there aren't a lot of things I haven't done. But I was never curious to go to the ordinary kind of nudist colony. There was something that didn't appeal to me about the secretiveness, about having to join up, and the feeling that you'd be somehow committed to a Cause. I've had my own crusades, but I hate being organised. This is different, I admit. This is a lot of people being allowed to do what they want to do, and taking advantage of it, and yet really doing it on their own. But—'

'You think there is something queer about us?'

'To be honest, I half expected to see a rather freakish-looking bunch of people. I was wrong about that. As a matter of fact, I'd say that on the whole they're a hell of a lot better-looking than the average of what you'd find on any ordinary beach. I'm glad there's a place like this for them, since this is what they want. But as a way of life it doesn't mean the same to me that it does to Uncle Waldo.'

'Then if we are not queer, we are foolish.'

'Not that, either.' He crossed his arms over his knees and rested his chin on them, frowning into the glare. 'Maybe the rest of the world would be a lot better if it learned your kind of tolerance – about minding your own business and letting everyone do what they like as long as they aren't hurting anyone else. But I couldn't settle for just that simple Utopia. Perhaps that's my loss.'

'At least you don't despise Mr Oddington for liking it.'

'Not a bit. I think he's very lucky to only want what he can have, and to be able to have it.'

'His nephew despises him.'

'I'd just say, he disapproves.'

'He disapproves of me, too.'

'I don't think he can figure you out. If it comes to that, I've been trying to figure you myself. You speak English very well—'

'I taught in a school in England for three years.'

'Then you also have a better than ordinary education. And you have much better than ordinary looks, and an attractive personality. There must be plenty of other things you could do – things that most girls would like better.'

'But I like it here,' she said simply. 'And Mr Oddington likes it. And what he likes, I like even more. Is that so unusual where you come from?'

He nodded.

'Sometimes.'

'Why don't you say that you think there must be something wrong because he is so much older?'

'Even if I did, it wouldn't be any of my business. But you can understand why it might worry George.'

She looked at him without a trace of the coquettish mischief that played so easily on her face.

'Mr Oddington is a very good man. He is different from other people in his way, but he does nobody any harm. I have known young men who were not good at all.'

Simon held her eyes steadily for a few seconds. If anyone had ever predicted that he would one day hold a conversation like that with a sea-nymph sitting on a rock without a stitch on her, he wouldn't have believed it. This was what you could get for striking up conversations with strangers in bars, he thought.

He looked back towards the beach, where he could see Mr Oddington and his nephew still sitting together. McGeorge was still firmly enveloped in his shirt, while Mr Oddington poked restively at the stones with his spear-gun. It was too far to see any expression on their faces, but the abruptness of an occasional gesture suggested restrained violence in the discussion.

'I wish you luck,' said the Saint. 'But I don't think George will give you any blessing.'

'Then,' she said, with a toss of her head, 'it's what you call too bad about him.'

She stood up, straight and lovely, and then sprang from her toes and arrowed into the water.

The Saint watched her come up and start swimming towards the shore. The breeze which springs up in the Mediterranean almost every summer afternoon was chasing turbulent riffles even into the sheltered bay; and in the dancing water an increasing number of swimmers, nearly all of them equipped with the diving-masks and snorkel breathing-tubes without which even a nudist might have felt undressed for Mediterranean swimming in those days, cruised in all directions like a fleet of miniature submarines. Simon stayed on the rock and wondered whether he should follow her, not knowing exactly how he was meant to take her parting retort.

Then, as her blonde head drew near the beach, she found a footing and came upright with her shoulders clear of the water, and at the same time one of the swimmers near her also stopped and stood. The swimmer pushed his mask up on to his forehead to talk; but even without that distant sight of his face, by the development of his shoulders and the carriage of his head, Simon recognised the same persistent male whose arrival at the cove he had already noticed.

Even the Saint had a limit to how long he could curb his discretion, and at that point he reached it. No matter if that meeting was entirely accidental or to what extent it might have been engineered, Nadine and the man were talking again, and the Saint had to hear something of it. One word, or even a look passed between them, might be enough to decide whether he would agree or disagree with McGeorge's estimate of the situation. This time he couldn't help it if he seemed crudely intrusive. Nothing in the whole set-up was any of his business anyway, but curiosity had always been one of his major vices.

He dived in and swam towards them, as quickly as he could without too noticeable a churning of water, and keeping his head down as much as possible. But in that way, because of the rustle of water around his ears, he heard nothing until he stopped swimming a yard from them. And then he only heard Nadine say the one word: '*Demain*.'

Then Nadine saw him.

'I wish I'd brought one of those masks,' he said conversationally. 'The water here must be wonderful for them.'

'Yes, it is,' she said.

She was angry – it was easy to see that, although she had it under control. But whether it was because of the interruption, or because of what had been interrupted, he had no way to tell. He let his feet down to the bottom and stood smiling as if he were unaware of any tension at all, and looked at the other man in such a way that it would have been almost impossible for her to avoid making the introduction.

'This is Monsieur Pierre Eschards,' she said. 'Mr Templar.'

Eschards extended a hand, flexing his biceps.

'*Enchanté*,' he said, but he did not look enchanted. The stare that he gave the Saint was cold and insolent. Then, as if Simon had already passed out of his life again, he turned back to the girl and took her hand. The way he looked at her was quite different in its intensity. '*J' attendrai*,' he said.

He touched her fingers to his lips, pulled down his mask, and swam away.

Nadine followed him a little distance with her eyes, biting her lip.

Simon took a chance.

'That's the fellow you first came to the island with, isn't it?' he said casually.

'I suppose Mr Oddington told you.' The frown stayed on her brows. 'It makes him very cross that Pierre has come back. He does not even think I should speak to him.'

'You can't altogether blame him for that.'

'Pierre is my cousin. We have known each other since we were children. I cannot suddenly pretend not to know him.'

'But didn't you say you were – sort of engaged?'

'For a while. I cannot undo the past. But that is all over. It was over when I began to go with Mr Oddington. He should believe that.'

Simon shrugged.

'He might find it easier to believe if Pierre stayed away.'

'I did not ask him to come. He just came here, from Antibes, where he likes to spend the summer. He said that he wanted to see how it was with me. He should have stayed there. It is a much better place for him.'

'And full of consolations, if you can afford them.'

She gave him a slow measuring look.

'There are plenty of rich women who can afford them,' she said.

It fell into place with a click. The Saint knew now why something about Pierre Eschards had seemed vaguely familiar. He was a type. You could find three or four of his duplicates any day of the season at a place like Eden Roc – sleek and handsome young men, wearing their hair rather æsthetically long but with carefully cultivated and tanned physiques, lounging around like well-fed cats, with bold and calculating eyes.

'But I thought you couldn't afford to stay here unless you had a job. What attracted him to you?'

'Everyone thought my grandfather was rich, and would leave me money. But that summer he died, and he had lost it all in the stock market. After that, Pierre was not so much in love. I did not believe it at first, but I know now that he was only waiting for an excuse for us to break up.'

'But you said he came back to see how it was with you.'

'I did not say he was not fond of me at all. He said I should not be wasting my life here – that presently Mr Oddington would die, and I would not be so young, but I would have nothing. I told him that Mr Oddington had thought of that in his will, even before we are going to be married . . . You ask a lot of questions, don't you?'

The Saint needed no one to tell him that he had been grilling her almost like a prosecuting attorney, and only a feat of personality had let him get away with it that far. But he couldn't stop now.

'I can't help being interested in people's problems,' he said disarmingly. 'I'm afraid Pierre was rather upset when I butted in. You'd just been telling him something, hadn't you? I only heard you say, "Tomorrow".'

'I told him that Mr Oddington and I were going to be married tomorrow.'

Simon raised his eyebrows.

'Well, congratulations! I didn't know it was as close as that.'

'We gave our notice at the *Mairie* long ago. But only when we went to our siesta this afternoon, he said we must do it tomorrow, while his nephew is still here.'

'That ought to have made Pierre happy, if he was worried about you. But I thought he looked mad.'

'He pretends he is still in love with me,' she said slowly. 'He says if anything goes wrong I can still come to him. You heard what he said when he left: "*I shall wait*."'

She did not waver under the Saint's quietly judicial scrutiny, but the Saint knew exactly how little that could mean. It is only in fiction that no liar can look an interrogator in the eye. But everything she said seemed to hold together – or he had consistently failed to trip her up. He began to feel embarrassed about the impulse that had started him probing at all. Of all the places in the world where he should have been out of range of trouble, let alone looking for it, the Ile du Levant should have been the nearest to a foolproof bet.

He looked around to see what had happened to George McGeorge and his Uncle Waldo. They were not on the beach where he had last seen them.

It took him a little while to locate them, and ultimately it was a flash of McGeorge's white skin that ended the search. The family confab must have ended, with or without a decision, and Mr Oddington had finally succeeded in bullying or cajoling his nephew into the water to join him in trying out the new spear-gun. Whether McGeorge had also been coaxed or coerced into surrendering his last stronghold of modesty could not be determined from there, for both men had waded in above their waists and the surface of the water was choppy enough to interrupt its transparency.

'Well, if George hasn't decided to give you his blessing, at least he seems to have called off his sulk for the moment,' said the Saint, with an indicative movement of his head.

Nadine put a light hand on his shoulder.

'I suppose I should try to make him like me,' she said. 'If you really do care for people's problems, I think you could help.'

She began to walk through the water towards the shore and at an angle towards the other end of the beach where Mr Oddington and McGeorge were. As the water shallowed, her breasts came above it, full and yet taut. The ripples dropped to her hollow waist, then to her hips; and Simon Templar, wading up beside her, found that he still had to make an occasional conscious effort to keep his attention up to the levels that the philosophy of the island took for granted.

He disciplined himself to keep looking at Mr Oddington, who had fitted his own diving-mask on to McGeorge and was urging him to put his head down in the water and enjoy it. McGeorge also had the spear-gun in one hand, which seemed to be an added liability to a natural clumsiness. He eventually achieved a more or less horizontal position, in which he floundered rather like a drowning beetle.

'If Uncle Waldo is still a vegetarian, why does he want to spear fish?' Simon wondered idly.

'For the sport,' she said. 'It is not a moral thing, only because he thinks vegetables are better for health. When he catches anything, he gives it—'

Her voice broke in a gasp.

Out of the water where McGeorge was thrusting

something lanced like a streak of quicksilver, and then froze in the form of a slim shaft of steel that stood rigidly, grotesquely, out of Mr Oddington's chest. Simon saw it at the same time, very clearly and horribly, before Mr Oddington rolled over and fell with a soggy splash.

4

'It is only to be expected that he would say it was an acci-dent,' said the gendarme. 'Not many murderers are so ready to follow their victims that they confess at the first moment.'

The memory of McGeorge's statement was etched on the Saint's mind in especially sharp detail, for it had fallen to him to act as interpreter.

'I haven't the faintest idea what happened,' McGeorge had said. 'I heard him give a sort of yell, and looked up, and there he was with that spear thing sticking in his chest. I dropped the gun and struggled over to him – he was only a couple of yards away – and dragged him out on the beach. The gun came trailing after him because the spear's attached to it with a short length of line. It must have gone off all by itself.'

'Were you on good terms with your uncle?' the gendarme had asked.

'I was very fond of him. But I suppose you'll soon find out that we'd been having an argument today.'

'It was about something personal?'

'Yes.'

'Yet soon afterwards you were swimming with him, and playing with this *arbaléte* which you had brought him as a present.'

'The argument was over.'

'I shall have to ask what it was about.'

'All right. I'm sure everyone knows that he was going to marry Mademoiselle Zeult. I told him I thought she was only marrying him for his money. He didn't think so. Finally I suggested a way to settle it. I dared him to tell her that he'd deceived her and he didn't have any money at all, and see if she still wanted to marry him. If she did, I'd apologise and lick her boots – if she had any. He agreed. In fact, he was so sure of her that he was as happy as if he'd already won a bet. So he insisted on my playing with his toy, as if he wanted to show that he didn't bear any grudge. He was so eager that I had to give in.'

Simon could still hear McGeorge's clipped precise accents and see his blanched tight-lipped face. Without pretending to any inhuman nervelessness, he had handled himself with a cool competence that any lawyer would have applauded, neither evading nor protesting too much. But in spite of that, McGeorge was now locked away somewhere in the building, while the gendarme sat in his little office scanning the notes he had written in an official ledger in an extraordinarily neat and rapid longhand.

Simon gave him a cigarette.

'Do you always treat an accident as if it were a murder?' he inquired.

'When there are grounds to suspect that it could be, yes,' said the gendarme politely. 'That is the law.'

He was, Simon had gathered, the only civilian officer of the law on the island. He was quite a young man, with a pleasant face, but very serious. He wore a semi-military khaki shirt with informal tan shorts and sandals, but had not gone so far as to try to maintain the dignity of his commission in a G-string. The Saint had not been unhappy to be able to change back into the clothes he had worn on the ferry, and had also brought a grateful McGeorge his trousers: it was twilight now, and cool enough for the light clothing to be no hardship.

'Figure it to yourself, *monsieur*,' said the gendarme. 'You have a man of some means, because he lives here all the time in a good villa and does not have to work. He has a young girl who is his secretary and housekeeper and no doubt other things. That is all right. But then he is going to marry her. *Alors*, very soon comes his nephew, who does not want this. That, too, is natural. If the uncle is married, perhaps there is no more money for the nephew. He tries to tell the uncle that the girl is only marrying for money. They argue. At last, they agree on a test. But then, at once, the uncle is so happy that the young man is afraid. The uncle seems to be so sure, that suddenly the nephew thinks that the girl could love the old man after all – such things have happened – and the test will fail, and he will have lost everything. Perhaps, he thinks, an accident would be much more certain. And in his hand he has the weapon. It takes only the touch of a finger.'

'Just like that, on the spur of the moment.'

'The thought of murder may have been in his mind before. It needed only the opportunity, the right circumstance, to send a message down his arm to the trigger. A very carefully planned murder may be good, if it succeeds; but the more elaborately it is prepared, the more risk there is that the preparation may be discovered. A murder on impulse can be just as good, and even harder to prove. But it is still murder. I have thought a lot about these things.'

'But Mademoiselle Zeult told me that Oddington had already made a will in her favour. So killing him would get McGeorge nowhere.'

'Can you swear that McGeorge knew that? If not, the proof remains that he had motive.'

The muscles in the Saint's jaw flickered under the skin. It was all presumptive, all circumstantial; and yet under the French criminal code which requires the accused to prove his innocence rather than the prosecution to prove his guilt, it could be a wicked case to beat.

'What happens next?' he asked.

'I have telegraphed to Toulon. I do not have the equipment or qualifications to do any more here. In the morning an Inspecteur of the *Police Judiciaire* will arrive and take charge. If you wish to help your friend, I would suggest that you send for an attorney.'

'I'm not interested in helping anyone,' said the Saint grimly. 'I only knew Monsieur Oddington a few hours, but I liked him very much. If he was murdered, I want someone to go to the guillotine for it.'

The gendarme nodded.

'He was perhaps a little eccentric, but I think everyone loved him. And I am employed to serve justice, *monsieur*.'

Simon doubled his right fist into a tight knot and ground it slowly into the palm of his left hand. The exasperation that found an outlet in that controlled gesture went all the way up his arms into the muscles of his chest. His eyes were narrowed between a crinkle of hard lines.

It was a cut-and-dried case ... and yet something was wrong with it. The instinctive understanding of crime which was his special peculiar gift told him so, brushing aside superficial logic. The infuriating frustration came from trying to pinpoint the flaw. It wasn't a straightforward problem like listening to a musical recording with an expert ear and spotting one or two false notes that had been played. It was more as if one or two whole instruments were micro-metrically off key, playing perfectly consistently as units and yet infinitesimally out of tune, so that the entire performance was elusively discordant.

'There are still inconsistencies,' he said, groping. 'I heard McGeorge disagree with his uncle quite openly. Once or twice he was almost rude. He made sarcastic remarks that Monsieur Oddington might easily have resented. Would he have risked that if he was so anxious to stay in his uncle's good graces? . . . And about Mademoiselle Zeult. A man who is really infatuated is just as likely to fly into a rage with anyone who says derogatory things about his girl as he is to wonder if they might be true. Perhaps more likely. Why would McGeorge risk running her down so openly when he could have been much more subtle?'

'Perhaps because he was stupid.'

'But just now you thought he was rather clever.'

The gendarme lifted his shoulders and arms and opened his hands in the Latin gesture which says everything and commits itself to nothing.

'The investigation will decide which is true, *monsieur*.'

'Listen,' said the Saint. 'You told me you did a lot of thinking about these things. So I imagine that being the village cop in a place like this is not your idea of a life's career. You may never have a chance like this again. Instead of waiting for the boys from Toulon to investigate and decide everything, suppose you could hand them a case that was all wrapped up and tied with ribbons. Would that help you to get a transfer to some place where you could find some serious detecting to do?'

The gendarme studied him shrewdly.

'Because I am interested in crime, I know who you are, *Monsieur le Saint*. I will hear what you suggest, so long as it is not against the law.'

'I only want you to let me play a hunch,' Simon said, 'and stand by to cash in on it if it pays off.'

A new exhilaration surged into him like a flood as he walked back to Oddington's villa in the failing dusk. It was a lift of spirit with no more sober foundation than the fact that at last he had stopped being a spectator and had something to do. But there was an energy of wrath in it too, for he could not think of the death of Waldo Oddington as the mere impersonal data in an abstract problem. It is more common in stories that the murder victim is an evil character whom many people have good reason to hate. In real life, it is more often the well-meaning innocent who has the bad luck to stand in the way of some less worthy person's greed or ambition, and who dies without even realising that he had an enemy. But if only villains got knocked off, Simon thought savagely, there wouldn't be much incentive to try to convict murderers.

He went in at the unlocked door of the villa and fumbled for a light switch inside the living-room before he remembered that there was no electricity. He took out his lighter and struck it. From a chair near the terrace, Nadine Zeult looked at him unblinkingly.

'There is a lamp on the table,' she said.

He went over to it, raised the glass chimney, and tilted his lighter. Illumination spread out to fill the room as the lamp flame took over and he adjusted the wick.

The girl continued to watch him without expression. She had put on a plain black dress with only a touch of white at the collar. There were no tears on her cheeks, but her eyes were puffy and shadowed.

'Are you all right?' he said. 'The gendarme kept me answering so many questions.'

'What could you tell him?'

'I had a job to convince him that I scarcely know McGeorge at all.'

'Why did he do it?' she said, in a dry and aching monotone. 'Why?'

The Saint used his lighter again, on a cigarette. There was still one crevice in which a wedge could be started, which could open a split through which anything might fall. He saw nothing to be gained by waiting another moment to strike there. Win or lose, there would be no better time to try it – the test that Waldo Oddington had agreed to, but which had not been made.

'One thing came out,' he said flatly, 'it seems that everybody was wrong about Uncle Waldo – just like they were about your grandfather. He wasn't a rich man at all. It turns out he didn't have a dime.'

Her eyes stayed on him so fixedly that they seemed hypnotised. And then, faintly and hollowly, she began to laugh.

It was a thin racking laughter, almost soundless, that shook her whole body and yet had nothing to do with mirth.

'So you are just like the others,' she said. 'I expect you would believe that I wanted someone to kill him. Perhaps even that I somehow helped to arrange it. I thought better of you. Oh, you fool!' She stood up suddenly, straight and quivering. 'Let me show you something.'

She crossed the room to the desk and jerked open a drawer. If she had brought out a gun he would hardly have been surprised, she was shaken with such an intensity of passion; but instead it was only a cheap cardboard file that she spilled out on the top of the desk. The papers scattered under her hands as she skimmed through them, until she found what she wanted. She brought it back and thrust it at him.

'Read that!'

Simon took it. It was on a chastely discreet letterhead that said only INFINITE ENTERPRISE CORPORATION, above the address, with the words engraved even smaller in the left-hand corner: *Office of the Chairman*. He read:

Dear Uncle Waldo:

Please forgive me for being a bit late with the enclosed cheque for your usual quarterly allowance. I've had to do a lot of travelling lately, and I somehow lost touch with my personal calendar. I hope this hasn't inconvenienced you too much.

Regarding your wish to own the villa you are now renting, I'd like to advance you the price, and agree that it might be

*an economy in the long run; but in view of the rumours about
the French Navy's plans for the island, don't you think we
should wait a little longer until you're sure the investment
won't be jeopardised ... ?*

There was more of it, but the Saint's eyes were already
plunging to the foot of the page, where it ended:

> *Your affectionate nephew,*
> *George.*

Simon Templar was conscious of seconds that crawled by
like snails before he regained his voice.

Images unscrambled themselves and reassembled in their
proper place as if a complex of distorting prisms that over-
laid them had been snatched away.

'Of course,' he said huskily, almost to himself. 'May God
forgive me if I ever let myself think in clichés again. In books
it's always the rich uncle and the no-good pampered nephew
whose only idea of a career is to keep putting the bite on
Uncle. So everything that George said, I had to take the
wrong way. I couldn't even hear him properly when he told
me how fond his mother was of Uncle Waldo, and how she'd
made George promise practically on her death-bed that he'd
try to be like a son to the old boy. I was too clogged-up in the
brain to be able to remember that there could also be such a
thing as a penniless uncle with a rich nephew.'

'Yes,' Nadine said, with the resentment still burning in her
voice. 'George is very rich. Waldo told me all about him. He
buys and sells companies and manipulates shares. He is
called some kind of boy wonder in finance.'

'My second feeble-minded fatuity,' Simon went on scari-
fying himself ruthlessly. 'Because George is young, and
snotty, and stuffy, and in every way the type of jerk I long to

stick pins into, it never dawned on me that he could be fabulously brilliant in some racket of his own. Or that anyone I personally disliked could be extravagantly loyal and generous to his family.'

'He was. Very generous.'

'But when you came along, he wanted to be sure that he wasn't going to be fleeced at second hand, by way of Uncle Waldo. You can't blame him for wondering what he might have had to bail Uncle Waldo out of.'

'Waldo could have told him in a minute that I knew everything, and that we wanted nothing extra from him.'

'But you've seen what George's personality is like. I can imagine how it would rub Uncle Waldo the wrong way. Only he couldn't show it – he had to try to keep George happy, instead of it being the other way around. But when George proposed that corny and pretty insulting test, Uncle Waldo must have nearly bust a gut. It would have been a crime to tell him then that you already knew. It was much more fun to look forward to seeing George's red face when you told him yourself.'

'So,' she said, 'now you believe me.'

He nodded.

'That was my third blind spot. When one sees a pretty young girl like you with a man of over sixty, it's so easy to think of another cliché. I humbly apologise.'

She gazed at him for a long time, while the last of the fire slowly died down in her and was spent.

'It isn't your fault,' she said in a low voice. 'It would be hard for you to understand. But I told you how I had been disgusted with young men, through Pierre – and perhaps others. I loved Waldo – no, not in the romantic way that you would think of love, but with a full heart. With him I felt protected, and safe, and sure; and that was right for me.'

The Saint lowered his eyes to the piece of paper which he still held, and after a moment got it back in focus.

'Who else knew about this?' he asked.

'No one,' she said. 'He told me, because that was his kind of honesty. But he did not want anyone else to know, because that was his one harmless little pride, to let it be thought that what he had was his own.'

'And when you told Pierre that Waldo had made you his heiress—'

'It was partly to try to stop Pierre bothering me, and partly to build up Waldo. Pierre is the last person to whom I could tell the truth. How he would sneer!'

Simon's cigarette reminded him of itself when it burned his fingers. He crushed the stump into an ashtray.

The door opened at the front of the house, and Pierre Eschards came through the archway. He had on a pair of very short shorts that displayed his muscular thighs, and a dark mesh shirt open to the waist. His hair glistened with brilliantine. He gave the Saint a glance that barely condescended to recognition, and went straight across to Nadine and put an arm around her.

'I could not go to bed without being sure that you were all right,' he said in French. 'Is there anything I can do?'

'No,' she said quietly.

'*Pauvre petite.*' His lips brushed the top of her head. 'But you are young. It will pass. You must not let it spoil the rest of your life. And when you want me to help you forget, I shall be at your service.'

The Saint put McGeorge's letter down with the other papers strewn on the desk, slipping it sideways so that it would not be staring anyone in the face. All the rest of what he had to do seemed suddenly so straightforward.

'I was just going to tell Nadine the latest development,' he said, now speaking in fluent French himself. 'There are no fingerprints of McGeorge's on the spear-gun that shot Oddington.'

They both turned to him with sharply widening eyes.

'Fingerprints?' Eschards repeated. 'But of course there would not be any. It was in the water.'

'A greasy fingerprint wouldn't wash off so quickly,' said the Saint. 'And where people are using sun-tan oil, they usually have greasy fingers. There were other fingerprints on the gun, but none of his. And because he was new here and afraid of a burn, he had oil all over him.'

There were times when the Saint's facility of invention was almost incredible, but now he was hardly touching its resources. It was more like describing things that came to his mind by extra-sensory perception, which were separated from actuality only by a slight displacement of time and would soon become authenticated facts even if he took the liberty of anticipating them.

'Then they have not searched well enough,' Eschards said. 'In any case, why do they want fingerprints? The spear that killed Oddington was attached to the gun by a cord, so it was not fired from any other gun.'

'But the gun was not attached to McGeorge,' Simon said calmly. 'In his statement, McGeorge said that when his uncle was shot, he dropped the gun he was holding and went to help him. The gun was pulled in afterwards by the cord. Now, there are many *arbalètes* exactly like that, because the experts consider it the best. Suppose somebody with an identical gun swam beside McGeorge and shot his Uncle Waldo; and then, when McGeorge let go his gun, exactly as one could expect, and went to help his uncle, this other person grabbed McGeorge's gun and swam away with it under water – it would look as if McGeorge did it. And even McGeorge might believe that he had had an accident, *n'est-ce pas?*'

Nadine said: 'But the water was so clear—'

'No,' said the Saint. 'If you remember, it had turned a little choppy.'

'But it is absurd anyway,' Eschards broke out. 'Who else would have a reason to do that?'

Simon shrugged.

'That may be harder to answer. But the first thing is to find the other gun. My guess is that the man who did it would have hidden it somewhere around the beach, because with his guilty conscience he would be nervous about being seen with the same type of gun so soon after the killing. If we find it, it will have McGeorge's fingerprints on it besides the other man's, and that will be the proof. I came here to borrow a flashlight, and I'm going back to search.'

'Tonight?' Eschards objected. 'You will find nothing. Wait till tomorrow, and I will help you.'

'By tomorrow the murderer may have gone back himself and taken it away.' Simon addressed himself to the girl. 'Is there a flashlight here?'

Nadine seemed to be straining to read his eyes.

'Yes,' she said. 'In the top drawer on the left.'

Simon took it out and tested it.

'Just wish me luck,' he said, with a brief grin at them both, and went out quickly.

He walked out on the road over which Mr Oddington had led him so happily that afternoon, not dawdling but not rushing it. The night was full of a massed chirping of cicadas that could have practically drowned any other sound farther from his ears than his own footsteps; but he was not worried until he had turned off the road on the side path, and picked his way rather gingerly down the steepening slope, and come out at last on the narrow trail that edges down the sheerest stretch of the final cliff. That was where he heard the tiny scuff of sound that he had steeled himself to wait for, exactly where he had expected it, and he twisted to one side as something grazed the side of his head and thudded with sickening heaviness into the blackness beyond.

Then a weight clamped on his shoulders and an arm around his neck, and he was borne irresistibly down; but he was set for it, and he dropped the flashlight and threw all his strength into turning so that at the last instant it was his assailant who hit the rocky path first and the Saint was on top and cushioned. The attacker had the strength of a young lion, but the Saint was powered by a cold fury such as few crimes had ever aroused in him, a pitiless hate that could only be slaked by doing personal violence to the wanton destroyer of one simply happy man. He got one forearm solidly across his opponent's throat, clamping the neck to the ground, and drove his fist like a reciprocating piston into the upturned face . . .

'*Ça suffit*,' said the gendarme.

With a flashlight in his hand, he forced himself between the Saint and another potential corpse, and metal clicked on the wrists of the man underneath.

'I told you this was where someone would jump me, if my scheme worked out,' said the Saint exultantly. 'I only had to be found at the bottom there with my skull caved in on a rock, and it would look as if I slipped and fell in the dark. Another fortunate accident. Shall we really hunt for that other spear-gun now, or wait till tomorrow?'

'I saw him following you, and then I saw him attack you,' said the gendarme judicially. 'That requires a motive, and there is only one that is plausible.'

'You have the rest of it,' Simon said. 'It was only the kind of impulse, or inspiration, that you spoke of this afternoon, but he saw how to kill Monsieur Oddington so that McGeorge would surely be convicted of it, and therefore would not be able to inherit anything. And in that way Nadine would become rich, and he was sure that after a while he would be able to win her again and marry her.'

The swollen eyes of Pierre Eschards glared up into the

flashlight beam out of his bruised and bloody and no longer handsome face.

'It is not true,' he croaked. 'It was my gun that killed Oddington, and then I was frightened and I let go of it and took the gun that McGeorge dropped and swam away with it so that he would be accused instead of me. But I had not meant to fire the gun. It was an accident!'

'I think it is you, instead of Monsieur McGeorge, who will now have to convince the *juge d'instruction* of that,' said the gendarme.

5

They buried Waldo Oddington in a shaded corner of the tiny flower-grown cemetery on the island.

'That is what he would have chosen,' Nadine said.

Later, after they had walked most of the way back to the village in silence, George McGeorge said, in his stiff awkward way: 'I suppose you'll soon be wanting something to occupy yourself. I've been getting involved in one or two deals with European connections lately, and I'll need a secretary here who speaks languages. Perhaps you'd like to think about the job.'

She looked at him uncertainly for a moment, and then put out her hand.

'Thank you,' she said, with a very small smile. 'I think I would like it.'

Simon wondered if there might be some unforeseen changes in the future of Mr McGeorge.

The Lovelorn Sheikh

I

The BOAC manager located Simon in the bar of the Cairo airport, and said: 'I'm awfully sorry, Mr Templar, but I still haven't been able to get you confirmed beyond Basra on this flight. So you'll have to get off there, and hope they'll be able to put you right back on the plane. If not, they can definitely put you on the Coronet flight to Karachi on Tuesday. So you'd only be stuck there for one night – and two days. You might find 'em interesting. Or of course you could just stay here. I can book you all the way through to Tokyo on this flight next week.'

'I'll take a chance on Basra,' said the Saint amiably. 'I've nothing against this charming place; but I've already been here a week.'

'I've been here for six years,' said the manager neutrally. 'But I'm surprised the Saint couldn't find any excitement in Egypt.'

Simon Templar grinned lazily.

'I leave this territory to Sax Rohmer,' he murmured. 'I liked it better in Cinemascope, anyhow – in a nice air-conditioned theatre. Your ruins are wonderful, but the Nile just doesn't send me without Cleopatra. Maybe I'll come back when you start running time machines.'

'Well, if I'm still here, I hope I can be a bit more help to you then.' The manager fumbled out a carefully folded sheet of paper and a pen. 'I know it's a frightful bore, but would you mind very much doing an autograph? I've got a young son who thinks you're the greatest man who ever lived, and I'll never hear the last of it if I let you get away without a souvenir.'

'You should have brought him up with more respectable heroes,' Simon said, writing his name.

'And that little stick-figure drawing with the halo – your Saint trade-mark . . . Would you?'

'Sure.' Simon drew it. 'How do you feel about a drink?'

'Thanks, old chap, but I've still got a spot of work to do.' The manager recovered his pen and paper, and put out his hand. 'The station officer will be looking out for you at Basra. Have a nice trip, Mr Templar, and come back and see us.'

'Just as soon as you can make me that date with Cleopatra.'

Simon sat down again as the manager hurried away. The friendly smile faded from his tanned face as inevitably as the memory of that whole encounter would presently fade. It had been pleasant indeed, but it was still only part of the routine of travel.

And exactly three seconds later, as a direct result of it, nothing could even remotely be called routine.

His hand was grabbed off the table and practically taken away from him by a little man whom he had never seen before in his life, who pumped it and clung to it with the almost hysterical fervour of a parent greeting a long-lost son or a politician looking for a vote.

The little man beamed from ear to ear, and his little brown eyes were bright with terror, and he said in a frantically pleading undertone: 'My name's Mortimer Usherdown. Please pretend you're an old friend of mine. Please play along with me. Honestly, it's one of those life-and-death things . . .'

'Well, Mortimer,' said the Saint automatically. 'Long time no see.'

He patted Mr Usherdown on the shoulder, and gently reclaimed his other hand. The little man with the big name sank into the nearest chair as if his knees had melted. He had a round button-nosed face that made one think of a timid gnome, topped with thinning wisps of mouse-coloured hair; he might have been five years on either side of fifty. His trembling could be felt rather than seen, as if he were sitting on some kind of delicate vibrator.

'Gosh, this is a break, running into you here, Simon,' he said, still with that fixed and desperate grin. 'If I could have picked anyone out of the whole world to run into now, I'd have asked for you.'

He looked up abruptly, and Simon looked up with him, as two other men loomed over them, crowding close to the table with unmistakable intent to be noticed.

'Oh,' Mr Usherdown said, as though he had momentarily forgotten them. 'These are two friends of mine—'

The two men did not look like friends of anyone, except possibly some Middle Eastern Ali ben Capone. They were Arabs of some kind and did not care who knew it, since although they wore conventional Western suits of fascinatingly inaccurate fit, with what appeared to be striped pyjama tops taking the place of shirts and hanging gaily out below the hem-line of their coats, their heads were still shrouded in the traditional red-patterned cowls bound to their brows by what looked like two quoits of heavy black rope. But even making allowance for the fact that the typical seamed and aquiline Arab face, especially when bearded, has a cast of intolerant cruelty that only a Toureg mother would have no misgivings about, the two specimens that Mr Usherdown introduced exuded less natural kindliness than any couple of their race that Simon had seen up to that date.

'This is Tâlib,' the little man said, indicating the taller and lankier of the two, whose suit was a couple of sizes too loose. 'And Abdullah.' The other was shorter and broader, and his clothes were too tight. 'This is Mr Templar, a very old friend of mine,' Mr Usherdown said, completing the introductions.

The two Arabs also sat down.

'I'm glad everyone's so friendly,' murmured the Saint. 'Who's got the cards? Shall we cut for partners, Mortimer, or do you and I take these two on?'

'Tâlib speaks English,' Usherdown warned him quickly.

'How you do?' said the tall lanky one, to prove it.

'Mr Templar is in the same business that I am,' Usherdown explained – or it was apparently intended for an explanation.

'Ah,' said Tâlib, with interest. 'He is a hot dog, I bet.'

He leaned his elbows on the table with a solidity which not only underlined the impression that he was there to stay but added a certain air of possessiveness to his presence which spread out to include the Saint in its orbit.

Simon lighted a cigarette while he tried to make sure of his cue. Although Mr Usherdown had most of the conventional earmarks of a Milquetoast type, his current state of suppressed panic reached an almost psychopathic intensity. But Tâlib and Abdullah, for their part, had none of the reassuring air which might have been expected even of the local counterpart of the men in white coats. They were not actually as conspicuous as their description might sound to anyone who has not seen that cosmopolitan crossroads which shuffles together not merely the costumes and countenances of Europe and Arabia but also Afghans, Indians, Pakistanis, Burmese, Thailanders, Malays, Chinese, Japanese, and every sect and subdivision in between, in what is probably the maddest mixing-bowl of this airborne age; but the aura of self-confident menace about them was as internationally obvious as that of any two dead-pan goons in a gangster movie. Yet it seemed preposterous that they could reduce even such a mild-looking person as Mr Usherdown to something so close to quivering paralysis in such a crowded and brightly-lighted modernism as the Cairo airport bar.

Simon glanced calculatingly around the swirling jabbering room, adding up a little knot of transient American GI's, a trio of British officers identifiable even in mufti, and a couple of Egyptian policemen in uniform quietly studying everyone, and found it hard to believe that even such a frightened goblin as Mr Usherdown wouldn't have dared to call the bluff of two goons who tried to crowd him in such a setting. But it was still a wild possibility that had to be methodically disposed of.

He estimated the extent of Tâlib's idiomatic accomplishments with another blandly analytic glance, and said: 'Spill it, Mortimer. Do you want me to clobber these fugitives from a road show of *Beau Geste?*'

'Oh, no,' said the little man hastily. 'Not on any account, please. Their religion doesn't allow them to drink. But I'll have a brandy, if I may.'

He was quite fast on the uptake, at any rate, or perhaps fear had lent wings to his wits as it might have to another man's feet.

Simon stopped a passing waiter and relayed the order, along with another Peter Dawson for himself.

'What on earth are you doing here, Mort, old boy?' he asked, trying to offer another opening.

'I've just been up to Greece. For Hazel.'

'And how is the dear girl?'

'Who?' Mr Usherdown looked blank for a moment. 'Oh, do you mean my wife? Violet?'

'Of course,' said the Saint. 'How stupid of me. I knew the name was something vegetable.'

'She's fine. I had to leave her in Qabat.'

'That's too bad. Or is it? Does she know about Hazel?'

Light dawned at last on Mr Usherdown's anxious face.

'Now I get it. You're kidding. I was talking about *hazel twigs.*'

'Hazel Twiggs?' Simon repeated foggily. 'I'm sorry, I still can't seem to place her.'

'Stop pulling my leg, Simon,' pleaded the little man, with a nervous giggle. 'You know what I'm talking about. Hazel twigs – for dowsing.'

'Nothing like 'em,' agreed the Saint accommodatingly. 'Although I have heard that these new-fangled fire extinguishers—'

'People have tried a lot of new things,' said Mr Usherdown, with beads of perspiration standing out on his upper lip. 'Down in Jamaica I've seen it done with branches of guava. I met a chap in South Africa who did it with a clock spring. And I've read about a fellow in California who uses a piece of bent-up aluminium. But I still say that for sound, consistent divining, there's nothing to beat the old-fashioned hazel twig.'

It was Simon Templar's turn to receive a glimmer of illumination as at least a part of the dialogue suddenly lost its resemblance to an excerpt from the Mad Hatter's tea party and became startlingly rational and clear.

'I had to see if I could get a rise out of you, Mort,' he apologised. 'But you didn't even give me a chance to ask you "Witch Hazel?"'

Mr Usherdown cackled again with the giddiness of relief, and nudged Tâlib, whose piercing black eyes had been trying to follow the conversation from face to face like a tennis umpire watching a fast rally.

'Don't let Mr Templar fool you. He's one of the best dowsers in the business – perhaps even better than I am, and there's no one else I'd say that about. But always making a joke of it; anything for a laugh.'

'I get you,' Tâlib said. 'Very funny man. Very wise in cracks.'

He bared his teeth in what was doubtless meant to be an appreciative grin, and succeeded in looking almost as jovial as a half-starved wolf.

The arrival of the drinks, and the business of paying for them, gave the Saint a brief respite in which to digest the exiguous crumb of information which was all that he had to show for several minutes of mild delirium.

Mr Mortimer Usherdown, he had finally gathered, had a wife named Violet and was a water diviner by profession, and apparently wanted Simon Templar to pretend to be one too. But what this could have to do with Mr Usherdown's life-and-death problem, or the scarcely disguised menace of the two Arabs, was a riddle that Simon preferred to spare himself the vertigo of attempting to guess.

He sipped his Peter Dawson, while Mr Usherdown took a large and evidently grateful gulp of brandy.

'Seriously now,' said the Saint, 'what are you up to in these parts?'

'I'm working for the Emir of Qabat.'

'Should I know him too?'

'My boss,' Tâlib said, bowing his head and touching his forehead. 'The Sheikh Yusuf Loutfallah ibn Hishâm. *Yusuf* is like in English "Joseph". *Lòutfallah* means "Gift of God" – like Abdullah here is "Servant of God". *Hishâm—*'

'Never mind,' said the Saint. 'Let's just call him Joe.'

'Qabat is one of those tiny independent principalities the British helped to set up in the Middle East after the First World War,' Usherdown said. 'Like Kuwait. In fact, it's a whistle stop for some of the local planes from Basra to Kuwait. Say!' The little man's eyes dilated with a blaze of exaggeratedly spontaneous inspiration. 'I heard that BOAC man saying you might have to stop over in Basra. Why don't you fly over to Qabat with me?'

'I don't know,' said the Saint dubiously. 'I'm still hoping I'll be able to stay on to Karachi, and make a connection—'

'It's hardly anything of a side trip, by air,' Usherdown persisted, in a tone that was not so much persuasive as imploring. 'And it's something unique – something you'll never run into anything like again. Besides, you might even be able to help me!'

As if suddenly afraid that he might have gone too far, he turned quickly to Tâlib, who was staring at him with narrowed eyes, and said: 'Don't you think the Emir would like that? Honestly, in my racket, Mr Templar is really the greatest. If we could talk him into working with me, we might get twice as much done in half the time.'

The tall one turned and conferred in guttural Arabic with the Servant of God, whose qualifications for the job would not have been revealed by any superficial system of physiognomy; and Mr Usherdown said to the Saint, in a voice that almost broke with the pressure of its suppressed entreaty: 'If you turn me down, you can't be the man I've always thought you were.'

'Very good idea,' Tâlib said abruptly, while Abdullah nodded. 'I think the Emir will make him most welcome. You two working together must be better than one. Double or quitting, okey-doke?'

The PA system said: 'Your attention, please. British Overseas Airways announces the departure of Majestic flight 904 to Karachi, Delhi, Calcutta, Rangoon, Bangkok, Hong Kong, and Tokyo, now loading from Gate One.'

Names that had woven their iridescent thread through innumerable yarns of high adventure. Simon Templar knew most of them as they really were, in their underlying squalor even more than their romantic overtones, and yet he would never quite be able to strip their syllables of a music that echoed out of a youth in which other names like Damascus and Baghdad had been only the geography of fairy-tales instead of their modern sordid reality. It was positively unfair, he thought, to throw those mysteriously nostalgic sounds at him when he had only been trying to get transported from one place to another with a minimum of inconvenience on the way, and a total stranger with all the appeal of a scared rabbit was trying to sucker him into some fantastic situation which he hadn't yet begun to understand . . .

'Let's talk it over on the plane,' he said, and should have known even then that he was hooked.

He took a parting swallow from his glass, while Mr Usherdown drained the last drop from his, and stood up and led the way out.

Mr Usherdown followed, practically clinging to his coat-tails like a small boy trailing his mother through a department-store sale. And in a little while they boarded the plane in the same Siamese-twin proximity, except that in jostling through one of the bureaucratic bottlenecks which still seem to be inseparable from international air travel their positions had somehow become reversed, so that it was the Saint who trailed Mr Usherdown through the aisle of the Argonaut and was starting to follow him into a pair of seats when the tall Tâlib tried to push past him and take the other one. The Saint's resistance was as decisive as a gently-driven bulldozer, but it left him sitting in the chair next to Usherdown and gazing apologetically up at the Arab who glowered down at him.

'I sit here,' Tâlib grated.

'I don't mind sitting here a bit, pal,' Simon insisted innocently. 'You go on and get one of the *good* seats.'

'Plenty of room up front, gents,' sang out a cheerful steward, strategically posted to keep the passengers moving through the cabin.

Trapped between uniformed authority and the stubborn

push of other passengers, Tâlib squirmed furiously into the next pair of seats ahead. Abdullah promptly followed him, and in an instant the irresistible flow of following voyagers had sealed them irrevocably in their upholstered slot. They could do nothing but twist around and stare suspiciously over the backs of their seats – until the steward made them buckle their safety-belts and even that solace was denied them.

Nevertheless, the Saint waited until the plane was airborne and he could adjust the level of his voice with the certainty that no sudden fluctuation in the background noise would leave it audible to the two men in front, before he said: 'Okay, Mortimer, you can talk now. What the hell is all this? Are you in dutch because you haven't been able to find water for Joe's goldfish pond?'

'I wasn't trying to,' Mr Usherdown said, quite seriously. 'I haven't even thought about ordinary water divining for years. None of the top-notch dowsers bother with that any more, you know. There isn't enough money in it, and too many amateurs can do it.'

'What do wizards like you and I work at, then?'

'Well, I've dowsed for gold in South Africa and opals in Mexico, but mostly I specialise in oil. Had a bit of luck finding some new fields in Oregon and Nevada. Not for myself, of course – I just went over the land where these big companies had leases, and told 'em where to sink their wells. But I got a lot of publicity at the time, and somehow this sheikh got to hear of me, and one day he sent me an offer. It might have made me a millionaire, too. Except that I haven't been able to do a single darn thing for him.'

Simon frowned.

'You mean it turns out to be an "or else" deal? If it doesn't make you a Croesus, you think they'll make you a corpse?'

'It's likely to come to that.'

'Don't you believe it, Mortimer. You get off with me at

Basra, and tell those two Bedouin brigands to go jump on a camel.' The Saint smiled sweetly at the two pairs of scowling eyes that kept turning to peer suspiciously over the backs of the seats ahead. 'If they get rough, I'll hold 'em while you call a cop.'

'It isn't as easy as that,' Mr Usherdown said lugubriously. 'I told you, my wife's there in Qabat. Violet. She insisted on going with me – she had some crazy idea that if she didn't I'd be running wild in a harem, or something. So now the Emir's fallen in love with her; and whatever he does about me, he's not going to let *her* leave.'

2

It had been an hour past midnight when they took off from Cairo, so that only a few anonymous winking lights in a black carpet served as a parting glimpse of the land of the Pharaohs and their considerably less glamorous successors. It was soon after an orange-coloured dawn when they landed on the outskirts of the formless sprawl of habitation that is Basra. And it was dazzling beige high noon, after sundry inevitable delays, as the shuttle DC-3 from Basra slanted down towards the landing strip of Qabat.

Leaning over Mr Usherdown to get a partial bird's-eye view through the porthole, Simon Templar wondered philosophically if there would ever be a limit to the cockeyed places he could be dumped into by his constitutional inability to turn down anyone who looked helpless enough in the toils of a sufficiently unstereotyped predicament.

'The whole place only runs to about eight hundred square miles,' Usherdown had told him, 'and the only town, if you can call it that, would rate about four gas-stations back home. But for a few years it produced enough oil to've supplied half of Europe.'

'And I never heard of it.'

'No reason why you should. It didn't last long enough to get talked about much outside the trade. Then the flow started to dry up; and the big companies moved their main operations down to Kuwait and Bahrain. Don't ask me why. I'm not a geologist. But apparently the experts decided that

Qabat was only on the shallow edge of the underground oil pool, or something like that, and they decided to move on and drill somewhere else.'

'Which made Joseph rather unhappy.'

'You can't blame him too much for that. His royalties've been dwindling away until last year they only came to about sixteen million dollars.'

'Thank God for technological progress. The stains from my bleeding heart will rinse right out of this Dacron shirt.'

'I know, it sounds as if I was trying to be funny. But you have to remember that in the same length of time, the Emir of Kuwait's income has gone up to over three million dollars a *week*.'

At a figure like that, even Simon Templar was awed.

'If some Texans I've met heard about him, they'd blow their brains out,' he remarked. 'So I suppose every time Joe thinks about that, it burns him to a crisp.'

'He's about convinced himself that it's only because the oil companies have a personal grudge against him, because he was the first sheikh they made one of those fabulous percentage contracts with. He made up his mind he'd prove that their geologists were liars. First he hired some independent experts for himself. But eventually they gave him the same report. That only convinced him that they were afraid to buck the big companies. Then somebody must've told him something they'd read about me, and he thought I might be the answer.'

'But you weren't.'

'Look, a dowser can't *make* oil – or water, or anything else,' said Mr Usherdown, with a rather forlorn remnant of asperity. 'He can only help to find 'em when they're there. I've done my conscientious best, but so far I haven't been able to contradict the regular geologists. All the signals I've picked up were definitely of the declining type.'

The town below their wing-tip looked even more hopeless than Mr Usherdown's description had led Simon to expect. It sprawled in an approximate semicircle of which the diameter followed the blue-grey line of the Persian Gulf, which from that altitude had a leaden air of sultriness that suggested none of the cool relief of more hospitable seas. The most modern and efficient feature of its topography was the row of cylindrical silver-plated tanks, spaced and aligned along a section of the waterfront with the accuracy of guardsmen on parade, linked by identical patterns of catwalk and pipe, and centred symmetrically around the short-straight white finger of a concrete pier projecting a couple of ships' lengths from the shore. The most aesthetic thing about it was the large wedding-cake edifice of domes and minarets which lay a little outside the semicircle at the end of a straight black ribbon of road, like a flower on a stalk, with half a dozen smaller sugar-frosted buildings clustered around it like buds on lesser roads, and even traces of improbably nurtured greenery scattered among them to add vividness to the simile. But in between, in the untidy half-moon of muck from which these exotic blossoms grew, there was only a hodge-podge of vaguely cubist agglomerations of grey-brown mud, cheap wall-board, and rotting canvas, blended together into the uniformity of a mummy's wrappings, alleviated only by the occasional glitter of a patch of corrugated iron. And all around it, to the dust-fogged horizon, stretched the petrified ripples of a dead sea of sand, a faceless segment of the most utterly sterile desert in the world, its awesome emptiness and monotony interrupted only by the occasional stark skeleton of an oil derrick.

There was no evidence that any large percentage of the liquid wealth that had flowed out of that barren land had been spent on civic projects or the betterment of the Qabatis as a people. In fact, the bird's-eye view of Qabat seemed to illustrate the local division of Nature's bounty more graphically than any statistics. But Simon had been prepared for that.

'Yûsuf is the real old feudal type of sheikh,' Mr Usherdown had explained. 'His mind's still in the Middle Ages, even if he has a different coloured Cadillac for every day in the week. He owns Qabat body and soul because his father owned it before him and he inherited it like a farm. He wouldn't feel there was any call to split his royalties with his subjects – except his own nearest relatives – any more'n a Texas rancher would feel obligated to share his oil money with his cows. And the same way, he thinks he's entitled to take anything he wants, because that's something that goes with being an Emir.'

'But I thought the Koran was pretty starchy about adultery – that is, about trespassing on any other guy's four legal wives.'

'Yes, it is. But all you have to do to divorce your wife is to say "I divorce thee" three times, in front of witnesses. That's what Yûsuf wants me to do to Violet. If I'd only do that for him, he could marry her after three months. But if I'm stubborn, then something could make her a widow, and then he just has to wait four months and ten days.'

'Which doesn't give you a lot of cards to open with,' Simon admitted. 'But you've just been up to Greece, out of his bailiwick—'

'Of course, I made up that excuse about needing some fresh hazel twigs, because mine had dried out in the desert heat. But he isn't so easy to fool. He sent those two along with me – Tâlib and Abdullah. And any time one of 'em went to sleep, the other one stayed awake. I don't suppose either one of 'em, or both of 'em, would bother *you* very much, from some things I've read; but I'm only half your size, and I've never done any fighting. And you've seen 'em for yourself. Wouldn't you say they'd as soon cut a man's throat as talk to him?'

'Maybe sooner. But if you'd started yelling for help in the middle of Athens, in Constitution Square, right under the nose of a policeman, what could they have done about it?'

'I've read about these Mohammedans,' the little man said darkly. 'They're fanatics. If they die killing an unbeliever, they think they go straight to Heaven. And on top of that, these two have been brought up to believe it's their holy duty to do anything Yûsuf tells 'em. If he'd told 'em to kill me rather than let me start any fuss, they'd be even less likely to care what happened to themselves. I mean, it's all very well to say it's ridiculous and it couldn't happen, but it wouldn't do me much good to be saying it after I was dead and Violet was left for this sheikh to do anything he liked with.'

Simon had to concede that Mr Usherdown had a tenable argument. It was, after all, no different from the attitude of any average man who has ever submitted to armed robbery. And in this case there was certainly room for even more than ordinary uncertainty about how reckless the threateners might be.

While the Saint didn't suffer from any of those inhibitions, he realised that the comparatively easy step of stiffening Tâlib and Abdullah would not contribute much towards the resue of Violet Usherdown. True, Mr Usherdown would then be free to head for the nearest American consul and appeal for help. He might even, after a time, succeed in convincing the consul that his fantastic tale was true. But then the matter would have to go through Channels. And, in Washington, those Channels would be bound to filter it up to the very highest level. In a flash of absolute clairvoyance, Simon could visualise the gnawing of well-manicured fingernails that it would cause in the upper echelons of the State Department. For the days were long past, not necessarily for the better, when all the might of the United States stood ready to enforce the lawful rights of any American citizen anywhere. Simon could hear every word that a composite of all Official Spokesmen would say. 'My dear fellow, it isn't like it was when Teddy Roosevelt would send the Navy and the Marines into any banana republic that got too much out of line ... With the Russians grabbing every opening they can find to throw in a red rag about Colonialism ... And the United Nations ... And the trouble we're having trying to keep friends in the Middle East ... Well, suppose we steamed into the harbour at Qabat and started talking tough to this sheikh – can you imagine the kind of propaganda the Reds could make of it in all the other Arab states ... ?'

And so the Saint found himself landing at Qabat with some vague and fantastic idea of trying to do something about it single-handed. A sardonic quirk widened his mouth and turned the corners fractionally downwards at the same time. Indubitably, he would never learn ...

The local authority vested in Tâlib and Abdullah was amply demonstrated by the magical ease with which they marched Mr Usherdown and the Saint through four separate formality barriers manned by Qabati militia in facsimiles of British battledress but still capped with the square rope-bound cowls of their forefathers, who had every air of being set for an orgy of red tape at the expense of any unprivileged passengers. If this portentously lubricated transit was some-how uncomfortably reminiscent of the fast clearance which in other countries might be given to prisoners in the custody of police officers, rather than VIP's in the care of protocol expediters, Simon preferred to ignore the resemblance.

They had to wait only a few minutes outside the row of converted Quonset huts which served as airport buildings, until their baggage was hustled through the surging, shout-ing, screaming, and apparently almost homicidal mob which was merely a typical assortment of Allah-fearing citizens assembled to greet arriving friends and relatives, to bid departing others godspeed, or simply to pass a few idle hours observing the activity. Then Tâlib shepherded them into a salmon-pink Cadillac convertible which rolled majestically away with the uniformed driver playing an astounding symphony on an American police siren, twin Klaxons, and a Bermuda carriage bell.

The road from the airfield curved around the outskirts of the town, which at close quarters liberally fulfilled all the promise of tumbledown squalor which it had made to the sky, and dipped briefly into a *souk* where shapeless black-veiled women and biblically-gowned merchants brooded and haggled over mounds of dates and bowls of mysterious spices, baskets of dingy-hued rice and chunks of half-withered meat mantled with crawling flies, all of it spread out on the ground to be seasoned with the dust and dung stirred up by the passing populace and their sheep, goats, donkeys, camels, and Cadillacs. Of the last-named there was a concentration, in terms of car per yard of roadway, which could only have been matched in Miami Beach at midwinter. There was also a fair sampling of only slightly less expensive makes, all equally new, even if sometimes lacking a hood or a fender, and all in the most brilliant colours – together with an assortment of motor-cycles overloaded with rear-view mirrors and silver-mounted saddlebags, and even bicycles trying to get into the act with candy-striped paint jobs, tassels, pennants, windmills, and supernumerary bulb horns and reflectors.

'I suppose the biggest cars all belong to Joe's close relatives, the smaller ones to cousins and in-laws, the motor-bikes to the pals they do business with, and the pedal pushers are the lads who just manage to catch some drips from the gravy train,' Simon observed, raising his voice with some difficulty above the din with which every other vehicle on the road was enthusiastically answering the diverse fanfares activated by their own driver.

'Something like that,' Mr Usherdown yelled back.

'Only Emir can buy cars,' shouted Tâlib. 'He give them to big shoots.' He turned to scream a sirocco of parenthetic invective at some hapless nomad whose recalcitrant burro had forced their chauffeur to apply the brakes for a moment, and turned back without a perceptible pause for breath. 'He give me a car now, maybe. Me big shoot!'

'It sounds rather like that,' said the Saint discreetly.

Almost at once they turned off the seething aromatic street which presumably meandered to the heart of the town, and speeded up again through the bare desert on what Simon recognised as the straight stem of highway that he had seen from the air, leading towards the flower-arrangement of palaces. On contact, it proved to be a badly rutted and potholed road which taxed all the Cadillac's resources of spring and shock-absorber even at the death-defying velocity of about forty miles an hour at which their Jehu launched them over it, still tootling all his noise-making devices in spite of having no other traffic to compete with. In about a mile they reached the first touches of imported verdure – at first clumps of cactus, then a few hardy shrubs, then a variety of palm trees at increasingly frequent intervals, finally a hedge of geraniums with a miraculous sprinkling of pink blossoms.

'This is the nearest thing to an oasis in the whole of Qabat,' Mr Usherdown explained. 'There's actually a small natural spring, obviously where the first Emir staked out his private estate. It doesn't flow many gallons an hour, though. And after Yûsuf's relatives built their own palaces, with American bathrooms and everything, there wasn't much to spare. When he took up gardening, there was even less. The town gets whatever's left over. I don't think anyone ever dies of thirst, but that's about as far as it goes.'

'I should think Joe would have wanted you to do some

plain old-fashioned water divining before he sent you dowsing for oil,' said the Saint.

'What for? Right next door, in Kuwait, they had to spend fifteen million dollars on a sea-water distilling plant, and now they're going to put forty-five million more into a pipeline to bring water from the Tigris and Euphrates – more than two hundred miles. Yûsuf's got about all the water *he* needs, personally. All he's interested in is getting something more like the Emir of Kuwait's money.'

Seen at somewhat closer range from the royal boulevard, the minor mansions of the Sheikh's favourites looked considerably less than palatial, and in fact would not have sparked any fast bidding if they had been on sale in Southern California. The Sheikh's own palace, however, although falling well short of Cinemascope dimensions, would have comfortably met the standards of a producer of second features. The one feature of it which would not have been likely to occur to a Hollywood set designer was the wire-fenced area opposite the main entrance, about a hundred feet long and half as wide, shaded from the merciless sun by strips of cloth stretched between poles spaced around it, bordered by colourful beds of petunias and verbena, and displaying as its proud and principal treasure a perfectly flat and velvet-smooth lawn of incredible green grass.

'Every morning, after prayers, Sheikh Joseph walk there without shoes,' Tâlib said almost reverently, as they got out of the car.

This time the Saint's smile was a little thin.

Two uniformed sentries at the entrance came to sluggish attention as Tâlib led his charges through a small rat-hole door cut in one of the main doors, either one of which was big enough for a double-decker bus to have driven through and which Simon surmised were only thrown open in their full grandeur for the passage of the Emir himself.

Even the Saint had to admit that it was rather like stepping over an enchanted threshold into a very passable likeness of an averagely romantic man's idea of the Arabian Nights.

The spacious patio in which he found himself had a vaulted roof intricately patterned with pastel paints and gold, but cunningly placed embrasures admitted sufficient daylight while filtering out all the eye-aching glare of the desert. A tile floor in exquisite mosaic lay at his feet, and in the centre of it a fountain created three-dimensional traceries of tinkling silver. Silken hangings softened the walls, and archways with their peaks cut in the traditional onion shapes of Islam offered glimpses of enticing passages and courtyards. But even before those details the thing that struck him first was the coolness, whether from air-conditioning or nothing more than the massive protection of the structure itself, which was in such contrast to the searing heat outside that it supplied in its own tangible surcease the most fairy-tale unreality of all.

The Saint forced his mind to turn back from there, over the carpet of tenderly shaded and watered grass outside, across a scorching mile of barren sand, back to the sweltering teeming fetid cluster of desiccated hovels that was the rest of Qabat; and to anyone who knew him well enough his buccaneer's face would have seemed dangerously thoughtful.

No longer seeming to feel called upon to play the tour conductor, Tâlib hustled them unceremoniously along a labyrinth of corridors and cloisters through which Mr Usherdown was almost immediately the one to take the lead, toddling almost a yard ahead of the Saint with his short legs pumping two strokes to Simon's one. After a full five-minute hike they came to a doorway guarded by a gigantic Negro, naked to the waist and actually armed with a huge and genuine scimitar, exactly like a story-book illustration. Mr Usherdown, however, seemed to accept this extravagantly fictitious sight as a now familiar piece of interior decorating,

and stopped expectantly by the door in a way that was comic-
ally reminiscent of a puppy waiting to be let out.

'I only hope Violet is still all right,' he muttered.

Tâlib growled a command at the Negro, who stepped
aside from the rather theatrical pose he had taken before the
door. Then the tall Arab addressed the Saint.

'I send you luggage right away. You rest, wash up. I tell
Emir about you.' He turned to include Mr Usherdown.
'Sheikh Joseph send for you soon, I bet – *Inshallah!*'

'These are our quarters,' Mr Usherdown explained to
Simon. 'Come on.'

He opened the door impatiently, and went in. Simon
followed him. The door boomed shut on the Saint's heels,
with an ominous solidity which suggested a prison rather
than a guest suite; but Simon barely gave it the backward
flick of a raised eyebrow. The scarcely half-subtle prison
theme had been established long before that.

Simon had already accepted, quite phlegmatically by now,
a snapshot impression of a sort of living-room which fitted
well enough into the rest of the slightly stage-harem scenery
(but after all, he was starting to think, some initial scene-
painter must have had *some* authentic motifs to work from)
and the curiosity that fascinated him above any other at this
point was aimed whole-heartedly at the *femme fatale* who had
been content once upon a time to settle for a quaint little
husband like Mortimer Usherdown, and yet whose charms
were still capable of raising the blood of an untamed desert
chieftain to apparently explosive temperatures.

'Violet, my dear,' said the little man, disengaging himself
from her bosom, against which he had plastered himself in
connubial greeting, 'I want you to meet my friend, Mr Simon
Templar.'

'Charmed, I'm sure,' said Mrs Usherdown, in the most
gracious accents of the Bronx.

She had red hair and green eyes and the facial structure of a living doll; and in her very first twenties, Simon could see, she would probably have cued any typical bunch of sailors on shore leave to split the welkin with wolf whistles. She would have been a cute trick in a night-club chorus line – or even in a carnival tent-show, where her path and Mr Usherdown's could plausibly have crossed. Now, some ten years later, she was still pretty, but about thirty pounds overweight. But this excess padding by Western standards, to the Eastern eye might well seem only a divine amplitude of upholstery; and her colouring would have seemed so startlingly exotic in those lands that it was no longer an effort of imagination to see an unsophisticated sheikh being smitten with her as the rarest jewel he could covet for his seraglio . . . Suddenly the one element in the set-up which Simon had found the most mystifying became almost ludicrously obvious and straightforward.

'Mortimer has told me all about your problem,' he said conversationally. 'I see that for the present you're almost uncomfortably well looked after. Is that Ethiopian at the door a real eunuch?'

'I don't know, I never asked him,' Mrs Usherdown answered with dignity. 'I think a man's religion is his own business.'

'But Yûsuf hasn't bothered you?' persisted her anxious consort.

'Of course not. He's very correct, according to his religion. You should know that. Did you remember to get me that candy?'

'Yes, dear. It's in my bags, as soon as they bring them up. I just hope it hasn't all melted . . . But I suppose you've *seen* Yûsuf?'

'Naturally. He's had me in for coffee, and shown me his electric trains, and I've seen all his old Western movies three times. But he took me out for a picnic in the desert in the full moon, and we had silk tents with carpets, and camels, and everthing, and that was very romantic. He's going to buy a yacht, too, and I'm going to help him decorate it, and then we'll take it to Monte Carlo and the Riviera and everywhere.'

Mr Usherdown swallowed his tonsils.

'Violet, my love, I mean – he hasn't given up this crazy idea about you, has he?'

'I do not think it is so gentlemanly of you to call it crazy,' said his helpmeet, with a modicum of umbrage: 'And I don't think that is quite the way to speak of a genuine prince who has paid you more fees than you ever got before, and all he wants is not to be made a sucker out of. I am starting to wonder if you aren't only jealous because he is taller than you and looks so dashing; and after all he only wants his own way, which is what they call the Royal Purgative.'

The Saint cleared his throat.

'I'm here to try and find you a way out,' he said. 'I don't want to make any rash promises, but I come up with a good idea sometimes.'

'You know who Mr Templar is, dear?' Mr Usherdown put in.

'He'd better stay out of this if he isn't a better diviner than you,' said his wife, with a toss of her coppery curls. 'Or he might end up the way you will, if you don't divorce me. Yûsuf says he has thought of something that'll let him make me a widow quite legally, and I'm beginning to wonder if it isn't just selfishness if you want me to suffer like that.'

3

Except for his costume, the Sheikh Yûsuf Loutfallah ibn Hishâm, Emir of Qabat, would not have been instantly recognised as the prototype of the desert eagle and untamed lover immortalised in fiction by an English maiden lady earlier in this century, and brought to life on the silent screen, to the palpitating ecstasy of a bygone generation, by an Italian named D'Antongualla, better known to his worshippers as Rudolph Valentino. Although his nose was basically aquiline, it was also a trifle bulbous. His teeth were prominent, yellow, and uneven; and his untidy beard failed to completely disguise the contour of a receding chin. As a symbol of his rank, his head veil was bound with twin cords of gold running through four black pompoms squarely spaced around his cranium, instead of the common coils of dark rope; and as an index of his wealth and sophistication he wore no less than three watches on his left wrist – a gold Omega Seamaster, a lady's jewelled Gruen, and a Mickey Mouse.

He ate rice and chunks of skewered and roasted mutton with his fingers, getting hearty smears of grease on his face. Seated on another cushion at the same low table, Simon Templar tried to be neater, but acknowledged that it was difficult. On the opposite side of the Emir, Mr Usherdown juggled crumbs to his mouth even more uncomfortably and with less appetite, seeming irreparably cowed by the sinister presence of Tâlib on his other side. The Saint was similarly boxed in by Abdullah, who kept firm hold of a pointed knife, with which he picked his teeth intermittently while staring pensively at the area under Simon's chin. In a corner of the room, four musicians made weird skirlings, twangings, and hootings on an assortment of outlandish instruments, to the accompaniment of which three beige-skinned young women moved in front of the long table, rotating their pelvic regions and undulating their abdomens with phenomenal sinuosity. It was still quite unreally like a sequence from a movie, except that no censors would ever have passed the costumes of the dancers.

When Mr Usherdown looked at them, he did it furtively, as if he was afraid that at any moment his wife might loom up behind him and seize him by the ear. But Mrs Usherdown was not present, having been expressly excluded from the command invitation to dinner which Tâlib had brought.

'Not custom here to have wifes at men's dinner,' Tâlib had explained cheerfully; but Simon, remembering the moonlight picnic which Mrs Usherdown had mentioned, figured that the local customs could always be adapted to the Emir's convenience.

The Saint had hoped to achieve a more personal acquaintance with that lovelorn sheikh, and he was disappointed to learn that his host spoke nothing but Arabic, which was not included in Simon's useful repertoire of languages. He had to be content with an impression of personality, which added nothing very favourable to the character estimate which he had formed in advance. He no longer wondered whether the Emir's infatuation with Violet Usherdown's voluptuous physique might not have blinded him to her shortcomings as an Intellect: obviously Yûsuf could never even have been thinking of spending long evenings in enthralling converse with a cerebral affinity, and Simon doubted whether the Emir would have had much to contribute to such a session even in Arabic. But in a ruthlessly practical way he was probably a shrewd man, and certainly a wilful and uninhibited one. For perhaps the first time Simon realised to the full that his displeasure might be very violent and unfunny indeed.

It was characteristic of the Saint that the crystallising of that awareness made him, if possible, only a little more recklessly irreverent. As the dancing girls stepped up their performance to coax even more fabulous rotations from their navels, and Mr Usherdown's attention seemed to become even more guiltily surreptitious, Simon leaned forward to call encouragement down the table to the little man.

'Joe may think he's the Gift of God to women, Mortimer, but you can't say he's selfish with his samples.'

'Sheikh Joseph got three wifes,' Tâlib put in proudly. 'Also one hundred eighty concubines. Very big shoot.'

The Sheikh suddenly threw down the bone on which he had been gnawing, wiped his mouth and whiskers on the back of his hand, wiped that on the lace tablecloth, and uttered a peremptory command. The musicians let their tortured instruments straggle off into silence. The belly dancers slackened off their gyrations and stood waiting docilely.

The Emir burped, regally and resonantly.

Tâlib and Abdullah eructated with sycophantic enthusiasm in response, vying with each other in the rich reverberation of their efforts. The Emir looked inquiringly at Simon, who finally remembered something he had once heard about the polite observances of that part of the world, and managed to express his appreciation of the meal with a fairly courteous rumble. Everyone then turned to Mr Usherdown, who somehow contrived a small strangled kind of beep which evoked only a certain pitying contempt.

Yûsuf gave an order to Tâlib, and the big Arab fumbled in his robes and brought out a thick bundle of American currency tied with a piece of string. He slapped it on the table in front of Mr Usherdown.

'This pay for your work,' he said, 'all time since you come here to find oil. Okey-dokey?'

'Why, thank you,' said the little man nervously.

'Sheikh say, you take it.'

Mr Usherdown picked up the bundle uncertainly and stuffed it into his pocket.

Yûsuf made a short speech to Mr Usherdown, accompanied by a number of gestures towards the three supple wenches standing in front of the table, while the little man strained to appear respectfully attentive.

'Sheikh say, you choose which girl you like,' Tâlib said.

'Why, they're all very nice,' Mr Usherdown said, in some embarrassment.

'Okay, Sheikh say you take all three,' Tâlib reported, after relaying the evasion.

Mr Usherdown's eyes bulged.

'Who, me? Thank you very much, but I can't do that!'

'Here in Qabat, Muslim law allow you four wifes. Or if you no want to get marry, you keep for concubine, like Sheikh. You be little shoot.'

'I can't take *any* of them,' Mr Usherdown protested, with his face getting red. 'It isn't *our* custom. Please explain to the Emir – and the young ladies – I don't mean any offence, but my wife wouldn't like it at all.'

'You lose wife,' Tâlib said. 'Divorce wife, very quick. Give her the boom's rush. Then you keep dancing girl. Whoopee!'

The flush died out of Mr Usherdown's complexion, leaving it rather pale. But perhaps emboldened by the Saint's presence, he said quite firmly: 'Tell the Emir I wish he'd stop this nonsense. I'm not going to divorce my wife, and that's final.'

Tâlib conveyed the message. Yûsuf did not seem particularly annoyed, or even interested. He grunted a few words in reply which sounded as if they were little more than a cue.

'Sheikh Joseph say you have money what you steal,' Tâlib translated, as if from a prepared speech. 'You take money to find oil. But you not find oil. So you have stolen money. You goddam crook. Now Sheikh must give you the works according to the law of Muhammad. It say in the Qur'ân, in the Sûrah *Al Mâ'idah:* "From a thief, man or woman, cut off the hands. It is right for what they done, a good punish from Allah" – *Bismillâhi'r Rahmâni'r Rahîm!'*

Mr Usherdown's face was chalk-white at the end. He clawed the thick wad of greenbacks out of his pocket and dropped them on the table as though they had been red hot.

'Tell him he can keep his money. I only promised to do my best, and I've done it. But if he feels I haven't earned it, we'll call it quits.'

Tâlib did not touch the money.

'That all finish – you have taked already,' he said with a fiendishly happy grin. 'Thief cannot change to not-thief just because he give back what he steal. If he can, any thief get caught, he give back stealings, everything uncle-dory, nobody can be punish. But Sheikh say because he love you wife so much, you divorce her, you go free. Not get punish. But if you not divorce her—'

He made a sadistically graphic gesture with the edge of his hand against his own opposite wrist.

'What difference would that make?' demanded the Saint harshly. 'His wife still wouldn't be divorced.'

'No need, maybe,' Tâlib said. 'After hands cut off, without doctor, man often die.'

The Emir had been following all this with his eyes, as if he had a complete enough anticipation of the scene not to need to have it interpreted line by line. Now, as if he sensed that a psychological moment had arrived, he clapped his hands and called out something that seemed to include a name; and through the velvet drapes on the far side of the room stepped a bare-chested Negro who might have been a cousin of the one who guarded Usherdown's apartment, and who carried the same kind of gleaming scimitar. The man made an obeisance and glared around hopefully, lifting his blade; and the three dancers huddled together, their eyes round with horror. Beside Mr Usherdown, Tâlib stood up.

The little man leaned forward and looked at the Saint piteously.

'What am I going to do?' he croaked. '*He means it!*'

'You know, I almost think you're right,' said the Saint, fascinated.

Actually, he no longer had any doubt at all. It was all very well to call it fantastic, but he knew that the primitive Islamic law had been correctly cited, and that there were still backwaters in the world where a primitive and autocratic ruler could enforce it to the letter. It would not be much use protesting through diplomatic channels after the deed was done. If, in fact, there were ever a chance to protest at all. Simon Templar could vanish from the face of the earth in Qabat as easily as a far less newsworthy Mortimer Usherdown.

The Saint knew that the error of underestimation which he had committed was of suicidal dimensions. Now he reviewed the situation in a single flash, adding up the Emir and Tâlib and Abdullah, the four musicians, the ebony giant with the scimitar and an unknown number of other palace guards of his ilk, and an equally indeterminate but certainly larger number of the less picturesque but better armed and probably more efficient militia outside – and came up with a very coldblooded assessment. He had blithely accepted some extravagant odds in his time, but he hadn't lived as long as that by kidding himself that he was Superman.

But he did attain a modest pinnacle of heroic effrontery as he turned and tapped Yûsuf on the shoulder with a genial nonchalance that made Mr Usherdown's trembling jaw sag.

'Just a minute, Joe,' he said. 'You may be an old goat, but that doesn't mean you can jump all over the rules if you want everyone else to be stuck with 'em.'

The Sheikh stared at him with incomprehension mixed with indignation and incredulity, and then turned to Tâlib for enlightenment.

'Tell him,' said the Saint, 'that Mortimer isn't a thief yet, because at his own expense he's brought me here to finish the job. Joe will be satisfied if I make him rich, won't he? And until I've had a chance to show what I can do, nobody can prove that Mortimer hasn't delivered.'

Tâlib repeated the argument haltingly, but must have succeeded in conveying the general trend of it; for Yûsuf listened with a deepening scowl that was not without sharp calculation, and promptly came back with a question.

'Sheikh ask, when you do this?'

'Hell, I only just got here,' said the Saint. 'Give me a chance. I'll go to work tomorrow morning, if you like.'

Yûsuf stared at him for what seemed like an interminable time, from under lowered beetling brows. Simon could almost hear the wheels going round behind the beady and slightly bloodshot eyes, like the cogs of a laborious sort of cash register. He was betting that the Sheikh's tender passion was not quite so intoxicating that it would have obliterated the much longer established urgings of avarice. Besides, Yûsuf should figure that he might have his cupcake and his oil too, if he delayed just a little longer. And delay was what the Saint needed first and most desperately.

The Emir growled another question, through Tâlib: 'You take money?'

'I love it,' said the Saint.

Yûsuf spoke to the huge Negro, and pointed to the packet of currency in front of Mr Usherdown. The guard stepped forward, flourished his scimitar, and dexterously picked up the bundle with the flat of the blade, like a flapjack, and held it out towards Simon.

'Oh, no,' wailed Mr Usherdown. 'Then you'll be in the same mess as me. I can't let you—'

'But I'm one of the best dowsers in the business,' said the Saint. 'Maybe *the* best. You gave me the testimonial yourself.'

He took the parcel of money from the sword.

'Now if you not do nothing, you a big thief too,' Tâlib said unnecessarily. 'Can have hands cut off like him. Okey-dokey?'

Simon had slipped the string off the wad of greenbacks and was riffling through them for a rough estimate of their total.

'This is all right for a retainer,' he said coolly. 'But you can tell Joe that if I strike it rich for him he's going to owe us a lot more than this.'

'You find plenty oil,' Tâlib brought back the answer, 'Sheikh say, he be very generous. You betcha. But you get on the ball damn quick, skiddoo.'

'Fine,' said the Saint. He put the money in his pocket, lighted a cigarette, and indicated the neglected trio of diaphanously veiled beauties with a gesture of magnificent insouciance. 'And now can we go on with the floor show? And may I pick a girl too?'

4

'I still wish you'd kept out of it,' Mr Usherdown repeated miserably, for perhaps the eleventh time. 'You shouldn't have let them trick you into touching that money.'

'I wasn't tricked,' said the Saint scornfully. 'I just decided that if I was going in at all, I might as well go in with a splash. Didn't you ever play poker? If you were bluffing, in a no-limit game, would you expect to impress anybody with a two-bit raise?'

This was very much later, when they were back in the guest suite, on which the guards had been doubled – which Simon had been tempted to call a two-edged compliment.

'I'll never forgive myself,' moaned the little man.

'Phooey,' snarled the Saint. 'You invited me in, didn't you?'

'I just happened to hear your name, and I realised who you were. I never thought I'd have had the nerve to pretend to know you like that, right in front of Tâlib and Abdullah. But I was frantic. I thought you might be able to do something.'

'Well, I'm trying.'

'I mean, something sensational, like I've heard about you – like fighting our way out of here.'

'Too much of this is like a B picture already, Mortimer. Don't make it any worse. What did you think I was going to use for armaments?'

'I thought someone like you . . . you know . . . would have a gun.'

'I did. It's in the suit-case I left in bond in Basra. Did you think I'd try to sneak it into a place like this, when I'm supposed to be a peaceful water diviner? You should know how hysterical it makes little big shoots to think of anybody but their own trigger men having nasty toys that go bang. Do you think my overnight bag wasn't searched before they brought it up here, and Tâlib didn't paw me over himself while he was hustling us through the Customs?'

'Perhaps we should have jumped on them at dinner,' Mr Usherdown said weakly. 'We didn't talk it over enough beforehand. I could have distracted their attention while you got the sword away from that eunuch, if that's what he was, and then you'd have grabbed Yûsuf and taken him for a hostage, and we might've fought our way out ...'

Simon gazed at him in genuinely sympathetic amazement.

'My God, my public,' he said dazedly. 'You must have really seen it like that, with me whacking our way through the infidels like Errol Flynn in his prime ... Forgive me, Mortimer; but there was a moment when I dallied with an idea of that kind myself, only I sobered up in the nick of time. I suppose I might have wrought some havoc among the Saracens – with your help, of course – but I'd still have had to get all of us all the way out of this castle. Including Violet. And after that, where would we go? Take a running dive into the Persian Gulf and start swimming through the sharks? Leap on to three conveniently parked camels and gallop off into the dunes? Or just hitch a ride to the airport and talk our way past the local Gestapo on to the next plane out? ... Assume that we've busted loose, and we're running: how do you see us getting *out of Qabat*?'

'I deserve anything that happens to me,' Mr Usherdown said wretchedly. 'I think you should forget about us and try to escape on your own. I know we'd be a terrible burden, but perhaps you could make it by yourself.'

The Saint stood by a window and examined the ornamental iron grille across it with professional appraisal.

'Crashing out of this gilded cage is liable to be more than an overnight project, even for me,' he said.

Violet Usherdown helped herself to another chocolate cream from the box beside her.

'That's the first sensible thing I've heard from you for a long time, Mortimer. Mr Templar should not feel obligated,' she said, with remarkable cheerfulness. 'Anyway, you know now that you aren't in half as much trouble as you were afraid of.'

Mr Usherdown's eyes took on a slight glaze.

'Nothing worse than having my hands chopped off,' he chattered bravely. 'Lots of soldiers have had that happen. And you can get wonderful artificial limbs now. I've seen pictures of them. I wouldn't be surprised if I could even go on divining, with a bit of practice—'

'In a pig's eye,' said Mrs Usherdown trenchantly. 'You wouldn't be doing me any favours, wanting me to live with a man with nothing but a pair of hooks. I couldn't stand it.' She shuddered delicately. 'I mean, knowing it was on account of me, of course, even though he was most heroic. I would rather be divorced and taken into the Sheikh's harem.'

'But I love you, Vi,' pleaded her spouse. 'I couldn't sacrifice you like that.'

'What is a woman's life but sacrifice?' she asked. 'And it isn't as if I would have to put up with his old wives, because he has promised me he will give them away. And even if he is getting down to his last few millions we wouldn't starve to death. When I think of some of the things I've had to put up with since I married you, Mortimer Usherdown, I cannot say it is the worst fate that could possibly happen to me, although naturally it is always a shock to a lady to be put asunder.'

Both Mr Usherdown and the Saint looked at her in oddly similar ways for a moment.

Then Simon touched the little man's arm.

'I want some sleep before the performance tomorrow, chum,' he said. 'But before I turn in, you'd better dig out those hazel twigs and show me how to make like a real dowser.'

It was quite a large and colourful gallery that turned out in the still bearable warmth of the early morning to watch the Saint set forth on his quest, as if it had been the tee-off of a golf championship. There was a group of about three dozen VIP's, identifiable by their fine robes and arrogant bearing, whom Simon took for the squires of the smaller manors and their personal friends. There were, inevitably, Tâlib and Abdullah, with no less than four of the scimitar-bearing Negroes hovering close behind them to add muscle to their menace. At a respectful distance stood a sizeable crowd of sombre and ragged citizens from the town, summoned by whatever served as a grapevine in that grapeless land. A full platoon of the militarily-uniformed guards was deployed to keep the common herd at bay – and was also a sobering reminder of the unromantic improbability of the dashing kind of getaway that Mr Usherdown had dreamed of. From the palace entrance had spilled a heterogeneous collection of servants and minor functionaries, including the quartet of musicians; but the dancing girls were not with them, or in fact any other feminine members of the Emir's household. However, glancing up at the façade, Simon was sure that he could detect a stirring of veils behind every barred window. He might have imagined it, but he even thought that in one of the gratings he saw a timid flutter of pale fingers, instantly withdrawn . . .

The only woman in plain sight was Violet Usherdown; and the descriptive phrase was not strictly apt, at that, for she had tied a square of brocade over her head in a sort of babushka effect, and fastened what looked like a man's white handkerchief across the aperture in front in such a way that it masked her completely from the eyes down.

'I've got to obey the custom of the country if Yûsuf is going to respect me at all,' she had explained with dignity. 'Why, I've found out that the women here would rather expose *any* part of themselves than let a man see their face. That means, if I didn't wear a veil, all the men would be staring at me – and I know what men are like, Mortimer – as if I was stark naked! When I think how I used to let anyone here see me with a bare face, before I knew what it meant to them, I'm so embarrassed I could blush all over.'

The Sheikh Yûsuf Loutfallah ibn Hishâm, in conformity with his royal prerogative, was the last to appear; but his arrival was a welcome signal that the period of suspenseful waiting was over. The Sheikh confirmed this himself, barking a few words directly at the Saint which needed no interpreter to announce that they meant 'Okay, let's get going.'

'You want camel or jeep?' Tâlib amplified, with a lavish wave of his arm which embraced both forms of transportation, conveniently parked along the driveway.

Simon had already considered the possibility of stretching the reprieve to the limit by embarking on a safari to the remotest corner of Qabat; but after reckoning that that could hardly be more than forty or fifty miles, he had decided that the time he could gain would not be worth the discomfort involved.

'I shall begin *here*,' he said, pointing dramatically to the ground at his feet, 'where nobody before me has thought of beginning.'

From the buzz of comment that came from those within earshot of Tâlib's translation of that announcement, the Saint knew that he had at least scored a point of showmanship.

He raised the hazel branch which he carried and took hold of it very carefully in the way that Mr Usherdown had taught him. It was cut and trimmed in the shape of a Y with long arms, and he held it inverted, in a peculiar kind of half-backwards grip, with the ends of the arms of the Y in the upturned palms of his hands. The main stem of the Y pointed almost straight up, but seemed to be in rather precarious balance because of the way he was spreading and twisting the arms at the same time against the spring of the wood.

'You have to stretch it till it feels almost alive and fighting you,' Mr Usherdown had told him. 'And then you just concentrate your mind on oil, or whatever it is you're looking for. It's the concentration that does it.'

Simon could feel the almost-life of the twig, reacting against the odd strained way he held it; but his concentration fell far short of the prescribed optimum. He found, rather disconcertingly, that his mind was capable of simultaneous wandering in at least three directions. One part of it remained solidly burdened with the involvments of the basic situation; another maverick element insisted on leaning back and making snide observations of the percentage of ham in his own performance; while whatever was otherwise unoccupied tried to think about oil, found it an elusive subject after picturing black sluggish streams of it in which revolved ponderous cams and gears, which merged into the oscillating stomachs of harem dancers, so that he switched quickly to the smog-belching sexlessness of a California oil refinery, and the grey haze creeping out to the Pacific Ocean where the sybarites thought it was too cold to swim but it would be wonderful to leap into straight out of the blazing sand and sky of Qabat ... and he found that his intensely aimless circling had brought him smack up against the gate in the fence around the Emir's precious private lawn.

The impulse that seized him then was pure gratuitous devilment. Letting go the hazel twig for a moment, he indicated the barrier with an air of pained indignation.

There was an awe-stricken mutter among the spectators, and Tâlib seemed to swell up in preparation for an explosion; but the Emir cut in with half a dozen words that abruptly deflated him. The gate was opened, and Simon resumed the proper grip on his oddly shaped wand and walked in.

He went on trying to think about oil, because the effort helped him to maintain a convincing aspect of strenuous concentration, but a perverse slant of association insisted on linking it next with salad dressing, and then leaving only the lettuce, fresh picked and still jewelled with morning dew, like the drops that sparkled on the grass he walked on, relics of the mechanical sprayer which until a few minutes ago had been scattering its priceless elixir over the sacrosanct turf . . .

What happened next was that the hazel began to twist in his hands, the upright stem of the inverted Y trying to swing over to point downwards, so startlingly that he involuntarily fought against it. But it was as if the wood had become possessed of a will and a power of its own, so that with all his strength he could not hold it, and it writhed slowly and irresistibly over in his grasp until the stem pointed vertically down.

Simon Templar felt the sweat on his body chilled by a passage of ghostly wings, and would never know how he succeeded in keeping his face from looking completely fatuous.

He thought that a distant roar came to his ears from a hundred indistinguishable throats, though it might as well have been only a subjective amplification of the turmoil in his own brain; yet it seemed almost breathlessly quiet in the enclosure, where except for the Emir himself only Tâlib and one pair of sword-bearing guards had presumed to follow him. And in that brimming silence he released the forked twig and extended his forefinger imperatively towards the spot where it fell, almost in the geometrical centre of the Sheikh's most treasured enclave.

'Here,' said the Saint.

'You mean close here, outside, okay?' Tâlib said, shaken for the first time since Simon had known him into an almost incoherent dither.

The Saint's arm and pointing finger remained statuesquely rigid.

'I mean *here*,' he repeated inflexibly.

Yûsuf was studying him in thunderous gloom, his head on one side like an introspective vulture. Simon met the inquisitorial scrutiny without blinking, letting everything ride with the bet that the Sheikh's cupidity would be stronger than his interest in horticulture – or at least that he was capable of the arithmetic to realise that a new oil well would buy a lot more lawns. And finally Yûsuf spoke.

'Sheikh say,' Tâlib transmitted it, 'you deliver, you get rich, pronto. Not deliver no goods, we cut your bloody head off. What you say, Mac?'

'You've got a deal, schlemiel,' said the Saint blandly.

After that it became much less orderly – in fact, it rapidly lost all semblance of order. The Emir rattled off another cataract of injunctions, and stalked away. Tâlib began to shout supplementary orders in four directions. The privileged spectators who were inside the cordon of militia pressed forward, gesticulating and shrieking in friendly conversation until they reached the fence, which bulged and bent and then meekly disintegrated before the weight of their excitement. At a word from Tâlib, the two Negroes closed in on Simon and hustled him unceremoniously through the jabbering mob. Outside the remains of the enclosure, the two other scimitar-bearers had already sandwiched in Mr Usherdown, who looked limp and pallid with stupefaction. Simon's unit joined up with them, and the four guards formed a hollow square with Simon and Mr Usherdown in the middle and rushed them towards the palace entrance.

Simon caught one glimpse of Violet Usherdown, off to the side, with Yûsuf making gestures towards the palace, and a few of his nobles gathering curiously around, and Tâlib heading across no doubt to volunteer the assistance of his extraordinary brand of English; and then he was pushed through the great doorway and hurried into the labyrinthine route that led back to what he now felt it was somewhat euphemistic to call the guest quarters.

The massive door slammed shut and quivered with the clanking of bolts, leaving Simon and Mr Usherdown alone to gaze at each other.

At last Mr Usherdown achieved a shaky voice.

'Why did you do that, Templar?'

'I guess I was born ornery,' said the Saint. 'It was such a priceless chance to trespass on Joe's holy of holies, I just couldn't resist it. I was quite tempted to take my shoes off and do it in my bare feet, but I was afraid that might be going too far.'

'But you didn't have to pretend to *find* there.'

'I didn't. Your hazel twig did that.'

'Nonsense. You made it look terrific, but I knew you were faking.'

'I wasn't,' said the Saint flatly. 'I admit, I'd thought of it. But I hadn't quite made up my mind. I was still ad-libbing. And then that silly stick took over.'

The little man stared at him unbelievingly.

'It couldn't. You said you'd never done any dowsing.'

'I haven't. But there has to be a first time for everything. Maybe I have unsuspected talents.'

'Did it feel as if it was sort of magnetised?'

'It was the eeriest sensation I've ever experienced in my

life. I couldn't control the damn thing. I tried. It almost tore the skin off my hands, twisting itself over.'

'There's no oil under the palace – least of anywhere,' Mr Usherdown said stubbornly, but in blanker perplexity than ever. 'I've held a rod around here myself – not too seriously, but you were wrong when you said nobody had tried. You must've been trying so hard, you got a sort of auto-suggestion. I've heard about things like that.'

Simon shrugged.

'Could be. It doesn't matter much, anyway. All I wanted to do was stall for time, and give Joe a new place to dig. While he's busy with that, we can work at digging ourselves out of this Arabian Nightsmare. What will the next move be?'

Mr Usherdown shuffled to the nearest barred window, where the Saint joined him. The opening did not look out on the front of the palace, where the latest activity had been, but through it drifted echoes of clangings and hammerings and a natter of filtered voices erupting in occasional screeches of peak enthusiasm.

'Yûsuf has a well-drilling rig of his own now,' Mr Usherdown said. 'He bought it after the big company refused to put in any more wells, and he's only been waiting to be told where to use it. They must be setting it up already, where you told them to.'

'How long will it take 'em to find out if it's doing them any good?'

'I don't know. I never had to study that sort of engineering. It seems to me if they were good enough they could get it working in less than a week, because they don't have any union hours, and then of course they'd be expecting something from the minute the drill started to go down. I don't know how many feet a day this kit he's got could drill, but they wouldn't wonder how deep they might have to go, either—'

'All right,' said the Saint impatiently. 'We can figure we've got a few days, anyhow.'

'I wish I knew why they didn't bring Vi back with us,' Mr Usherdown said worriedly.

There was no answer to that for almost an hour, when the door was flung open again and Tâlib came in. He was accompanied by one of the possible eunuchs, an ordinary manservant, and a dumpy woman heavily swathed in drab veils; a militiaman armed with a Tommy-gun brought up the rear, and stopped in the doorway with his weapon at the ready and a very competent look in his eye. The woman bustled on through the apartment, located a suit-case, and began to stuff it with everything feminine that caught her eye. The manservant followed her, examining the articles which she discarded, opening drawers and cabinets, and occasionally tucking things away in his pockets.

'What's the idea?' bleated Mr Usherdown. 'And where's my wife?'

'Wife go live with Sheikh's other wife mothers,' Tâlib said. 'Sheikh don't want her live with you no more, no sir. But take yourself easy. Nobody hurt her. Sheikh only make sure you don't be like jealous husband, perhaps bump her over yourself. Or perhaps you and friend try run off with her. Not bloody like it.'

He spoke to the big Negro, who gave Tâlib his scimitar to hold while he made a quick but thorough search of Simon's and Mr Usherdown's persons.

The woman went out, lugging the heavy suit-case, with the manservant sauntering after her.

'Men starting to dig right now,' Tâlib said. 'You wait. Very soon we know if you full of balloons. We dig up oil, Sheikh Joseph make you rich somofabitches. Not find oil' – he bared his teeth, and drew the back of the blade luxuriously across his throat before handing it back to its owner – 'it's too goddam bad, you betcha.'

He strode out, followed by the Negro, and lastly the guard with the sub-machine-gun backed out and kept the room covered with it from the passage until the door was closed again.

'Lovable fellow,' drawled the Saint.

'What are we going to do?' whimpered the little man. 'Did you see what he did? I know you only made it worse by telling them to tear up the Sheikh's garden. Now they'll cut off our heads instead of just our hands.'

'I can't see that it makes much difference, Mortimer. But Tâlib is probably exaggerating. We should have asked him what it says in the Koran about making divots in an Emir's green.'

'And it wouldn't do us any good to escape now. Even if we got out, we wouldn't have any idea where to look for Violet.'

Simon lighted a cigarette.

'I don't think we're going to do any escaping for a while, anyway,' he said. 'Didn't you watch the valet character going through everything while the maid was packing up? And the Ethiopian who searched us didn't even leave me my nail file.'

He had no reason to correct his hunch after they had gone over the apartment virtually inch by inch. Every article of metal that had a point or an edge or even a sharp corner had been neatly removed from their possessions. And when the first meal of their incarceration was brought to them, it was a reminder that in a country where the fingers were still the accepted eating utensil there would not even be the ordinary remote hope of secreting a fork or a spoon. As for the possibility of scratching away the very modern concrete in which the window ironwork was set with a shard from a broken dish, Simon could not even delude himself into giving it a trial.

'There must be *something*,' persisted Mr Usherdown numbly.

'There is,' said the Saint, stretching himself out philosophically. 'You can tell me the story of your life.'

That was about what it came to, for the next five days, and some of it was not uninteresting either, once the desperate need for any kind of distraction had got the little man started.

It may seem a shatteringly abrupt change of pace to suddenly condense five days into a paragraph; yet in absolute fact it would be nothing but outrageous padding to make more of them. Mr Mortimer Usherdown's wandering reminiscences might have made a book of sorts by themselves, but they have no bearing on this story. Nor, in the utmost honesty, do the multifarious schemes for escape with which the Saint occupied his mind: since they were built up and elaborated only to be torn down and discarded, it would be a dishonest use of space for this chronicle to get any reader steamed up and then let down over them. It should be enough to say this time that if Simon Templar had seen any passable facsimile of a chance to make a break, he would obviously have taken it. But he didn't. The main door of the suite was only opened twice each day, when their meals were brought, and each time the operation was performed with such efficient precautions that it would have been sheer fantasy to think that it offered a loophole. The Saint was realistic enough to conserve his energy for a change that would have to come sometime.

It must be admitted, however, that when it came it was like nothing that he had dreamed of.

The first hint of it came around the middle of the sixth day, in the form of a vague and confused rising of noise that crept in on them even without any window that looked out on the front of the palace. When they noticed it, after the first idle surmises, they ignored it; then wondered again; then shrugged it off; then could not shut it out; then could only be silent and wonder, without daring to theorise in words.

It was an eternity later when the door was flung open, the four giant Negroes marched in, this time directed by Abdullah, and backed up by twice the usual detail of armed militia, and the Saint and Mr Usherdown were once again boxed in a square of herculean muscle and marched head-long around the corridors and courtyards and corners that led back with increasing familiarity to the main forecourt. Since Abdullah spoke no English, it was useless to ask questions, although Mr Usherdown ineffectually tried to; and so they hurtled eventually through the grand portals into the ugly stifling heat and glare of the afternoon without any warning of what was to greet their eyes.

Simon was prepared for the tall skeletal pyramid of the oil derrick that now towered starkly amidst the withered remnants of Qabat's only garden. The voices that he had heard from far off had also prepared him for the excited swarm of labourers, palace servitors, guards, and notables from the nearest mansions who were milling vociferously around it. Nor was it surprising to see the Emir himself as a secondary focal point of the group, or Tâlib hovering behind him – or even Violet Usherdown standing near the Sheikh, recognisable in spite of an orthodox veil by the copper curls which hung below a gold lamé turban which she had adopted.

What the Saint was incredulously unprepared for was the thick shining silvery column of fluid that shot up between the girders of the derrick and dissolved into a white plume of spray at the top.

For the first few dizzy seconds he felt only a foggy bewilderment at the colour of it. Then as the observation forced itself more solidly into his consciousness he wondered deliriously whether he could have topped everything with the all-time miracle of bringing in a well that gave only pure refined high-octane gasoline. But in another moment his nose gave crushing refutation to that alluring whimsy. There was no smell of gas. And as his escorts wedged him through the encircling congregation and delivered him beside the Emir, at the very base of the scaffolding, a shower of drops fell on him, and he caught some on his hand and brought the hand right under his nostrils and then touched it with his tongue and knew exactly what it was.

It was water.

5

As if it had been only six minutes ago, instead of six days, Simon re-lived the capricious insubordinations of his mind, when he had been trying to concentrate on oil, and had been wafted through refineries to the ocean and through salads to irrigation; and it became clear to him that his latest discovered talent would need a lot more disciplining before it would be strictly commercial.

It also dawned on him that he was not his own only critic.

'Sheikh know now, you one big goddam thief,' Tâlib bawled at him.

The Saint drew himself up.

In the superb unhesitating confidence of his recovery, he turned that flabbergasting moment into one of his finest hours.

'Tell Joe,' he said coldly, 'that he is one big goddam fool.'

Mr Usherdown gasped, and even Tâlib blanched as he blurted out an indubitably expurgated rendition of that retort.

'I didn't promise to find oil,' Simon went on, without waiting for the Emir's reaction. 'I can't find it if it isn't here, which you've already been told. I said I would make him rich. And I've done that. In Kuwait, isn't water worth more than oil?'

As that was repeated, a hush began to fall, and even the Emir's furious eyes settled into sharp and penetrating attention.

'Lots of places around here have oil,' said the Saint disparagingly. 'But I've given Qabat something that none of the others have. I was told that Kuwait is spending forty-five million dollars to build a pipeline to get water. Won't they be glad to save nearly two hundred miles of it and just bring the pipeline here, and give you the money instead? Is there any place around this Gulf that wouldn't trade you ten barrels of oil for one barrel of water? Let Kuwait and Dhahran sweat out their oil, while in Qabat you take their money and buy beautiful cars and jewels and walk about in grass up to your knees.' He swept his arm grandly towards the jet of pure and glistening H_2O that was roaring merrily into the parched and burning sky. 'This is what I've done for you, Joe.'

Tâlib was still stumbling over the last few words when Yûsuf demonstrated his lightning grasp of practical economics by enfolding the Saint in a grateful and embarrassingly affectionate embrace.

He then turned ebulliently towards Mr Usherdown, but concluded the gesture much more perfunctorily, as if a different and disturbing thought had obtruded itself midway in the movement.

Suddenly Mrs Usherdown's voice cut stridently through the rising babble around.

'I don't know what you're taking a bow for, Mortimer Usherdown,' it said scathingly. 'After all, *you* didn't do anything.'

The interruption was on such a rasping note that Yûsuf turned inquiringly.

Tâlib, whose expression had been getting progressively sourer as the atmosphere of congratulation and camaraderie seemed to be gaining the ascendant, brightened visibly as he translated.

The carnivorous gleam came back into Yûsuf's stare as he

stepped back and contemplated Mr Usherdown with a new and terrifying exultation.

But instead of quailing under that baleful regard, the little man was not even aware of it. Instead of trembling with fear, he was quivering with the stress of what Simon realised was a far more cataclysmal emotion. He straightened up to the last millimetre of his height, inflating all that there was of his chest until the veins stood out on his neck, and sparks flashed from his small watery eyes.

'Why, you nasty creature,' he squeaked indignantly. 'I know what you're trying to do. But you needn't bother.' He stuck out a straight skinny arm ending in a wrathfully pointing finger. '*I divorce you, I divorce you, I divorce you.* There!'

'Well,' said Mrs Usherdown tartly, 'you're very welcome, I'm sure.'

She turned, with a toss of her head, and strutted away towards the palace, bouncing her ample hips.

Tâlib construed the passage in the tone of voice that he might have used to bring tidings of a major disaster, and this time the hug that the Emir gave Mr Usherdown was unmarred by any reservations.

'Sheikh say,' Tâlib droned gloomily, 'you ask anything you want, you get it, if not too much.'

'We'll settle for the price of one small oil well,' said the Saint. 'And our tickets on the next plane to Basra,' he added casually, wishing that he knew more about geology, and vowing not to uncross his fingers until whatever freakish artesian source they had tapped had proved that it was capable of keeping the gusher flowing at least until he had taken off.

'Okay, dough kay,' Tâlib said. 'But tonight, Sheikh order big feast and whoopee.'

Mr Usherdown winked at the Saint, slapped the Emir on the back, and poked the outraged Tâlib in the ribs, while a broad beam of ineffable rapture overspread his lumpy little face.

'That's what I'm waiting for,' he crowed. 'Bring on the dancing girls!'

The Pluperfect Lady

I

Simon Templar stayed at the Raffles Hotel in Singapore for sentimental reasons. Although more modern and more luxurious caravanserais had been built in the many years since he had last been there, the Raffles was one of the places that was simply synonymous with Singapore to him, as it always will be to the real Far East hands from away back. And as to why that one particular place had won out over two others almost equally traditional, Major Vernon Ascony had a theory.

'I just looked at the name on the front and felt sure you couldn't have resisted it,' Ascony said.

'Since you couldn't possibly have been thinking of A. J. Raffles, the immortal Amateur Cracksman of fiction,' said the Saint, 'I wonder what there can be about me that reminds you of Sir Stamford Raffles, the illustrious pioneer and Empire builder, whose name is commemorated on so many landmarks of this romantic city.'

Major Ascony permitted the vestige of a smile to stir under the shadow of his closely clipped moustache.

'Nothing, old chap. Positively not one single thing.'

'And why were you trying to find me anyway?' Simon inquired.

'I'm with the Police,' Ascony said, and modestly refrained from specifying that he was an Assistant Commissioner.

The Saint sighed.

'One day I'm going to have this printed on a card,' he said. 'But if you'll accept it verbally, I can save you a lot of time.

No, I am not here to stir up any trouble. No, I am not looking for any crime or criminals. Yes, I am just an ordinary tourist. Of course, if something irresistibly intriguing happens under my nose, I can't promise not to get involved in it. But I don't intend to start anything.'

'What made you decide to come here? This is a bit off your beat, isn't it?'

'It wasn't always. As a matter of fact, one of my first big adventures started not far from here, though it came to a head in England. But that was an awful long time ago. And the other day, out of the blue, I had a sudden crazy belt of nostalgia: I just had to come back and see how much the place had changed. I hadn't anything else in mind for a couple of weeks, and BOAC flies here awful fast. I remember the first time – took me six weeks on a freighter from Lima.'

Ascony proffered his cigarette case, and Simon accepted one.

'How about a drink?'

'I'd like it,' Simon said.

They sat down at a table on the terrace overlooking the bustling Esplanade, and a soft-footed 'boy' came quickly to dust it off.

'A *stengah*, or something fancier?'

'Peter Dawson will be fine.'

'*Dua*,' ordered the Major. He rubbed his moustache thoughtfully. 'I suppose you've already noticed a lot of difference?'

'Quite a bit,' Simon grinned. 'The plumbing, especially. And air conditioning, yes. And no more rickshaws.'

'Yes, there've been a few improvements. But a lot of things are worse, too.'

'I've heard about that. You're pretty high on the Russian list of places to make trouble in.'

'It's not too bad right here. We've had a few nasty riots, but nothing so far that we couldn't handle. But it's a bit rugged for the blokes up-country sometimes.'

'You've still got those Red guerrillas? I thought a namesake of mine cleaned 'em out.'

'General Templer? Only he spelt it with an E. You know, when he was sent here, one of the London papers ran a headline about "The Saint Goes to Malaya". And people used to ask him if he was any relation of yours. I never found out whether it really amused him or not.'

'I thought the manager gave me an odd look when I registered.'

Ascony nodded.

'Templer – Sir Gerald, I mean – did a darn good job. But there are still a few too many of those lads at large, with guns hidden away that we dropped to 'em during the occupation, and others that they captured when the Japs gave up. Every now and again they go on a rampage and shoot up a mine or a plantation, so the chaps up there still have to keep armed guards and barricade themselves in at night.'

'Sort of like Africa with the Mau Mau?'

'Sort of. Or like America with the Redskins, judging from what I've seen in the pictures.'

The boy returned and served them their highballs.

'Well, cheers,' Ascony said.

'Cheerio,' said the Saint accommodatingly.

Ascony drank, put down his glass, and lighted another cigarette.

'I suppose you wouldn't be interested in seeing that sort of thing,' he remarked.

His tone was impeccably casual, so that it would have seemed embarrassingly hypersensitive to attempt to read into it a challenge or a sneer. Yet something deep inside the Saint prickled involuntarily.

'I hate to miss it,' he replied. 'But I don't suppose the

Chamber of Commerce is featuring it as part of a guided tour.'

'I could arrange it,' Ascony said; and Simon knew then that he had given Ascony precisely the opening that Ascony wanted.

Simon said: 'Is it worth all that trouble to get me out of town?'

The police official's infinitesimal smile was permitted to make its tiny diffident movement under the scrubby moustache.

'I won't deny that I'll have a load off my mind when you leave. But I do have another ulterior motive. You could be quite a godsend to a pal of mine up there, while you're having a spot of fun for yourself. Chap by the name of Lavis. A real good egg. Has a place up in Pahang, miles from anywhere, in one of the worst areas.'

'What makes you think I'd be a godsend to him?'

'He's been having a rather rough time – ulcers, and fever on top of it. He ought to be in the hospital, actually, but he won't leave the plant. I can't blame him, in a way. You see, up till about a year ago he was doing very well for himself, in fact he was one of the most successful business men in Malaya, and then one day his partner simply skipped out with every penny he could raise on their assets. It was a shocking business. Ted Lavis was practically wiped out overnight. This plant up in Pahang was about all he managed to salvage, and he's trying like the devil to make a go of it, but if anything happened to it he'd really be sunk. He's got a white assistant, of course, and the usual native foremen and guards, but with Lavis himself laid up and his wife having to nurse him it's no picnic for anybody.'

'His wife's there with him?'

'Naturally, old chap. A stunning woman – used to be married to a doctor here. The assistant's a bit of a bounder, in my private opinion. But you'll see for yourself. How does it appeal to you?'

Simon was used to the unconventional hospitality of the tropics, but he knew that Major Ascony must have something more in mind than mere friendliness. But since Ascony was obviously not planning to put any cards on the table, the Saint decided to play along with equal inscrutability.

He said blandly: 'I'd love it, if you think they'd put up with me.'

'I'm sure they'll be glad to. I'll send them a wire at once.' Ascony signed the chit which the boy had tucked under the ashtray, and stood up. He seemed to be a very decisive man, in his own way. 'Sorry I have to run along now, but I'll ring you first thing in the morning.'

Simon waited fatalistically to see what the call would bring. He was sampling his *ketchil makan*, the ritual eye-opener of tea and buttered toast without which the Englishman in the East Indies is not supposed to have the strength to get dressed for breakfast, when the telephone rang.

'Mrs Lavis wired back that they'll be delighted to have you,' Ascony said. 'The train leaves in a couple of hours. I hope that isn't rushing you too much. If I can get away, I'll drop by the station and see you off.'

With an odd sensation that he was already on an express train hurtling towards some unrevealed rendezvous with destiny, Simon dressed and breakfasted and re-packed the few things he had taken from his bag.

He was just settling himself in the corner of a first-class compartment when Major Ascony came along the platform, looking very military in a crisply laundered uniform with a swagger stick tucked under his arm, and stopped by the open window.

'Ah, there you are, Templar. I see you made it.'

'That's a relief,' said the Saint seriously. 'I wasn't altogether sure that I was here myself.'

The Major looked a trifle puzzled, but disciplined himself to suppress it.

'You shouldn't have anything to worry about on the trip,' he said. 'They haven't wrecked a train for ages.'

'I'm sorry to hear that. I've always wanted to be in a good train wreck.'

'Give my best to Teddy and Eve, will you? And tell 'em I mean to come up myself the first chance I have to take a few days off.'

'I will.'

There was a blowing of whistles and a rising tempo of shouts and jabbering around the second- and third-class carriages as the train crew struggled to separate the travellers from the farewell deputations and pack the former on board so that the train could start. Ascony handed a book through the window.

'Thought you might like something to read on the trip.'

'Why, thank you.'

'Not at all. You can return it when you come back.'

It was a bulky volume entitled *Altogether*, by W. Somerset Maugham, and a glance inside showed that it was a collection of short stories.

'I believe I've read some of these before,' Simon said.

'Well, you get more out of some of 'em the second time, I think. Besides, it's more fun to read 'em right where they're supposed to have happened. Might give you a feeling about some things, if you know what I mean.'

'They're almost historical now, aren't they?' said the Saint, trying not to sound captious. 'Maugham was here long before even my last time, wasn't he?'

'Yes, I dare say he was. But human nature doesn't change much.'

The whistling and shouting and jabbering reached a crescendo, and the train gave an authoritative clattering jolt and began to creep forward. Ascony strolled along with it for a few steps, beside the window.

'There's one story especially I'd like to get your reaction to,' he said.

'Which one?'

'You'll come to it. Hope you have a good time. So long, old chap.'

And merely by ceasing to walk, with a cordial gesture that was half wave and half salute, Ascony made an incontestable exit, being left behind in a moment as the train drew away from him.

2

Simon did little reading on the trip, for he had barely started to turn the pages of the book when he was sociably conscripted by three planters in search of a fourth for bridge. Then there was lunch, the inevitable curry, and afterwards almost everyone fell into a doze, and the Saint himself found it lazily easy to fall in with the custom of the country. He awoke with one of the Malay guards shaking him gently by the shoulder, as he had been enjoined to do, and saying: 'The next stop will be Ayer Pahit, *tuan*.'

During such opportunities as he had had to let his mind wander, he had tried to figure what could lie behind Major Ascony's peculiar behaviour, and had had conspicuously negative success. He was reasonably certain that Ascony was not dreaming that the Saint would personally solve the problem of the Red guerrillas, when a prolonged and large-scale military operation had not completely succeeded in eradicating them. It had to be something much less farfetched and more limited than that. But the only further assumption that seemed safe was that it must be something involving the personalities he was going to meet, and Simon stepped out on the platform not quite literally like an outlaw entering a hostile city, but with a similar feeling of keeping his weight lightly on his toes and his eyes alert for more than the ordinary visitor would see.

Almost as soon as he stepped off the Malay guards clambered aboard again with their rifles slung, some of them

riding on the engine, and the train tooted its whistle and
was off again with its usual disjointed preliminary lurch. As
it pulled out it revealed on the other side of the tracks a
half-dozen *atap*-thatched ramshackle buildings, one of
which had double doors wide open and from what could
be seen of its murky mysteriously cluttered interior
appeared to be a combined general store and saloon, and
behind those buildings was the solid jungle, crowding in on
them obtrusively as if it actively resented the few square
yards that they had usurped from it and was impatient to
absorb them again: this was all that could be called the
village, if it could be dignified even by that name. On the
side of the tracks where the Saint stood was the Lavis
estate, the centre and only reason for existence of the settlement called Ayer Pahit or its railway station, which consisted
of a ten-foot-square wooden hut at the side of the platform.
Close behind that was a very large corrugated-iron shed
like a warehouse, and a little farther back still was a large
rectangular building of smoke-streaked concrete topped
with an incomprehensible tangle of pipes, with an incongruously modern and industrial look to it. The concrete
building was set right into the side of a cleared hill that rose
away from the railroad. A little above it were two long stark
buildings like barracks, recognisable as coolie quarters, and
much farther up was what had to be the manager's house,
also of wood and *atap*, but set up on pilings and with a
long, shady, screened verandah running the whole length
of it. Even the big house was not on the very hilltop, but
some thirty feet below it, the crest itself being taken up
with something with square low white walls which at first
sight looked like a kind of fortification but which Simon
reminiscently identified as the top of a water-storage tank.
There were a couple of small individual cottages, probably
for native foremen, on the flanks of the hill between the

barracks and the big house, and for background again the dense dark green all-smothering jungle.

Simon took in the essential topography with one deliberate panoramic survey before he lowered his gaze to explore the vicinity of the platform. He saw a handful of idlers of the nondescript and seemingly purposeless kind who can be found hanging around every wayside railroad station on earth, and two smart-looking young Malays in khaki shorts and shirts who carried Lee-Enfield rifles and who at first he thought must be guards left over from the train until he realised from their rather more informal uniforms that they must be constabulary attached to the estate; and then he saw Eve Lavis coming towards him from the hut that served as station office, and for a definite time thereafter he had no eyes for anything else.

Ascony had called her 'stunning,' but the cliché was not truly descriptive at all. She was not an impact, she was an experience, which from being more gradual was all the more enduring in its effect. His first impression of her, foolishly it seemed at the time, was one of coolness. Even at a little distance he noticed that the plain white skirt and shirt that she wore had a crackling fresh look, and yet the holster-belt with a revolver hanging low on the right side did not look as if it had just been put on. She had very fine ash-blonde hair of the natural kind which often looks almost grey, yet in spite of the sweltering humidity there was nothing dank or bedraggled about it. As she came closer still he saw that her wide-set level eyes were another grey, clear and cool as mountain lakes under a clouded sky.

The experience continued to build impressions into an inevitable structure. He had only observed at first that her figure appeared to be pleasantly normal in size and proportions: it became a conviction later that the only right word for it was 'perfect'. Because it was so perfectly without deficiencies or exaggerations it was not immediately striking, but after a while you were aware of it as the most symmetrical and shapely and desirable body that a woman could have. In the same way her face was not beautiful with the startling prettiness that snaps heads around and evokes reflex whistles. You became fascinated one by one with the broad brow, the small, chiselled nose, the delicately contoured cheekbones, the wide firm-lipped mouth that opened over small teeth like twin rows of graduated pearls, the strong chin and the smooth neck that carried it with queenly poise, and presently you felt that you were looking at Beauty itself made carnal in one assemblage of wholly satisfying features.

'You must be Mr Templar,' she said. 'I'm Eve Lavis.'

She put out her hand, and it was as cool and dry as she looked, so that the Saint was aware of the stickiness that even his superbly conditioned body had conceded to the heat.

'I'm a fairly housebroken guest,' he said. 'I never smoke in bed, and I seldom shine my shoes with the bath towels. Sometimes I don't even wear shoes.'

'I'm sorry I kept you waiting,' she said. 'I was sending a wire to Vernon – the railway ticker is our telegraph station. I told him you got here all right.'

The reversal of ordinary sequence, that she had waited to complete a telegram and mention his arrival before even greeting him, renewed and redoubled the sense of abnormal coolness that had first struck him. Yet there was nothing chilly or unfriendly about her manner. He had a sudden sharply-etched feeling that it was only her way of doing things, a disconcertingly direct and practical way.

'Shall we go up to the house?' she said. 'The boy will take your bag.'

She beckoned a Chinese who had been patiently waiting, who took the Saint's suit-case and hurried away with it straight up the hill. Mrs Lavis started to walk in an easier direction, and Simon fell in step beside her. The two Malay guards followed at a discreet distance.

'I may as well point out the sights as we pass them,' she said. 'Did Vernon tell you anything about what we do here?'

'Not very much,' Simon admitted. 'He did mention a plant, but I wasn't too clear whether it grew or made things.'

'Vernon can be terribly vague. It's a wood distillation plant.'

'I'm still not much wiser.'

'You might call it charcoal making. But when you do it the modern way, the by-products are actually worth more than the charcoal, so we call it wood distillation. The coolies cut wood in the jungle, and bring it down here in trucks.'

They were passing the rectangular concrete building, and as they turned a corner Simon saw rows of sooty wheeled cages, like skeleton freight cars, on short lengths of track which ran into black tunnels in the base of the building. There were heavy iron doors that could close the tunnels. Some of the vans were piled high with logs of all sizes, and others were still empty.

'The wood goes in those cars, and they go into the ovens and get baked. When it comes out, it's charcoal.'

They climbed a stairway to the roof of the building, where the confusion of pipes was.

'The smoke goes through various distillations, and it's separated into creosote and light wood oils and wood alcohol. It's all very scientific and industrial, but once the plant's built almost anybody can run it.'

'If only the guerrillas leave them alone, you mean,' Simon remarked.

From the roof of the building, another flight of steps led up to rejoin the steeply graded road that coiled up past the coolie quarters to the house above.

'Yes,' she said calmly. 'They couldn't steal anything that'd be worth much to them, but they'd get horribly drunk on the alcohol and then anything could happen.'

Just beyond the barracks one of the Malays overtook them to open the gate in a nine-foot fence topped with barbed wire which crossed the road and stretched straight around the hill.

'You're now in our inner fortress,' she said. 'It's locked at night, and patrolled, and we've got floodlights we can turn on, and if the Commies try to attack we can put up quite a fight. But I hope there won't be any of that while you're here.'

'I'm not worried,' said the Saint. 'I've seen it in the movies. The good guys always win.'

She did not even seem to be hot when they reached the house and she led the way up the steps to the screen door in the centre of the verandah. A little way along one wing of the verandah she opened another door, disclosing a bedroom where the Chinese boy was already unpacking the Saint's bag.

'This is your room,' she said. 'I hope you'll be comfortable.' There was an automatic in a shoulder holster which the boy had taken out of the suit-case and placed neatly on the bedside table. Mrs Lavis picked it up, examined it cursorily, and handed it to the Saint. 'I don't want to sound jittery, but while you're here you ought to get in the habit of not letting this out of reach.'

Simon weighed the gun in his hand.

'I hope I won't be just a nuisance to you,' he said.

'Not a bit,' she said. 'I expect you'd like to have a shower and freshen up. Charles Farrast is out with the coolies now, but they'll be knocking off soon. We always meet on the verandah for *stengahs* at six. And whatever you've seen in the movies, we *don't* usually dress for dinner.'

'Major Ascony sent you the usual greetings,' Simon remembered, 'and he said he'd be coming to see you as soon as he could get away for a few days.'

'That'll be nice.'

'He told me about your husband having been ill. How's he coming along?'

She turned in the doorway.

'My husband died early this morning, Mr Templar. That's what I was sending Vernon the wire about. We buried him shortly before you got here. In the tropics you have to do that, you know.'

By six o'clock it was tolerably cool. The houseboy had asked '*Tuan mau mandi*?' and Simon recalled enough of the language to nod. The boy came back with an enamel pail of hot water and carried it down into the bathroom, a dark cement-walled compartment under the pilings. Simon stood on a grating and soaped himself with the hot water, and then turned on the shower, which ran only cold water which was not really cold. Even so, it was an improvement on the kind of facilities he had encountered on his first trip up-country, when the cold water was in a huge earthenware Ali Baba jar and you rinsed off by scooping it out with an old saucepan and pouring it over your head. Arrayed in a clean shirt and slacks he felt ready to cope with anything. Or he hoped he could.

The communal part of the verandah, where he had entered, ran clear through the depth of the building from front to back, forming a wide breezeway which in effect bisected the house into two completely separate wings of rooms. Through the screen door at the back Simon could make out dim outlines of the cook's quarters and kitchen – a separate building, as is the local practice, connected to the rear of the house by a short covered alleyway. At that end of the breezeway there was a table already set for dinner, but the front three-quarters of the area was furnished as a living-room. A man was mixing a drink at the sideboard. He turned and said: 'Oh, you must be Templar. My name's Farrast.'

They shook hands. Farrast had a big hand but only a medium firm grip. He was almost as tall as the Saint, and seen by himself he would have been taken to have a good powerful physique, but next to the Saint he looked somewhat softer and noticeably thicker in the waist. He was good-looking, but would have looked better still with a fraction less flesh in his face. He had a thin pencil line of moustache and sideburns whose length was a little too plainly exaggerated to be an accident.

'*Stengah?*' Farrast said.

'Thanks.'

Farrast poured for him. He wore a tee shirt and a native sarong, which the old-timers used to affect for informal evening comfort; but he could not have been past his middle thirties.

They moved towards the front of the verandah with their glasses.

'This is a hell of a time for me to land here,' Simon said. 'Mrs Lavis should have wired and put me off.'

'That's what I told her,' Farrast said. 'But the plant has to keep running, and it's not a bad idea to have another white man around, just in case anything happened to me. That was her argument, anyhow.'

'She's certainly got herself under control,' Simon said. 'She must have been with me for half an hour, giving me the two-bit tour and playing the perfect hostess, before she even mentioned that her husband had died and you'd just buried him.'

'That would be just like her.'

'What sort of a guy was he?'

'A nice fellow.'

Simon noted to himself that he did not say 'One of the best' or any of the other stereotyped superlatives that might have been expected in the circumstances. He made no comment;

but even Farrast seemed to realise that such grudging restraint might be unduly conspicuous, and added: 'Made a frightful mess of everything, though. I expect Ascony told you.'

'The way I heard it,' said the Saint, 'he was unlucky enough to be robbed by his partner.'

'Unlucky, yes. But he was supposed to be a smart business man. How smart is a fellow who gives anyone – anyone at all – a blank cheque on everything he owns, and trusts to luck the other fellow won't be tempted? If you ask me, he must have been pretty lucky to make that much money in the first place.'

'You didn't believe he was going to make a comeback, then?'

'From a place like this? Not in a thousand years. It's a nice little business, but it couldn't ever put him back where he dropped from. When you come right down to it, popping off the way he did was probably the kindest thing that could have happened to him.'

Farrast lifted his glass and drained it.

'You must have been very fond of him,' said the Saint expressionlessly, 'to have stuck with him like that.'

Farrast gave him an odd uncertain glance.

'A job's a job,' he said, and went back to the sideboard to pour another drink.

'What will Mrs Lavis do now?'

'Sell the place, if she has any sense. And the buyer won't get me with it.'

'It wouldn't be a job any more?'

'If you want to know all about it,' Farrast said, 'I don't have to worry much longer about jobs. In about three more months I'll have a birthday, and I'll come into eighty thousand quid that my old man left in trust for me, and then it's good-bye to this stinking jungle and home to England and the life of a country squire for me.'

There was a rustle of skirts along the verandah, and then Eve Lavis was with them. She had put on a very plain cotton dress, cut low but not indiscreetly low in front, with a single strand of pearls around her neck, but with her face and figure and bearing she looked ready to receive royalty. The only incongruous touch was her gun-belt; but she was not wearing it, she carried it with her and hung it over the arm of a chair.

'I'm sorry,' she said. 'I should have been out here first to introduce you.'

'We managed,' said the Saint.

'How do you feel, Eve?' Farrast asked.

'I feel fine, Charles,' she said evenly. 'Make me a gin *pahit*, will you?'

Her face was smoothly composed, and her cool grey eyes were dry and bright with no trace of redness or puffiness.

'Is your room all right, Mr Templar?' she said. 'I'm afraid the plumbing's not quite what you're used to; but you should have seen it when Ted and I first came here.'

'Everything's fine,' he said. 'I'm only sorry I had to come at such an unfortunate time.'

'It isn't a bit unfortunate. I couldn't help hearing the end of your conversation just now. Of course I'm going to sell the place. But it won't fetch anything like its value if it isn't a going concern. So we've got to keep it running, exactly as if nothing had happened. And having you here will be good for our morale. Sometimes it's good for people to have to keep up appearances.'

Farrast brought her a wineglass half full of pink fluid and an ice cube. She took it and glanced at the Saint's glass.

'Will you help yourself whenever you're ready, Mr Templar?' she said. 'Don't wait to be asked. I want you to feel absolutely at home.'

'Thank you,' said the Saint.

'Charles,' she said, 'Mr Templar never even met Ted, you know. So he hasn't suffered any bereavement whatever. So there's no reason why he should have to pretend he's in mourning. For that matter, it isn't your personal tragedy either. Now I'll feel much better if you'll both avoid lowering your voices when I'm around and acting as if I were a kind of bomb that's liable to explode. I assure you I won't, if you'll only stop being so damned concerned about me.'

'Right-o, Eve,' Farrast said. 'If that's how you want it.'

There was a light flush on his cheeks and his complexion had become faintly shiny.

Eve Lavis looked at the Saint and at Farrast and at the Saint again. The shift of her eyes was not as pointed as the description sounds, but to the Saint's almost psychic perception it was startlingly clear that in her cool detached way she had made a comparison, and the fact that her gaze returned last to him and stayed on him had a very direct implication. Farrast turned and went back to the sideboard and could be heard replenishing his glass again.

'And what kind of justice is the Saint going to bring to Ayer Pahit?' she asked.

'I don't think Major Ascony expects me to do that,' Simon said lightly.

'Have you known him long?'

'No. In fact, only since yesterday.'

'He said in his wire that he'd just met you, and he thought we'd like you, but I didn't know if he was kidding.'

'Would that be his idea of kidding?'

'It might be. He likes to do mysterious things. After all, even I recognised your name, so he must know all about you. I didn't think he'd send you here without some reason.'

'I told him I was trying to keep out of mischief, but I put in some time up and down the peninsula a long while ago, when at least there were no guerrillas to worry about, and I was curious to see what it was like today.'

The houseboy came in and began to light the lamps, and they moved idly towards the front of the verandah.

'We'll show you the rest of the place tomorrow,' she said. 'Not that there's much to see. But no guerrillas, I hope.'

Looking down the hill, he could still see the barracks below as blocks of blackness.

'Your coolies seem to be barricaded in already,' he remarked. 'I suppose being outside the fence they're more nervous.'

'No, they're not there at all. Those quarters were built for the Chinese who used to work here. But most of them were scared away when the trouble started, and you couldn't be sure that those who wanted to stay weren't in league with the Reds. Most of the guerrillas are Chinese, you know, but most of the Malays hate the Commies. The only Chinese we have now are the cook and the boy and an *amah*, and Ted had had them for years. We're using Malay labourers, from a village a mile away. They don't get half as much work done, but we feel a lot safer with them.'

'I wouldn't go on saying that too loud,' Farrast put in.

He had sat down on a sofa with his feet up on the coffee-table and was flipping over the pages of an old *Illustrated London News*.

'Why?' Eve Lavis turned. 'Is anything wrong?'

'It's been getting worse for several days,' Farrast said. 'Every day a few more of 'em haven't been showing up, and the ones that do come have been more jittery. Even the excuses are half-hearted. When I got back to the wood-cutting gang this afternoon after – after the funeral, more than half of 'em had gone home. Just dropped their tools and wandered off as soon as my back was turned.'

'Couldn't the *krani* stop them?'

'They wouldn't pay any attention to him. They only accept him as a foreman when they can see me standing behind him. He said the *pawang* had been talking to them.'

'That's their sort of witch-doctor,' Mrs Lavis explained to Simon.

'I think the Commies have converted him, or they've bought him,' Farrast said. 'Anyway, he's been spouting a mixture of propaganda and mumbo-jumbo. His latest yarn is that the spirits have taken sides against the white colonisers, as witness the way Ted was struck down, and anyone who works for us is due to fall under the same curse.'

'They can't possibly fall for that nonsense!'

'I'm afraid they do, my dear. These are jungle Malays, remember, not like the ones you were used to in Singapore. They're as superstitious as any savages.'

'Then we'll just have to sell them a better fairy-tale, Charles.'

'If I catch that *pawang* around tomorrow,' Farrast said darkly, 'I'm going to take a stick to him, and let 'em see if his spells can do anything about that.'

The boy had been bringing in plates of soup and lighting candles on the dining-table, and now he stood waiting patiently beside it. Mrs Lavis put down her empty glass and turned to the Saint again.

'Are you ready?' she said, and put her hand under his arm, so that he had to escort her to the table as formally as if they were going to a ceremonial banquet.

The soup was chicken. The main dish after it was steamed chicken, to accompany which the boy passed a platter on which was a great mound of rice smothered with successive sprinklings of fried onions, grated coconut, and chopped hard-boiled egg. The rice when dug into proved to be liberally mixed with peanuts and raisins.

'I hope you like it,' Mrs Lavis said. 'We're terribly limited in the supplies we can get here, and I can't stand curry more than once a week, though we usually seem to have it at least twice. But we must stop boring you with all our problems.'

'That's what I came for,' said the Saint cheerfully. 'And I've been wanting to taste this dish again for more years than I want to count. I'll make a deal with you. If you don't want us fussing over you, will you stop apologising to me?'

Her face lighted with a more spontaneous smile than he had seen on it yet.

'You're absolutely right. I promise I won't do it again.'

Thereafter the conversation was as unstrained as it could be amongst a threesome of whom one was a virtual stranger. Even Farrast relaxed from the dour mood which had started to overtake him sufficiently to ask some questions about London, which he had not seen for four years. But he drank another highball with his meal, and his face seemed to become a little ruddier and shinier, while in repose the sullen cast of his brow became more pronounced and a surly undertone always seemed ready to edge into his voice. Simon diagnosed him as a man of uncertain and violent temper who had probably made no little trouble for himself with it in his time, and was careful to avoid being drawn into any argument.

Eve Lavis became more of an enigma to him as the time went on. In every technical detail she was a perfect hostess. She was unfailingly ready with the anticipation, the interjection, or the explanation that would save the stranger from an instant's embarrassment or perplexity or a feeling of being left out. Yet that very perfection of poise and graciousness might have made someone less relaxed than the Saint uncomfortably conscious of his own gaucheness. She was a good and appreciative listener, and yet her complete attentiveness could seem exacting, as if she required in return that what the speaker was saying should be informative or intelligent or witty enough to justify the attention she gave it. There was no suggestion that she would cease to be polite if you failed to measure up to her, but her politeness could be more crushing than anyone else's open contempt. The proof that she could live up to her own standards was in the fact that Simon had to keep reminding himself that her husband had died that morning and been buried that afternoon.

The Saint had been trying to guess her age. She wore no make-up except lipstick, but not even the closest scrutiny would support a guess as high as thirty. The combination of such poise and self-control with such youth was almost frightening, and yet at the same time strangely exciting.

After dinner they adjourned to the front part of the breeze-way for coffee, and Mrs Lavis was pouring it when a sound of footsteps and voices approaching made them all silent in sudden tension. In a moment she resumed pouring without a tremor, but her eyes had flicked once to the holster on the arm of her chair, and Simon had a feeling that thereafter she could have drawn the gun without looking.

Farrast stood up, with a hand on the revolver tucked in the waist fold of his sarong, and went to the front door, standing up to it with his legs truculently apart and his face close to the screen to see out better. The Saint rose quietly and moved only a little to the side, so that if it were needed the gun in his hip pocket would be less obstructed.

One of the rifle-carrying guards came into the overflow of light at the foot of the steps. With him was a very old Malay, wearing nothing but a sarong drawn up under his protruding ribs. The old man hung back as they approached and squatted down, tucking the sarong between his skinny legs.

The guard looked up and said: '*Tabeh, tuan. Itu penggulu mau chakap Mem.*'

'You talk to him, Charles,' Mrs Lavis said. 'It's better if they have to talk to a man.'

She put down the coffee-pot and picked up a cigarette. Simon struck a match for her.

'It's the *penggulu* – the headman of the village where our labour comes from,' she said.

The *penggulu* had stood up again and was talking lengthily in a plaintive singsong. When his mouth was open it showed only three teeth, with no apparent relationship between them.

'Can you understand him?' Mrs Lavis asked.

'My Malay's pretty rusty,' said the Saint. 'Just a few words come back to me now and then.'

'At the moment he's just saying how wonderful my husband was and how sorry he is for me.'

Farrast said something impatient, promptingly, and the *penggulu* launched out on another extensive speech.

'Now he's getting to the point,' Mrs Lavis said. She listened with her head bent, staring at the end of her cigarette when she was not putting it to her mouth. 'His people have got out of hand, they don't respect him any more, they mock him when he tries to assert his authority . . . They don't want to work for us any more. He would like to make them work, but he is a feeble old man and they laugh at him . . . The *pawang* has taught them to do this . . . The *pawang* has told everyone that if they go on working for us the guerrillas will come after them, and the demons will haunt them, and none of them will escape. The *pawang*—'

Farrast roared in sudden anger: '*Mana bulih!*'

'And that,' Mrs Lavis said, 'is what I think Americans mean when they yell "*For Christ's sake!*"'

Simon grinned.

'That's one phrase I do remember.'

Farrast was still shouting indignantly in Malay, and no interpreter was needed to convey the idea that he was profanely inquiring whether the *penggulu* was a man or a mouse and why the hell didn't he get another *pawang*.

The *penggulu* heard him out respectfully, and then embarked on another long quavering apologia.

Farrast turned his head.

'What shall I tell him, Eve?'

'You should know better than I, Charles,' she said steadily. 'You're in charge now. Make your own decision.'

Farrast turned again with his under lip jutting. He interrupted the old man with another tirade in Malay, but this one had a harsher finality. Mrs Lavis stirred her demitasse and drank some of it.

Farrast swung around on his heel and rejoined them at the coffee-table. He picked up his cup, deliberately keeping his back turned to the steps. The *penggulu* stood outside still looking up, mumbling despondently. After a moment the guard unslung his rifle and prodded the *penggulu* with it, not ungently. The old man turned slowly and shuffled away into the darkness, with the guard following him.

'Well, that ought to settle something,' Farrast said.

'What did you say to him?' Simon asked.

'I told him that I'd expect a full crew on the job tomorrow, and if I didn't get it I'd come looking for the *pawang* and personally beat him to a pulp, and he could tell his precious *pawang* that with my compliments.'

Mrs Lavis finished her coffee.

'I hope that was right,' she said impersonally, and stood up. 'I think I'll go to bed now, if you'll excuse me. It's been a long day, and I was up most of last night.'

She gave Simon a friendly smile all to himself.

'I'll see you at breakfast,' she said. 'And I hope you sleep well.'

'Good night,' said the Saint, hardly capable of being amazed any more. 'And the same to you.'

Farrast made another of his trips to the sideboard.

'Care for a nightcap?' he asked shortly. 'We don't stay up late here. Have to get up too early in the morning.'

'I don't think so, thanks,' Simon said pleasantly. 'I wouldn't mind catching up on some sleep myself.'

'Night-night, then,' Farrast said.

'See you tomorrow.'

The Saint sauntered away to his room.

He stripped down to his shorts, brushed his teeth, and then lighted a last cigarette, enjoying the taste of it on his freshened palate. He paced soundlessly up and down the polished hardwood floor in his bare feet, trying to put his impressions in some sort of order.

He had met an extraordinary woman and a more ordinary man of a type that he felt he could easily learn to dislike. But beyond observing and trying to analyse them as personalities, he did not know what he should have been looking for. It was frustrating that he had arrived just too late to form his own impression of the third member of the triangle. He thought of it unconsciously as a triangle, and only after he had done so was aware that his intuition had already drawn one conclusion.

He heard Farrast walk heavily past and open a door farther down the verandah, and then he heard him through the partition wall. Farrast, then, had the adjoining room to his, and the other wing of the house would be the master suite. The wall was not much of a sound insulator. Simon heard Farrast moving about, opening drawers and closets, getting ready for bed, and presently the fall of his slippers and the creak of springs.

The Saint put out his cigarette, took off his shorts, lay down quietly, and turned out the lamp. But for some time he lay with his hands behind his head and his eyes open, staring up at the ceiling.

When two people have slept together, there is a kind of transmutation between them which, no matter how carefully they behave, without a single false step that could be specifically pinpointed, can reveal the fact to a sensitised intuition as baldly as if it were branded on them.

The Saint dozed.

Presently, he judged it was about half an hour later, he was wide awake again, and the sound that had aroused him was still clear in his recollection. It had been the creak of a board outside on the verandah. Instinctively he dropped one hand to the butt of the automatic which he had tucked under the edge of the mattress, but he made no other movement, and made himself breathe regularly and heavily. And after a few seconds he heard the almost inaudible scuff of stealthy footsteps moving away. That was when he let go the gun again, for his praeternaturally acute hearing told him that the feet were shod. It was hard to follow them very far: the surrounding night crowded in on his ears with its competing antiphony of innumerable frogs and insects and small beasts of unimaginable variety, a background orchestration that you could forget entirely until you wanted to listen for something else and then it seemed to swell up into deafening volume. But after a while he heard, with unmistakable clarity, the soft turning of a latch, and perhaps felt rather than heard, conducted through the joists of the building, the muffled closing of a door, far down in the other wing of the house.

He went to sleep.

When he woke up again it was as if his brain had not stopped working. It was daylight enough to read, and he reached out at once for the book on the bedside table. He could not wait any longer to find out what Major Ascony had wanted him to read in it. But it was a very thick book, and to work through it from the first page in the hope of coming upon something that might fit in would be a marathon task.

He riffled the pages methodically in search of a clue, and suddenly came to one that was turned down at the upper corner. It was a very neat turn-down, no bigger than the diagonal half of a postage stamp, but it was the only one in the volume, and it was on the first page of a story. He had a feeling that Ascony might almost have measured it with a micrometer, making it just big enough not to be overlooked permanently, but small enough not to be found prematurely.

The story was called *Footprints in the Jungle*. As he started on it he had a vague recollection of having read it before, and as he went on it all came back to him. It was about a woman whose lover, with her encouragement, murdered her husband, and then married her.

4

When he went out on the verandah he carried the book with him. Eve Lavis was sitting at the coffee-table in the living area, sipping a cup of tea. She looked up with a ready smile and said: 'Good morning. Did you sleep all right?'

'Like a baby. No, that's wrong. Babies wake up at ungodly hours, bawling their heads off. I didn't.'

She was wearing light tan jodhpurs and a pastel yellow shirt, and her ash-blonde hair was pulled plainly back and tied with a yellow ribbon on the nape of her neck. It made her look even younger than the day before. Her grey eyes were clear and unshadowed.

'I don't need to ask you how you feel,' he said. 'You look merely wonderful.'

'I can't help that. But I'm afraid it shocks you.'

'It shouldn't. I ought to know better than anyone that death seems a little less important each time you see it.'

'You mean that this isn't the first husband I've lost and I'm getting hardened to it.'

'Well, Ascony did mention the doctor. But he didn't go into any details.'

'Dr Quarry,' she said. 'Donald Quarry. He committed suicide.'

'You don't have to talk about it.'

'I don't mind. You're curious, aren't you? It's natural. I was on a cruise boat that stopped here. It suddenly came over me that if I had to make one more sightseeing trip with the same crowd of people saying the same things about everything I'd go out of my mind. I decided to drive out to the Golf Club and ask if they'd let me play a round and be by myself for the first time for weeks. But I met Donald on the first tee and we played the round together, and then we had drinks, and he asked me to dinner, and it was something at first sight, I suppose, and when the cruise boat went on I wasn't on it. We were married for two years. And then he did an operation that went wrong and his patient died, I don't know why, but he got very depressed and thought he was no good any more, and soon afterwards he took a shot of morphine and put himself to sleep. I think I cried a little that time.'

Simon looked down the hill, across the railroad tracks to the dense greenness that reached back towards a horizon of blue haze. The damp air still had a deceptively spring-like freshness.

'The first time is always the worst, isn't it?' he said.

'You really do understand,' she said.

'If you won't accuse me of going back on our pact, Mrs Lavis, I think you may be the most remarkable woman I've met.'

She was pleased, and did not pretend to hide it.

'I'm glad you came here,' she said. 'And I think you could drop the "Mrs Lavis" stuff. Do you mind if I call you Simon?'

'I was waiting for a chance to suggest it, Eve.'

She put a hand on the teapot to test its temperature.

'Would you like a cup of tea? It's still hot.'

'I'd rather have breakfast. I'm the horribly healthy type.'

She glanced at a clock across the room.

'We'll give Charles another five minutes, and then I'll ring for it, whether he's here or not.'

He was still trying to visualise her in bed with Farrast. There was nothing prurient about the effort: it was more like an exercise in abstract mathematics. Intellectually, he had no doubt left that his assumption was correct; but to translate it into a picture that he could believe emphatically was a form of confirmation that eluded him. Could that invulnerable air-conditioned poise really melt in the warm confusion of sex, abdicating its pedestal to lie with a cheaply handsome, spoiled, wilful and surely less than fascinating mortal like Charles Farrast?

'Isn't he up yet?' Simon asked.

'Good heavens, yes. We literally get up at the crack of dawn here. *Ketchil makan*, and out to get the coolies started at six o'clock. Then back to breakfast after everything's running.'

He still had the book in his hand as he sat down beside her, and he put it down on the table in front of him.

'I didn't know how long it might be till breakfast, and I didn't know I'd have better company,' he explained.

She leaned a little towards him to look at the title.

'Maugham,' she said. 'I don't think I know that one. Is it new?'

'No, it's a collection. Ascony lent it to me.'

'Vernon? I never thought of him as the bookish type.'

'He said there was a story in it that he'd like to get my reaction to.'

'Really? Which one?'

'A thing called *Footprints in the Jungle*.'

She passed him a tin of cigarettes and took one herself.

'What's it about?'

'Well, Maugham never does go in for very sensational plots, and this one certainly isn't the newest one in the world. It's about a woman whose husband is murdered, supposedly by robbers, and soon afterwards she married his best friend, and the presumption is that they were the ones who actually arranged to knock off Hubby.'

She took a light from the match he held, without a wrinkle in her smooth brow. She was enjoying a civilised conversation, nothing more.

'It isn't exactly original, is it?'

'It's all in the writing. He makes you see them as quite ordinary people that you might meet anywhere, instead of monsters out of another world.'

'But I wonder why Vernon wanted your opinion of it.'

'The inside story is supposedly told by a police chief,' he said. 'The policeman finds enough evidence to be fairly convinced that they did it, but he also knows that he could never get enough to stand any chance of convicting them. So he's never done anything about it.'

She met his gaze with level untroubled eyes.

'I wonder if Vernon has a problem of that kind and can't make up his mind what to do. But I can't imagine Vernon not being able to make up his own mind about anything. But of course, if he didn't have enough evidence, there's nothing he *could* do anyway, is there?'

Simon shrugged.

'He didn't tell me anything, and I didn't read the story until this morning.'

'I'll have to read it myself.' She glanced at the clock, and stood up. 'Let's not starve ourselves any longer.'

She went to the dining-table and rang the silver hand bell that stood in front of her place; but they had hardly settled themselves when Farrast stomped up the front steps and shouldered blusterily through the screen door.

'Sorry if I'm late,' he said perfunctorily.

He sailed a terai hat into an arm-chair as he marched through to the table and sat himself down heavily, his boots scraping the floor. He had the kind of complexion on which sunburn never loses all its redness, and it seemed more inflamed now, perhaps because he was warm. His khaki shirt was already wilted and clinging.

'Trouble?' Eve Lavis asked.

'Plenty,' Farrast said. 'And I'm going to make more.'

'You'll be able to do it better with a good breakfast under your belt,' she said practically.

It was a good breakfast, staunchly British, with bacon and eggs and sausages and toast and marmalade and strong tea to wash it down, as was to be expected, for that is one tradition on which no proper Colonial even in the remotest outpost of the Empire would make any concession to local cuisine. At other meals he may without protest eat bird's-nest soup or stewed buffalo hump, and may even become an addict of semi-incandescent curries; but breakfast under the British flag is incorruptible from Hampstead to Hong Kong.

After the boy had finished serving and gone out, and they had started eating, Farrast said: 'I went down to the plant. The *krani* was there, but no men. They were supposed to clean out a couple of the stills. I waited twenty minutes. Then I loaded him in the jeep and drove out where they were last cutting wood. The other *krani* was there, with a truck, but no men. I gave it another ten minutes. Nobody showed up. So you know what I did? I made the *kranis* pick up a saw and start cutting wood themselves. I said if they couldn't get their crews on the job, the only way they could earn their pay was by doing it themselves.'

'Do you think that was wise, Charles?' Mrs Lavis asked. 'You want to keep them on your side.'

'You told me last night to show who was boss,' Farrast answered belligerently. 'If the *kranis* had been tougher themselves, perhaps we'd never have had this trouble. This ought to teach 'em a lesson. I told 'em not to come in till they could bring the truck full of wood, which is all we need to complete a batch that's waiting to be baked. And then I hiked off to the Malay village.'

'By yourself?'

'No, I had a friend with me.' He drew his revolver, held it up for a moment, and thrust it back in the holster. 'I was just hoping somebody *would* start something, so I'd be given a chance to use it. But when I got there there wasn't a grown man in sight. They'd all sneaked off into the bush when they heard me coming. Except the *penggulu*.'

'Poor old man! I hope you didn't hurt him.'

'I made him show me the *pawang's* hut. I threw everything out of it that was movable, his personal possessions as well as his charms and concoctions – broke everything that was breakable, and trampled the whole shebang into the mud. Then I told him to see that all the men saw it when they came back, and he could ask 'em how they thought the *pawang's* magic could be any good if I could do that to him. And I told him to give the *pawang* a message, in front of plenty of witnesses, that I dared him to show his face anywhere around the estate, because wherever I found him I'd give him a public thrashing.'

Eve Lavis buttered some toast.

'Well, that ought to lead to a showdown,' she said. 'What do you think, Simon?'

'I don't see how the *pawang* can help losing face if he doesn't do something about it,' said the Saint. 'On the other hand, if he does something, it's liable to be something unhealthy for Charles.'

'Don't worry about me, Templar,' Farrast said. 'I'm pretty handy at taking care of myself.'

Mrs Lavis frowned thoughtfully.

'I can't help wondering if we aren't missing the target,' she said. 'You said yourself that the *pawang* must have gone over to the Reds. Doesn't that mean there must be a bigger Commie agent somewhere around here who's giving him his orders? If you could find him, you'd get the trouble out by the root.'

'Perhaps Templar can detect him,' Farrast said.

'I'll think about it,' Simon said amiably. 'But with your

local knowledge you'd do it better. I think Eve's got something, though.'

'Well,' Farrast said grudgingly, 'if I catch that *pawang* I'll see what I can beat out of him.'

They had finished eating and were smoking cigarettes at the table when one of the guards came up the verandah steps and knocked on the frame of the screen door. Farrast got up and went over there, and the guard spoke briefly.

'He says the *pawang* and a couple of his pals are in the Chinese shop across from the station,' Mrs Lavis translated to Simon.

Farrast returned to pick up his hat, and also a stout Malacca cane.

'This is what I've been looking forward to,' he said grimly.

Simon folded his napkin and stood up.

'Would you like me to come with you?' he asked.

'Suit yourself.'

Farrast opened the door and went out. Simon followed him.

The tropical day was getting into its stride, and as they stepped out from under the shade of the roof the sun hit them through a mugginess that was almost palpable. Farrast marched down the hill in ominous silence, the set of his jaw proclaiming one implacable preoccupation. But at the gate in the fence that ringed the upper part of the hill he stopped the guard and told him to wait there.

'*Jaga baik-baik, tuan,*' the guard said; and Farrast glared at him as if the man had insulted him by merely urging him to be careful.

They went on down past the plant and the warehouse and across the station platform, without another word being spoken until they had crossed the tracks. Then Farrast stopped a few yards from the open entrance of the store and looked carefully to left and right, as though satisfying himself that he was not walking into an ambush.

He said: 'You can come in with me if you like. But don't interfere unless you're quite sure that I've had it. I'm the fellow who's got to go on running this show. They've got to be afraid of me all by myself, and not thinking they can start up again as soon as you've left.'

'Whatever you say, Boss,' murmured the Saint.

Farrast went in, and Simon followed again and stepped off to one side, keeping his back to the wall.

There were three Malays gathered around an antique pinball machine at the rear of the shop. Two of them, with bottles in their hands, were watching and boisterously encouraging the third, who was playing. But as Simon and Farrast walked in they abruptly stopped laughing; one of them muttered a warning, and they stepped back a little. The one who was playing seemed to pay no attention. He remained huddled closely over the machine, without looking around, concentrating intently on his shot. He could only have been the *pawang*, though he was dressed no differently from the others, in a much-mended shirt and a sarong.

Farrast strode straight over to him, without hesitation, his boots thudding on the bare floor in defiant announcement of his approach; but the third Malay did not move until Farrast grasped his shoulder. Then the *pawang* turned, like a twisting snake, and a *kris* flashed in his hand at waist level where he must have been holding it all the time under cover of his crouch at the machine. Simon saw the glint of the wicked wavy-bladed knife, but the Malay was so quick and Farrast was so close to him that even the Saint could have done nothing about it. But Farrast himself must have been anticipating the attack in precisely the way it happened, and he was countering it almost before it started, pushing the Malay back and bringing his already lifted cane down in a vicious cracking blow on the man's wrist which undoubtedly broke a bone. The knife fell to the ground and Farrast put his foot on it. Then he grasped the *pawang* by the collar and began to rain merciless blows with the stick on his back and buttocks.

The *pawang's* attempt had been made and foiled so instantaneously that it hardly seemed like an interruption at all, and his two putative sycophants were left winded and dumbfounded by the speed with which their prospective hero had been disarmed and reduced to squirming impotence. Simon kept them under close observation, but it was obvious that their role had been meant to be that of witnesses and admirers, and that they had no ambition to join the fray after the tables had been so catastrophically turned on their champion. They watched open-mouthed, until with a scream and a still more violent plunge the *pawang* tore himself free, leaving half his patched shirt in Farrast's hand, and raced out of the shop like a terrified cur; and then, as Farrast turned speculatively towards them, they sidled around behind a counter with increasing velocity that culminated in a panic-stricken bolt for the door.

Farrast picked up the *kris* and examined it.

'This'll make a nice souvenir,' he said.

'You earned it,' said the Saint, who could seldom withhold approbation when it was due. 'When I saw him pull it I thought he had you, but you handled him like a commando.'

Farrast looked pleased with himself, rather than with the compliment.

'I told you I could take care of myself.'

They went outside again. All three Malays had disappeared.

'Two of 'em are on their way back to the village to tell the story right now,' Farrast said. 'I don't think the *pawang*'ll have much prestige left when they've finished. In fact, I'll be surprised if he ever shows his face in Pahang again.'

'Unfortunately,' Simon remarked, 'you didn't get a chance to ask him who he was taking orders from, after all.'

'Probably it doen't matter much now.'

Farrast squinted up at a haze of dust drifting around the shoulder of the hill. 'Those *kranis* have brought the truck in,' he said. 'I hope for their sakes it was full of wood.'

He started to walk briskly up towards the distillation building, and the Saint tagged quietly along. Farrast swung his cane as if he was enjoying the feel of his recent use of it in retrospect, and would be happy to repeat the experience. His lower lip began to tighten and protrude again.

The truck had pulled into the loading area in front of the ovens, where the cage-like carts received their cargoes of raw wood. The two *kranis* were heaving billets from the truck into the last car of a row of previously filled ones. They were Tamils, and they had started the day in white shirts and trousers as befitted their position as supervisors of common labour, but now their clothes were soiled and soaked with sweat. They did not look at Farrast or the Saint, but went on working steadily, with masks of undying resentment on their thin-featured black faces.

Farrast measured the size of the load they were handling with his eye, and seemed disappointed that he could find no fault with it.

'I've good news for you,' he said in English. 'I think I've fixed the *pawang* and you'll have all your men back tomorrow morning. But I don't want this to happen again. So to make sure you remember what happens when you let 'em get out of hand, I'm going to let you fill in for 'em for the rest of the day. After you finish loading that train we'll run it in and start cooking, and you can try yourselves out as stokers. Then this afternoon we'll go back to the coils and tanks that your men were supposed to clean. Between you, you ought to be able to make up some of the time that's been lost. And I'm going to watch you do it. Unless you'd rather go back to India and look for another job.'

The two men stood still for long enough to appraise him with inscrutable faces of sweat-glazed jade, and then stolidly resumed their work.

'Those two speak English as well as I do,' Farrast said carelessly, 'but they still need a bit of educating.'

He found himself a place in the shade, sat down, and played with the captured *kris*.

Simon Templar lighted a cigarette and wandered idly around, finding what he could to interest himself. Farrast was plainly no casual conversationalist, and was content to glower intermittently at the toiling *kranis* and watch for the next excuse to lay a verbal lash across their backs. Simon found himself liking Farrast not one particle better, even though the man had surprised him with a demonstration of physical courage and capability of no insignificant order. It was a revelation that a form of genuine respect could be so sharply limited.

The Saint endured Farrast's inexorable dourness until his last three cigarettes were smoked and he could stand it no longer, and then he said: 'Eve must still be wondering what happened. I'll go back and tell her how you smote the ungodly, hip and thigh.'

'Go ahead,' Farrast said curtly, and glanced at his watch. 'I'll be along soon for tiffin.'

Eve Lavis was sitting on the verandah with the Maugham book open on her lap. She looked up at Simon with eager but restrained concern.

'What happened? You've been such a long time.'

'I know, I should have come back before. I was watching them getting ready to run a load of wood through the cookshop. The *pawang* was taken care of long ago.'

He gave her a sufficiently graphic account of one of the

few brawls in which he had ever been an entirely superfluous spectator.

'Farrast was terrific,' he said. 'I can be very frank now, and admit that I hadn't expected that much from him. You know how one tends to think that a guy who makes a lot of threatening noise, which Farrast is rather inclined to, won't be half so tough when the time comes to deliver. This was an eye-opener. Maybe he was a bit brutal, but he was quick as lightning and he was all guts.'

'I can't blame you for not liking him. He's been quite boorish with you — I can't think why.'

'We haven't exactly become bosom pals yet,' Simon acknowledged tolerantly. 'But I'll give him a testimonial any day for courage. It gave me a rather different slant on his character. You can tell a hell of a lot about a man's character from a few minutes like those.'

'You've probably had lots of practice.'

'All right, from the criminal point of view: Suppose Farrast had an enemy, or someone he wanted to get rid of. Farrast would probably challenge him to a fight, or at least give him some token chance to defend himself. Suppose Farrast were a murder suspect. I might believe it if they said he met the victim face to face and shot him down. I wouldn't believe that he slowly poisoned him to death.'

She stared at him, her eyes widening fractionally.

'What an extraordinary thing to say!'

'Why? Poisoning is the most cowardly kind of murder. No killer feels as sure as a poisoner that he can't be caught. And it's the easiest thing to do to someone who trusts him. Even the lowest gangsters have hardly ever sunk to using poison. The victim doesn't even have a chance to duck.'

'No, no,' she said, with the nearest he had yet seen her come to impatience. 'I mean, why would you ever think of Charles as a murderer?'

Simon grinned.

'Force of habit,' he said blandly. 'I think of all sorts of people like that. It's like a game. And maybe the stuff I've been reading set me off again.'

It was a moment more before the shadow of a frown ironed itself out of her forehead and she looked down at the book.

'Oh, yes, I read your story, and I went on and read several others.'

He lighted a cigarette.

'What did you think of it?'

'It wasn't bad. And nobody's poisoned in it, either.'

'That's true.'

'I still can't imagine what Vernon has on his mind.'

'Maybe he has his own views on what the policeman in the story ought to have done, or would have done according to regulations, and he wants to have an argument with me.'

'But what *could* the policeman do?'

Simon shrugged.

'Damn if I know. In that particular case, I don't even know what I'd do myself. It was such a private, almost humane little murder.'

'I thought you'd be understanding about that.'

'I might be. But a callous murder for profit is something else. For instance, take the Bluebeard type. I met one of those not too long ago, in England. He married one woman after another, taking care they had money or insuring them if they didn't, murdered them in a number of ingenious ways, and after a decent interval went on the woo for the next. It was a completely coldblooded business operation.'

'And you couldn't have any sympathy for him.'

'I helped to get him hanged,' said the Saint.

She closed the book and put it on the table, and studied him again with those sober and profound grey eyes.

'I like you very much,' she said. 'You know exactly what

you believe and what you'd do about it. If we got to know each other better we might disagree about lots of things, but we'd always speak the same language.'

He knew it for as open a promise of eventually more than friendship as any strumpet's moist mouth and skilfully disarranged skirt, but it was made with such queenly dignity and for such a discreetly indefinite future that even at her last husband's funeral it would have been in perfect taste.

'Coming from you, Eve,' Simon said quietly, 'I take that as a rare compliment.'

Farrast came tramping up the steps and kicked the screen door open with an exuberant toe.

'Well, Eve,' he said, 'should I put in for a raise?'

She stood up, her face lighting with eager appreciation.

'Simon told me all about it,' she said. 'You must have been wonderful.'

'I told you I'd do it,' Farrast said, flinging down his hat and cane. 'And the two *kranis* are learning how much better it is to keep other people working than have to do it yourself. When the Malays come back tomorrow morning, everything will be running like clockwork again.'

He was flushed and hot, but the satisfaction of meting out punishment seemed to have finally put him in a good humour.

'I'm going to have a drink,' he announced, and went to the sideboard.

Eve turned to the Saint.

'Aren't you thirsty?'

'I could use a cold beer, if you have one.'

'Of course.'

She rang the bell on the dining-table; and the houseboy came in, took the order, and went out again. Farrast raised his glass.

'Excuse me if I don't wait,' he said. 'Cheerio.'

He drank deeply, putting down two-thirds of the highball

at one long draught. As he lowered the glass, a strange expression came over his face, and quickly turned into a dreadful grimace. He retched and choked, and then doubled up as if he had been hit in the solar plexus. The glass fell from his hand as he clutched his stomach, and then his knees buckled under him.

Eve Lavis gave an inarticulate cry.

Simon sprang forward and rolled Farrast over. Farrast's muscles were cramped in knotted rigidity, his teeth were clenched and his lips drawn back from them in a horrible grin. The colour of his face was darkening towards purple. Simon tried to force the mouth open so that he could physically induce vomiting, but he knew it was no use.

'Those devils,' Mrs Lavis said, in a clear unnatural voice.

Charles Farrast was finished. Technically there might still have been a flutter of pulse or breath to quibble about, but he was dead beyond human reversing. Nevertheless the Saint went on trying for a few seconds, stubbornly reluctant to give up.

He heard Eve's footsteps cross the room, pause, and then pass quickly behind him. The rear screen door slammed.

Simon looked up, puzzledly. And then from the direction of the cook's quarters at the back he heard a man's wordless yell, which was instantly cut off by the first of two crashing shots.

The Saint took off from the floor like a sprinter from a crouch, plunged through the rear door, and raced down the covered alley outside, his automatic already out in his hand.

He saw Eve Lavis through the first doorway he came to; and a moment later, as he braked his headlong rush, the picture was completed. The room was a sort of serving pantry, with china cabinets and an ice-box. On a table in the centre stood an empty beer bottle, and a freshly filled glass on a Benares tray. The houseboy lay on the floor, quite still, with his eyes rolled upwards and two holes marring the front of his immaculate white jacket. Mrs Lavis held her revolver still pointing at him, as though considering whether to fire it again.

'I knew it,' she said in a flat mechanical tone. 'I knew it. It came to me one-two-three. It couldn't have been anyone else. And then if he poisoned the whisky he could have been slowly poisoning Ted all that time, and perhaps he didn't have ulcers at all. And then if he was poisoning people like that why should he stop there? I could see it all in a flash. I grabbed my gun and ran out here. I caught him red-handed. Just as I thought, he was pouring something into your beer. And when he saw that I'd seen him, he picked up that knife. Look.'

Her gun pointed at a small brown bottle on the floor by the houseboy's feet, and a kitchen knife near his right hand.

There was a faint scuffling sound from the back of the building, and Eve Lavis turned abruptly and hurried out of the door. Simon went after her. A fat Chinese and a little woman were galloping wildly away down a stretch of slope. From their clothes and appearance, they could only have been the cook and the *amah*.

Eve raised her revolver.

'I'll kill them all,' she said coldly.

Simon caught her wrist in a grip of steel.

'You don't know that they had anything to do with it,' he said. 'The boy was the one you caught in the act. They're probably just scared to death.'

He took the gun away from her without much difficulty. She struggled only very briefly, until her complete helplessness against his strength was obvious. Then she became still, and presently sagged a little against him.

'I'll be good,' she said. 'I'm sorry.'

'Come back to the house,' he said.

As he took her through the rear door again she averted her eyes from the body of Farrast on the floor. Simon let her go, and took a napkin to lay over the man's congested face. She sat down in a chair and put her hands over her eyes; but it was a rigid gesture suggestive of intense concentration rather than collapse.

Other footsteps came pell-mell to the front of the veran-dah. The uniformed guard appeared at the top of the steps, with the staring faces of the two *kranis* a little below and behind him. Simon went and let them in. He recalled what Farrast had said about the Tamils having learned English, and was grateful that he did not have to struggle through a narrative in halting Malay. He stated what he had seen for himself, and what Mrs Lavis had told him, lucidly and concisely; and one of the *kranis* translated it for the guard. Mrs Lavis did not move or speak.

Then Simon led them through to the back and showed them what was in the serving pantry.

He said to the elder *krani*: 'Tell the guard he is to stay here. He must not go in or touch anything. He is to stand at the door, and he is not to let anyone in for any reason – not even myself or the Memsahib. When he is tired, one of the other guards will take his place. This will go on until the police get here.'

He returned to the house with the two Tamils, and nodded at the body by the sideboard.

'One of you help me take him to his room.'

One of them did so, the other going along to open the door. When they came back, Mrs Lavis was still sitting where they had left her. The only difference was that she had dropped her hands to the arms of the chair. Simon went to a small desk that stood against one wall, found a sheet of paper, and wrote on it briefly but carefully.

'Send this to Major Ascony in Singapore on the railway telegraph. If he can't come himself, he'll have someone sent on the next train from Kuala Lumpur or Ipoh.'

'Yes, sir.'

'Do it at once,' Mrs Lavis said.

'Yes, *Mem*.'

The *kranis* went out.

Simon paced thoughtfully back, picked up the round yellow tin of cigarettes from the coffee-table, and chose one from it.

'I'm sorry,' Mrs Lavis said. 'I went off the deep end for a few minutes. I won't do it again.'

Her face was again stoically controlled, her eyes dry and clear and unwavering.

'That's all right,' he said. 'The stiff upper lip can get slightly petrified if it never lets up.'

'It was just too much,' she said. 'Ted swore by the boy Ah Fong. It was so true what you said about poisoning, how mean it is. To think that Ah Fong could have been bringing him poisoned food and drinks day after day, watching him suffer and waste away, all the time pretending to be so sympathetic . . .'

'You're quite sure he was doing that?'

'If Ted was being poisoned, it'll show in an autopsy, won't it?'

'Probably.' Simon looked around for a match. 'But if Ah Fong took so long over your husband, being so subtle and trying to make it look like natural causes, why did he suddenly decide to knock off Farrast in one dose that nobody could mistake for anything but what it was?'

'Remember what Charles did to the *pawang*. It was a setback to the whole Red operation in this district. They were furious, and desperate. They had to show the Malays at once that nobody could beat up a Commie and get away with it. And they'd have given it to you at the same time just because you'd been with Charles.'

'But it wasn't at the same time. Ah Fong saw Farrast mixing a drink when he took the order for my beer. Why would he think it was any use poisoning the beer, when Farrast would have started his drink before I got mine, and after what happened to him I obviously wouldn't drink anything?'

'He must have hoped that Charles would wait for you. Or at least he mightn't have expected Charles to drink so fast. Did you notice how he gulped down most of that drink without stopping? If he'd sipped it like anybody else, there might have been plenty of time for you to get your beer and take a good swig at it before the poison hit Charles.'

Simon lighted his cigarette at last, and took a long drag deep into his lungs. He let the smoke out slowly, looking at her quietly through it. He wanted to print her on his memory like that, sitting with her hands folded placidly in her lap, the dainty symmetries of her figure subtly rounding her blouse, the patrician composure of her intelligent upturned face framed against the silver-ash softness of her hair, all the astounding proud loveliness of her as it had become familiar to him feature by feature. He had never known anyone like her, and he was not likely to again.

'It's no good, Eve,' he said. 'It's clever, but it won't sell.'

The lift of her finely delineated eyebrows was only a flicker. 'I don't understand.'

He held the spent match above an ashtray, corrected its position with an estimating eye, and dropped it for a dead-centre hit.

'I'm sure,' he said, 'that you poisoned the whisky. Then, when I was trying to do something for Farrast – as you knew in advance I certainly would be – you rushed out to the pantry and shot Ah Fong. You had the poison bottle in your pocket all ready to drop beside him, and it only took another second to snatch a knife out of a drawer and throw that down beside him too. Who'd make a better fall guy than a Chinese houseboy who was too dead to be able to even try to deny anything?'

For the first time he saw her statuesque calm jarred by a tremor of shock. But even then it was more as if she winced over a breach of good manners that he had been guilty of.

'I don't think that's very funny,' she said primly.

'It wasn't meant to be.'

'Then the heat must have done something to you.'

'I'm only wondering,' he said, 'what would have happened if I'd decided to join Farrast in a *stengah*. Would you have let me die with him, and framed the houseboy a trifle differently but still shot him before the police got here? Or would you have delayed me, or upset my glass, and saved me somehow so that I could still be a witness? I'm afraid that'll always torment me. You'll never tell me; or if you did, I wouldn't believe you.'

She laughed, a little faint brittle sound.

'You're very charming,' she said. 'And would you care to tell me what you think I did it for? Am I a Communist agent?'

'That's one thing I'd never suspect you of. I'm certain you're strictly in business for yourself. You did it mainly to cover up the poisoning of your husband.'

'Oh. I did that too?'

'Both of them, as a matter of fact.'

Her eyes widened momentarily.

'This is fascinating. It's a good job I'm not the hysterical type, otherwise I think I'd be screaming.'

'Would you like me to run through it from the beginning?'

'You might as well. I couldn't be any more baffled than I am now.'

He sat on the arm of a chair and reached over to ease the cylinder of ash off the end of his cigarette.

'I'll only go back as far as the things I've heard about,' he said reflectively. 'You were on a world cruise. I've no doubt it was a speculative investment. A cruise of that length is expensive enough to guarantee some fairly well-to-do passengers, and ships are renowned incubators of romance. But for some reason that trip wasn't paying off: by the time you got to Singapore you'd methodically investigated all the prospects, and the right man or the right situation just wasn't aboard. So you weren't merely bored – you figured you might still get something out of it by doing some prospecting in port. That's why you ducked the sightseeing tour and went to the Golf Club. And that's where you met Donald Quarry, a doctor with an excellent practice, and it was no problem at all for you to knock him dizzy.'

'Thank you.'

'Of course, he was only a stepping-stone. Even a very successful doctor could hardly make enough money to be more than that, to a really ambitious woman. But he was an entrée to local society, and a splendid meal ticket until something better came along. And in due course you met Ted Lavis – one of the richest and most successful business men in these parts. So Quarry had to be disposed of. That wasn't hard. You only had to wait until one of his patients died, which happens regularly even to the best doctors, and then start whispering to your friends about how morbidly depressed he was in spite of the brave front he tried to keep up. Once that idea had been well planted, it was easy for you to steal some morphine from his supplies and switch it for any other shots that he might be taking. And you already knew you could blitz Lavis as soon as it wouldn't look too blatant – in fact, you'd probably had him on his knees already.'

'After all, there's not so much competition in these outlandish places.'

'I think you could get almost any man you wanted, anywhere. And you've always known it. But you wanted position and money with him: you were heading for the top. Lavis was a prize. You might have been satisfied with him for a long time. But as Farrast said to me, maybe he really was more lucky than brilliant. Anyhow, he suddenly lost everything, in an amazingly stupid way. You were not only disgusted with him for letting you down, but you were convinced that he was a goose who'd never lay another golden egg. Slow poisoning disguised as intestinal troubles was a neat and plausible way to get rid of him. And meanwhile Charles Farrast had shown up on the scene, with a legacy of eighty thousand pounds waiting for him only a few months away.'

'While you're building up this fantastic story,' she said, and now she was patiently coping with a rather tiresome lunatic, 'you ought to explain why I have to murder my husbands instead of simply divorcing them.'

Simon drew at his cigarette again meditatively.

'I will if you like,' he said. 'You have a fetish about tidiness and correctness, and a phobia about any kind of emotion – both carried to psychopathic extremes. You couldn't bear to have your reputation soiled with the kind of nastiness you'd have had to admit to give them cause to divorce you, and you'd have died rather than go through the scenes that would have been necessary to make them agree to let you divorce them. Murder, to you, was so much less messy.'

She took a cigarette from the tin near her.

'Give me a light, please,' she said.

He struck a match and leaned forward with it. She put her cigarette in the flame and brought it to a steady glow.

'Thank you,' she said, and took the cigarette from her mouth to exhale with an absolutely smooth and tremorless movement.

Her luminous grey eyes dwelt on him with tremendous absorption, while he lighted another cigarette for himself.

'Now,' she said, 'about Vernon Ascony.'

'He must have thought all along that there was something not quite kosher about Quarry's suicide,' said the Saint. 'Then, when Ted Lavis was taken sick – not long after losing most of his money – his hunch got stronger. But there was nothing that he could prove, no action that he could take. And he might even be totally wrong. Then I happened to show up in Singapore, and he had a brain-storm. If I spent a little time up here, and there was anything funny going on, I might be able to spot it – if I was looking.'

'And the Maugham story was to make sure you looked.'

'It wasn't an exact parallel, of course – but that would scarcely have been possible. It was close enough. And maybe it was even better, because if necessary Ascony could always invent some other case and deny that he had you in mind at all . . . He probably had another angle too. He knew you'd recognise who I was, and he figured you might think I was part of a trap, and that might panic you into making a fatal mistake. Which it did.'

She frowned.

'You mean like finishing Ted off in a hurry before you got here and saw him? Naturally you wouldn't believe me if I said I didn't.'

'That was only the start of it, anyway. The important thing is that it gave you a scare when Ascony asked if he could send me; but you were more scared of making it look worse if you tried to get out of it. After a little verbal fencing, and reading the Maugham story this morning, you were sure you were in trouble. So was I; but it was still mostly intuition. And at first I couldn't decide what was Farrast's part in the deal. Not even when I heard him go to your bedroom last night.'

She half closed her eyes, with a little shudder of distaste.

'Really,' she said, 'are there any lengths you won't go to?'

'Oh, I don't think you invited him. Not last night, I mean. You'd never be as crude as that. But he could be. And I'm guessing that started you thinking that he was expendable. But after I saw him in action this morning I'd never buy him as a poisoner, and I said so, and you realised it was no use playing with that idea. So you went ahead with Plan B.'

'I'm quite certain two people never had a conversation like

this before,' she said. 'But since we're doing it, you'd better finish. What was this fatal mistake I made?'

Simon picked up the gun he had taken from her a little earlier – it was in its holster slung over the other arm of the chair on which he had thoughtfully perched himself – and toyed with it idly.

'The Ah Fong job was the first one you've ever had to do in a hurry,' he said. 'And anyhow I got out there too quickly for you to have been able to set the stage with your usual care. That's why I posted a guard at the pantry door and told him that nobody, not even me – or you – was to go in there or move anything. I'm betting that when the cops go to work they'll find your fingerprints on the knife Ah Fong was supposed to have attacked you with—'

'Why shouldn't my fingerprints be on a knife in my own house?'

For the first time her voice seemed to rise a little.

'And on the poison bottle beside him—'

'I snatched it out of his hand!'

'I mean *only your fingerprints.*'

There was an absolute silence.

The Saint had shifted his eyes from her before he spoke, and he did not move them back.

A very long time, an eternity, seemed to pass. His cigarette burned down between his fingers, and he put it out.

At last Eve Lavis said, in a very cool, very even voice: 'Would you mind if I had a drink?'

He still did not look at her. It was as if an iron hand closed on his heart. Perhaps after all he was an incurable romanticist. In spite of all the statistics, he preferred to think of crime as men's business. A beautiful woman should be a damsel in distress, for a knight errant to rescue, or a heroine, to ride squarely side by side with him. No man should ever have to meet one like Eve, so lovely and so damned.

'No,' said the Saint. 'Help yourself.'

She stood up, and crossed to the sideboard. He heard her over his shoulder, and the clink of glass and the soft plash of liquid. It made no difference now that the four murders that he knew of were almost certainly not the only ones she had done, that she had very likely started long before she reached Singapore. There was a fathomless pain and anger in him that would never be wholly stilled.

'This,' she said, 'is to the only man who ever turned me down.'

He did not turn his head, he could not, even when he heard her fall.

The Sporting Chance

I

Cowichan Lake was a sheet of silver under a cloudless sky that was slowly warming into blue after the recent pallor of dawn, but rising trout were still dimpling the glassy sheen of the water. Simon Templar had already caught three of them, and four of that size were as many as he wanted for his lunch: he didn't want to kill one more fish than he could use at that moment, and so he was in no hurry to end his sport by taking the last one. He was really working on the perfection of his cast now rather than trying to take a fish, waiting for a rise no less than twenty yards away from his boat and then trying to place his fly in the exact centre of the spreading concentric ripples on the surface, as if in the bullseye of a target.

Somewhere in the distance, so faint at first that it seemed to come from no actual direction, he heard the hum of an aeroplane engine.

There was nothing intrinsically noteworthy about the sound. Simon permitted himself a moment of detached philosophical astonishment at the random reflection that there could be hardly a corner of the globe left by that time where the sound of an aeroplane overhead would attract any general attention; in such a few years had man's domain extended to the stratosphere, and so easily had the miracle been taken for granted. Up there in the heart of Vancouver Island beyond the end of the last trail that could be called a road, a plane was merely commonplace, the most simple and obvious vehicle to convey prospectors, timber surveyors, hunters and fishermen to the remote destinations of their choice. The fantastic contraption of the Wright Brothers had become the horse and buggy of their grandchildren.

A nice sixty feet away, a young uncomplicated rainbow rose lazily to ingurgitate some insect that had fallen on the surface. Simon picked the tiny vortex of its inhalation as his next mark, and his rod rose and flipped forward again in a flowing rhythm. The line curled and snaked out like a graceful gossamer whip, and at the end of it the artificial fly settled on the water as airily as a tuft of thistledown.

The young trout, perhaps pardonably thinking it had left something unfinished, must have turned in its own length to rectify the omission. The fly went under in another little swirl, and instantly Simon set the hook. He felt his line become taut and alive, and the fish somersaulted into the air, the blade of its body shimmering in the clear morning light.

The drone of the plane had grown rapidly louder, and it seemed to the Saint's sensitive ear that there was a kind of syncopated unevenness in its pulse. Almost as soon as he had localised it somewhere behind him and to his left it was bearing down lower, but he was too busy for the moment to turn and look at it. For a few minutes he was entirely absorbed in balancing the vigour of the fish against the strength of a filament that one sharp tug would have snapped. The struggle of the fish came through the fragile line and limber rod all the way into his hand, as if he were linked to it by an extended nerve. And the aeroplane engine roared in an approaching crescendo and then suddenly stopped, but the rush of its wings through the air went on, coming closer still, blending with the whine of a dead propeller and punctuated by an occasional spastic hiccup of erratic combustion. It wooshed over his head suddenly like a gigantic bird, seeming to swoop so low over him that involuntarily he ducked and crouched lower in the boat.

That momentary distraction and the slack that it put into his line were all that the spunky young trout needed. It was gone, with a last flashing leap, to await some other rendez-vous with destiny; and Simon ruefully reeled in an unresist-ing hook as the cause of the trouble touched down a little farther on, striking two plumes of spray from the water with its skimming pontoons.

He laid his rod down and lighted a cigarette, looking the seaplane over in more detail as it coasted towards the nearby shore. It was painted a dark grey that was almost black, its lines were not those of any make that he could identify, and it seemed to carry no identification numbers or insignia of any kind – he made those basic observations in approximately that sequence, although in less sharply punctuated compart-ments than the summary suggests.

Also it had definite engine trouble, as had been hinted by the irregular thrumming sound of its approach and the bron-chitic coughs it had emitted as it glided down. Now the propeller was turning again, making strained uneven revolu-tions with recoils and pauses in between: the pilot was for-cing it with the starter, but the motor refused to fire. Already the seaplane had lost the momentum of its landing speed; it needed power to steer and taxi even on the water, but it was not producing any, and a breeze that had barely started to ripple the smoothness of the lake was beginning to waft it sideways in undignified but inexorable impotence.

The plexiglass canopy opened, and the pilot squirmed out and wriggled down on to one of the pontoons. He reached under into a trapdoor in the plane's sternum and hauled out a light anchor with a line already attached and let it drop with a splash, and presently the plane stopped drifting and slewed around at the end of the line with its nose pointed aloofly at the playful zephyr.

The pilot stood on the pontoon and looked around with a

kind of studied nonchalance, almost pointedly refraining from more than a glance in the direction of Simon Templar in his skiff. It was as if he intended to disclaim in advance even the suggestion of an appeal for help – as if, in fact, he would have denied that anything was wrong.

If that was the way he wanted it, Simon was in no hurry either. He snipped off the fly which the escaped trout had mauled severely in the tussle, and concentrated profoundly over the selection of another from the assortment in his pocket case. Finally he settled on one with grey hackles, a red body, and a yellow-brown wisp of tail, and began to tie it on to his leader with leisured care.

There was no outward change in his demeanour, any more than there is any visible change in the exterior of a radio when it is switched on. But already the mysterious circuits which had made the Saint what he was had awakened to silently busy life, telling him with dispassionate certainty that even in those last few moments, with no more overt symptoms than the facts which have just been narrated, the delicate tendrils of adventure had made contact with him again, even in that placid Shangri-La of the North-west.

From the city of Vancouver on the west coast of Canada it was two hours and a quarter by ferry to Nanaimo on the east coast of Vancouver Island; from Nanaimo it was a roundabout sixty miles to where the Cowichan Lake road ended at the Youbou lumber settlement; beyond that, it was almost ten more miles by boat to the cove near the north-west tip of the lake where Simon Templar had been fly-casting when the grey-black seaplane swooped down to shatter the peace of the spring morning with its spluttering engine and drag him rudely back out of his own brief moment of tranquillity. Even there at the very edge of outright wilderness, it seemed, the Saint's destiny could not spare him for long. Adventure was still as near as it had ever been. It was only up to him whether he should answer or ignore its beckoning finger.

But of course it was no accident that the invitation met with him there. The first pass had been made weeks ago, on the other side of the Pacific.

2

At the Raffles Hotel in Singapore, Major Vernon Ascony, the Assistant Commissioner of Police, said: 'It isn't coming through here, old boy. If it were, I couldn't help getting a whiff of it. I personally don't believe it's even coming from India. From what I hear, the new governments of India and Pakistan have pretty well snuffed it out. And I don't think it's coming down from Indo-China either. We'd have been bound to find a link somewhere along the route. I just don't think it's our pidgin at all. But you can't tell that to the international bigwigs. They're still stuck with the ideas they got from Fu Manchu. Drugs are peddled by sinister Orientals; Singapore is one of the Orient's gateways; therefore this must be one of the ports it clears from. So when an unusual amount of the stuff turns up in Los Angeles or Toronto, this here is one of the most likely places it came from. Then everyone wants to know why *I* don't bloody well personally put a stop to it.'

The Saint smiled.

'A policeman's lot is not a happy one,' he murmured. 'Could that be set to music, or has someone already done it?'

'Don't be too disappointed if someone got ahead of you, old chap. At least you've done more than almost anyone else to make it true.'

'Have I given you any trouble?'

'No. But I'm jolly well keeping my fingers crossed till your plane takes off ... Seriously, old man,' Ascony said, 'why don't you do something about it? I don't mind telling you, when I was a bit younger you were quite a hero of mine. *You* know, the Robin Hood of modern crime, the knight in shining armour – all that sort of rot. A lot of us in England used to think of you like that, when we read about you in the papers. But lately, you seem to have become rather different.'

'The world has become a little different too,' said the Saint.

'I know. And I'm sure that everything you've been doing has been important enough, in its own way. But I can't help wishing that once in a while you'd take on something more like the old times, I mean some simple racket that we all understand and agree about, and do it up good and proper without making a dollar out of it for yourself, just because it ought to be done. Like this dope racket, for instance.'

'You're not a boy now,' said the Saint, almost harshly. 'You're a policeman. You know how big and complicated the dope racket is. You know how many man-hours and dollars, how many elaborate organisations in how many countries, are trying to fight it. But you just want me to fix it all by myself, by tracking down one dastardly master-mind and punching him on the nose.'

'Yes, of course I know it isn't so simple. But there actually is a flood of dope reaching North America on a bigger scale than it ever did before. Anyhow, that's what I gather from the memoranda that end up on my desk. Well, a thing like that *could* have one simple source, which a fellow like yourself might be able to dig out, if he was lucky. You get around a lot. I suppose I'm talking out of turn. But I wish you'd try.'

Simon Templar frowned at the beading of dew on his *stengah* glass. It was a long time since he had been reminded of certain truths as bluntly as Major Ascony's incongruously genuine eagerness had stated them.

'Maybe I'll have to do that,' he said darkly.

And by the next morning he might have preferred to forget

the easy boast; only some of the backwash of memories that had stung it out of him would not be so easily dismissed.

But in Hong Kong, Inspector Stephen Hao said: 'If it's coming from Red China, it isn't shipped from here. Would you like to see how we search everybody who comes in from the mainland these days? After we get through frisking 'em, five thousand of 'em couldn't be carrying enough dope to give an addict one good fix. Why don't you look around in Japan?'

But in Tokyo, at his favourite *tempura* restaurant on Yodobashi Avenue, Master Sergeant Ben Johnson, of the Office of Special Investigations, said: 'Sure, the Secret Service and the FBI have been riding our tails about it for months. They know that most of the supply these days is moving from west to east, from the Pacific Coast. But I'll swear it isn't coming from Nippon. Hell, we've got it licked here to the point where the domestic traffic is about ready to die from starvation, and the prices are out of sight. So where would anyone find that sort of quantity to export? What do you say, Nikki?'

Inspector Geichi Nikkiyama, of the Tokyo Metropolitan Police, nodded owlishly over a fried shrimp bearded with golden batter.

'Ah, so. More likely criminal technician in United States having discovered how to make synthetic dope in bathtub, like so profitable Prohibition gin.'

But in San Francisco, in Johnny Kan's restaurant on Grant Avenue, as the Saint dipped his chopsticks into a dish of *tung gee bok opp*, a succulent squab marinated in exotic spices and rose liqueur and dressed with a quite improbable sauce, Johnny told him: 'If I were you, I'd go on up to Vancouver. From what I hear, that's the easiest place to get it in all North America. If my name was Charlie Chan, I'd deduce that where it's most plentiful would be the place nearest the source. I'd like to see you do something about it, Saint.'

'So would I,' said the Saint. 'And it can't be much harder than catching hold of a rainbow.'

'You might look into that too, while you're up there,' Johnny Kan said confusingly.

Simon figured that some minor idiomatic cog had slipped somewhere between them, but wrote it off as not worth a laborious exploration. Yet for the first time he felt that he might be getting warm, and in Vancouver he made no more direct inquiries.

Most of what he did there would make rather tedious story-telling, except for certain individuals who might have nefarious motives for a too detailed curiosity about the Saint's methods. It was quite a few years since the Saint had last slipped into the underworld and disappeared without a ripple, like an otter into a dark pool; but he did it as easily as if the last of the old days had been yesterday, and none of the persons he moved among during that time ever dreamed who it was that had passed through their stealthy lives more stealthily than their utmost caution could conceive.

He forgot all about Johnny Kan's bland *non sequitur* until one day in the devious labyrinths he followed there was the echo of a name, Julius Pavan, and with it a reference to what seemed to be a stock joke about Mr Pavan's passion for fishing. And at long last a bell had rung as Simon remembered that among truly dedicated fishermen the word 'rainbow' primarily suggests a species of fish, the rainbow trout, after which the lighting phenomenon in the sky may possibly have been named.

And so a hint and a hunch had eventually led him to where he had just seen a seaplane of unfamiliar design and with no identification markings landing on the waters where Mr Pavan fished; and now it all seemed as clear and sure as Fate.

3

At the edge of the pines on the north shore of the cove there was a log cabin no bigger than a double garage. It was the only sign of human habitation within sight of that remote corner of the lake. It was crudely but solidly built of hand-hewn timber, and mellowed into the landscape with the weathering of many seasons. Perhaps some trapper of a generation ago had built it for his headquarters, before the swaths cut by commercial logging had driven the game even farther back into the dwindling wilderness. But now it was the fishing camp of Julius Pavan, who lived alone in a big house in the heights of West Vancouver, and drove a big car and invested in buildings and real estate.

A man in a red plaid shirt and drab trousers came out of it and hurried down to a rough floating dock where a small motor-boat was tied up. He cast off and cranked it up and chugged across to the seaplane at an unspectacular but useful speed.

He stopped the boat beside the pontoon where the pilot stood, and the pilot got in. There was some discussion or explanation or argument, in which the pilot took the more gesticulatory part. Presently the pilot climbed up on the short foredeck, and from that elevation managed to open a cowling over the plane's single engine, while the man in the plaid shirt steadied the motor-boat by holding on to the plane's propeller. The pilot peered and probed lengthily into the engine's innards, and finally closed the cowling again and lowered himself back down into the boat with another outburst of gestures.

The man in the plaid shirt shrugged, and cranked his motor again, and the boat swung around and headed back towards the dock below the lonely cabin.

Their course took them within fifty yards of the Saint, and both men looked at him as they went by. But neither of them waved a casual greeting as is the friendly custom of the back-woods; and the Saint, having left it to them to make the advance, did not belatedly take the initiative. When they had finished looking at him they returned to their private discussion; and with reciprocal indifference to their existence and their problems Simon Templar plucked his fly from the water where it had been resting and freshened it a little with a couple of false casts and sent it floating downwind towards another imaginary target.

Out of the corner of his eye, he watched the motor-boat tie up at the dock, and the two men get out and walk up to the cabin and go in.

Simon decided to allow himself just three more casts, each to be made and properly fished without unseemly haste. Through one circumstance and another, several summers had gone by since he last practised that pin-point accuracy with a trout rod, and he was ingenuously delighted to discover that his wrist had lost little of its cunning. But on another level of his mind those three casts were only a convenient way of estimating a period of time which he felt he should let go by, and simultaneously a way of occupying the time which might lull any suspicions of the two men who were now in the cabin, if perchance they were still keeping him under observation.

His third cast happened to be the first to fall several inches wide of its mark, but he disciplined himself sternly against the temptation to try just one more. He picked the line up on the reel, secured the fly, and put the rod down with the resigned air of a man who has decided to concede a temporary triumph to the caprices of the finny tribe. He even moulded exactly the right expression on his face, just in case he might be playing to an audience equipped with powerful binoculars.

As a matter of fact the sun had risen high enough by that time to send the fish down to cooler and shadier depths, and the rises had stopped almost as if some piscine curfew had sounded. It was a perfectly normal and convincing time for any angler to pack up until the evening.

Simon hauled up his anchor, moved back to the stern seat, and pulled the starter of his outboard.

It was one of the new silent models which were just then beginning to reduce the traditional machine-gun racket of outboard motors to little more than a horrible memory. It came to life with no more obtrusive a purr than an expensive automobile, but the skiff shot away as if springs had uncoiled behind it. And because of this epoch-making mechanical improvement, which made it impossible for anyone to trace his course and progress by ear, he was able to turn the skiff in towards the shore and cut the engine the moment he had passed the first promontory that shut off the cabin from his view, with complete assurance that the men in the cabin would hear nothing to suggest what he had done.

He let the skiff glide the last few yards under a steeply sloping bank, and moored it to a tree on which he also swung himself ashore. He climbed the slope at an easy slant and came to the top of a low ridge. From there he could look down to the waters of the cove which he had just left, and the seaplane riding at anchor farther out on the lake. The roof of the log cabin was below him, almost hidden among the trees.

The same trees and bushes provided a perfect screen for his approach, and he moved between them as silently and invisibly as any Indian ever crept upon a pioneer's home-stead. He only had to expose himself in the very last eight feet, and those he covered in a low crouching leap that brought him up against the widest span of blank wall on that side and still kept him well under window level. The man-oeuvre seemed even excessively cautious, for he felt quite sure that anyone in the cabin who was keeping a lookout at all would be watching the approach from the lake and not the back of the building.

Rising flat against the wall, he slid along it to the nearest window and with infinite care raised one eye just above the sill in one bottom corner of the opening.

The inside of the cabin was one big room for sleeping, living, and cooking, with the black iron wood-burning range which is standard equipment in the North-west placed squarely and starkly in one corner. Other amenities, however, had been introduced to alleviate the Spartan simplicity in which the original builder had probably lived. There was a good carpet on the floor, a modern radiogram in another corner, chrome-tube chairs with plastic-covered rubber cushions at the big all-purpose table, and a couple of big luxurious-looking armchairs with gay chintz slip covers. The pilot of the seaplane sat in one of them, gazing out at the lake through the opposite window.

The sleeping accommodation consisted of double-decker bunks built against the wall at one end of the room. Peering around at an acute angle, Simon could see about half the structure. But what he saw was the half where the girl sat.

She would have been no more than twenty-five, he judged, if you discounted the tired pallor that had sabotaged the young contours of her face. She wore blue jeans and a form-fitting cardigan that plainly sculptured youthful curves of hip and waist and breast. Her short hair was midnight black but her eyes were clear blue like mountain lakes. She sat on the lower bunk and leaned against one of the smooth posts that supported the upper berth, with her cheek resting against it and one arm wrapped around it. As she wore it the attitude had an unconsciously pathetic grace, but she could not have changed it much if she had wanted to, for her two wrists were handcuffed together where they met in her lap.

He did not see Julius Pavan.

But he heard Pavan say, behind him: 'Put your hands up. Don't make any other move, or I'll blow you in half.'

4

'Well, well, well,' said the Saint. 'Now I know what they mean by overpowering hospitality. Did I really look so lonesome, or were you just desperate for someone to make a fourth at bridge?'

He glanced mildly around the cabin with his hands still in the air, and Pavan kicked the door shut behind him without taking his repeating shotgun out of the Saint's spine.

'Just as I figured,' Pavan said. 'He ran his boat around the point and got out and came sneaking over the hill. All I had to do was stand still in the bushes and get the drop on him when he was jammed up against the house, peeking in.'

'What did you do that for?' the pilot asked Simon with curious gentleness.

He was under six feet tall, but immensely broad, with the neck and shoulders of a wrestler. His bullet head was covered with blond hair cropped so close that at first sight it looked shaved. He wore blue trousers and a grey turtle-neck sweater that somehow combined to give him a faintly nautical appearance. His age might have been anywhere in the thirties; the hardness of his features made it difficult to guess more accurately. His eyes were yellowish and very pale.

'I thought it would give an opening to anyone who wanted to ask silly questions,' said the Saint.

'Search him, Igor,' Pavan said impatiently. 'I don't want to have to hold this gun on him all day.'

The pilot ambled closer and passed his big hands

competently over the Saint's body. He showed no surprise at the automatic which he felt under the Saint's armpit and pulled out from the shoulder holster under Simon's shirt. He checked the action matter-of-factly and stuck the gun in his own hip pocket.

Beyond that, the Saint's pockets yielded only a small amount of money and some cigarettes and matches, which the pilot put on the table, and a wallet, which the pilot opened and began to browse through.

Pavan's shotgun muzzle prodded the Saint viciously in the kidneys.

'Get over to the bed. Hook your arm around the post, like the girl's is, and put your wrists together.'

Simon obeyed. To get his arm around the post he had to put it around the girl's arm as well, and he had to sit on the end of the bunk with his body half turned away from her.

Pavan produced another pair of handcuffs and snapped them deftly on the Saint's wrists. Simon looked down at them with reluctant approval.

'So much faster and safer than tying people up,' he murmured. 'I've often wondered why you crooks didn't make more use of them.'

Pavan stared at him broodingly. Pavan was middle-aged and a little paunchy where the plaid shirt was tucked into his pants. He had lank black hair thinning back from his forehead, a long swarthy clean-shaven face, and thin lips clamped around an unlighted cigar. His black eyes measured the Saint for a retort, but debated at unhurried length whether it should be verbal or physical.

'His name is Simon Templar,' the pilot announced, from his study of the identification cards in the Saint's wallet.

The name did not seem to mean anything to him; but Simon felt the girl recognise it, without looking at her, in the involuntary tensing of her shoulder where it rested against his, and he saw the reaction that first widened Pavan's eyes for a moment and then started something smouldering in them like hot slag.

Pavan uttered it.

'The Saint!'

'What is that?' asked the pilot.

'He's no cop,' Pavan said. His eyes were fastened on the Saint with the unblinking malevolence of a snake's. 'He's worse. He's a guy who set out to be the cop and the judge too. He gives out that he hates crime – so that gives him an excuse to commit crimes himself against anyone with a racket. According to some people, this makes him a Robin Hood. According to me, he's just a robber *and* a hood.'

'So now that I've been so elegantly introduced,' Simon said to the pilot, 'what's the rest of your name, Igor?'

'Igor Netchideff,' said the pilot amiably.

Simon nodded, and turned his head to the girl.

'Since we're all getting so chummy,' he said, 'won't you tell me who you are?'

'Marian Kent,' she said.

Her voice was low but steady, and he liked the candid appraisal of her gaze.

'Are you trying to pretend you don't know each other?' Pavan snarled.

Simon looked at him and then down to the shotgun, and drawled: 'Pappy, I'd be proud to marry her, but I am not the father of her child.'

Pavan moved the gun abruptly and hit Simon across the ear with the barrel. Pain and shock stabbed a kaleidoscope of fire through the Saint's brain and for an instant almost dissolved into blackness. As he fought to clear his vision, he heard Netchideff laughing.

'You are upset, Julius,' the pilot said. 'Two of such people on your trail, so close together – it *is* upsetting. But if what you say about Templar is right, obviously they would not be friends. Now go and bring back Templar's boat, before it may be noticed by some other fisherman.'

Pavan put the shotgun down in a corner by the door and went out.

Slowly the sharp agony in the Saint's ear died down to a dull throbbing, and the sequins stopped dancing in front of his eyes.

Netchideff stood at the window, gazing out, rubbing his square jaw on his clenched fist, apparently deep in thought.

'How did you get into this?' Simon asked the girl quietly. 'Don't answer if it's any help to the enemy.'

'They know,' she said. 'I'm in the Royal Canadian Mounted Police.'

'What – with no horse? No red coat?'

His flippancy was as cool as if they had been making conversation at a cocktail party. Tired and desperate as she must have been, it still managed to bring the wraith of a smile to her lips.

'These days, we're also a Canadian FBI,' she said. 'And they haven't advertised it, but they've let a few women in. There are cases sometimes when they can do more than men.'

'And they tried you on Julius.'

'I got a job as his secretary.'

'So he'd already been tabbed as the main dope source that everyone's been looking for?'

'Oh, no. It was much more like a wild suspicion. Until I had a couple of lucky breaks, that is. But I guess this unlucky one wipes them out.'

'I followed you up from Nanaimo last night,' Simon said. 'I'd been watching you and wondering about the set-up before that, of course. I saw the two of you pile into his motor-boat and push off from the dock where he keeps it, and somehow I felt that something was wrong and that you were scared deep inside. But it was only a feeling, and there were too many facts against trying to get a boat and follow you in the dark. I stopped at a motel and figured I wouldn't have too much trouble locating you after daybreak, but I'll admit I didn't sleep too well.'

'Were you after the same thing that I was?'

He nodded.

'Ever since a bloke in Singapore reminded me how long it was since I last did anything really valuable and altrustic to the human race.'

'I was damned scared,' she said. There seemed to be so much that they had to tell each other, even though a strange understanding had grown from nowhere between them that made the most skeletal explanations full and sufficient. 'I had a sixth sense telling me that something had gone wrong and Pavan was on to me, but I tried to tell myself it was only nerves. This was my first important assignment, and I wanted to be a hero. I figured that if I wasn't being brought here to be murdered, this might be the big break. I just had to take the gamble.'

'What was the reason he gave for bringing you up here?'

'To work on the prospectus of a housing development he's interested in.'

'You couldn't possibly have believed that that was all he meant to work on, at least.'

'I wasn't afraid of what you're thinking,' she said. 'This was one of those jobs I mentioned where it was an advantage to be a woman. I have news for you. He's queer.'

'That's a switch,' said the Saint. 'Now you may have to protect me.'

They had been ignoring the pilot unconsciously – it didn't seem that anything he heard now could do more harm, and indeed he had appeared to be completely immersed in his own cogitations. But now they saw him looking at them again with sphinx-like intensity, and became aware that he had never stopped listening.

Suddenly he thumped his chest.

'I am not queer,' he proclaimed proudly.

'Well, congratulations,' said the Saint.

Netchideff stalked closer, with an almost feral compactness of movement for a few footsteps.

His course trended towards the girl. He stood looking down at her, studying separate details with his pale eyes. Then, as if to confirm his observation, he cupped a hand over one of her breasts.

Marian Kent kicked at him savagely, but he turned skilfully and her foot only struck him in the thigh.

Netchideff slapped her face hard, but by no means with his full strength. Then he put his hands on his hips and roared with laughter.

'You son of a bitch,' said the Saint.

He couldn't kick Netchideff effectively himself because of his position around the corner of the bunk, but he hoped that the pilot might be tempted into a move that would remedy that.

Netchideff regarded him thoughtfully; but then the door opened again and Pavan returned.

Pavan carried the Saint's fly rod and tackle box. He put the tackle box down by the wall and waved the end of the rod up and down, feeling the action of it, before he stood it up in the corner.

'Nice rod,' he said. 'That's all he had in the boat. He must have rented it from a camp down the lake.' His dark eyes shifted from one direction to another, and made certain deductions. 'Were they giving you trouble?'

'No,' Netchideff laughed again. He moved back to the table, took a cigarette from the Saint's package and lighted it, then looked a second time at the match booklet he had used. 'Lake Cowichan Auto Court,' he read from it. 'That is where he stayed last night.'

'Very likely. It looks like one of their boats.'

'When will they wonder why he does not come back?'

'Not before dark – and probably not even then.'

'Good. Then we do not have to worry all day. I will look after them while you take your boat down the lake and buy the part that will mend the engine of my plane.'

Pavan's heavy brows drew together.

'Why me? I don't know anything about engines.'

'It is a very simple part. I will write it down for you. It was invented by Russian engineers, but the spies of Henry Ford stole the design from our trucks which they saw in Europe and they now use it in all their cars. That is what it says in my emergency instructions.'

Simon exchanged fascinated glances with Marian.

'I'd probably still have to drive to Duncan for it,' Pavan said. 'And that's another twenty miles.'

'But you know the way, and you will know where to go, and no one will wonder about your accent,' Netchideff insisted jovially. 'You need not be afraid for me. I have been listening to them talk, and I am quite sure they are alone and do not expect any friends to come to rescue them very soon. You should be back in three hours, and I shall not be bored. But that is no reason to waste time, Julius. You will start at once, please.'

5

The pilot came back from seeing Pavan off with Simon's three rainbows dangling on a string. He held them up and admired them.

'This is very nice of you,' he said. 'I shall enjoy them for lunch.'

'I hope you choke on a bone,' said the Saint pleasantly.

Netchideff chuckled with great good humour. He could not have made it plainer that he knew that he could afford a robust invulnerability to mere verbiage.

He took the fish to the sink and began to clean them, humming to himself in a rich voice that swallowed up the last receding mutter of the departing motor-boat. He seemed to have forgotten about sex as capriciously as a child might have been distracted from a toy.

Simon tried tentatively to keep it that way.

'I guess it's a lot better than the lunch you'd get on your submarine,' he remarked.

The pilot stopped humming.

After a moment he said: 'The Russian Navy is the best fed in the world. But did you know I came from a submarine, or did you guess?'

'It was a fairly simple deduction,' said the Saint. 'Your clothes have a sea-going look. Your seaplane is painted a naval colour. But all the insignia and identification marks have been painted out. Therefore you're on a secret mission. Your seaplane is a type that could be launched from a large submarine. The safest craft to come sneaking close enough to this coast to launch it would be a submarine. So I bet on the submarine.'

'You are most intelligent.'

'The secret mission, of course, isn't so glorious. The great well-fed Russian Navy is bringing supplies to a common dope peddler. But it isn't so easy to deduce why.'

'I was told that he had a good organisation, and he pays well.'

'Does he pay you?'

'Of course not. I do not know how that is done, but I suppose he pays one of our agents here. Then I am told when to make delivery.'

'And that doesn't bother you a bit.'

'I am a good officer. I do what I am told.'

'I forgot, I'm sorry. Where you come from, you're not encouraged to think.'

Netchideff had finished cleaning the fish. He washed his hands under the faucet and came towards the Saint, drying them on a dish-cloth.

'I think,' he stated complacently. 'It is not my business, but I think I know why we supply Pavan. This dope is a popular vice in the bourgeois democracies. It is one of the vices that weakens them. So it is good for us to encourage. Anything that helps to keep you weak is good, because it will be harder for you to make the attack on us that your Wall Street leaders are planning. And the money we get helps to pay our friends and agents who keep us informed of your imperialist plans. So in all ways this is very good for us.'

'I begin to see the advantages,' Simon admitted. 'Only you can't help getting the aggressive and defensive angles reversed.'

Netchideff frowned.

'I do not quite understand that, but what you say is not

important anyhow. Because of your bourgeois education, you cannot think clearly and correctly like a Russian.'

'But you just said I was most intelligent.'

'When you make a correct deduction, you are intelligent. When you repeat capitalist lies, you show that you are too stupid for anything except fishing.'

The pilot's eyes drifted towards Marian again.

'Now you're really talking as if you'd been hit on the head with a hammer and sickle,' Simon said desperately. 'Maybe you invented everything from Ford cars to fleas, but I'll bet there isn't one good fisherman in the whole Soviet Union.'

Netchideff turned back to him with a sort of irritated incredulity.

'Now you are merely ridiculous. How do you think we make the caviar that even your Wall Street bankers will pay any price for?'

'By catching a poor pregnant sturgeon in a net,' Simon scoffed. 'That isn't what we call fishing. I mean with a rod and line.'

'We have people who catch fish with a rod and a hook too. I have done it myself, often.'

'And what did you use for bait?'

'A piece of bread, or meat, or a worm.'

'That's what I thought. You wouldn't even know what to do with a rig like mine.'

Netchideff glared at him in an uncertain way. Then he stomped over and snatched the Saint's rod out of the corner where Pavan had stood it. He shook it as if it were an inadequate club, then pored over it from end to end like an inquisitive ape.

He unfastened the fly from where it was hooked into a little keeper ring near the butt, and held it up in his huge paw to squint at it.

'This is what you catch fish with?' he demanded.

'That's right,' said the Saint. 'It's an artificial fly.'

'It is only some little feathers on a hook.'

'That's all. But you see, the kind of fisherman I'm talking about would be ashamed to catch a fish with anything that a fish could actually eat. You don't have to be very clever to make a fish take a bite at a good meal. The only time you prove that you're really smarter than a fish is when you can fool it into taking a bite at a piece of tin, a few feathers, or an old shoelace – anything that no fish would dream of eating if it wasn't for the way you offered it.'

Netchideff shook his head puzzledly.

'But why do you want to do that when it is much easier with a worm?'

'A Communist couldn't begin to understand,' answered the Saint. 'But the idea is to give even a poor fish a sporting chance.'

The pilot's glower darkened.

'I don't not believe you. It is some kind of bourgeois propaganda.'

'Comrade, you've just cleaned three fish that swallowed it.'

'How do you make fish eat these feathers?'

'You cast the fly out on the water, and if you do it right a fish comes and takes it. But as I said, no Russian could ever do it.'

'A Russian can do anything that you can,' Netchideff said violently.

'One rouble will get you fifty dollars that *you* can't.'

Netchideff hefted the rod, as if he had half a mind to hit Simon across the face with it. Then he looked at it again, and at the little red-bodied fly dancing at the end of the leader. A confused sort of anger twisted his face in a way that was incongruously suggestive of a baby preparing to cry.

'I will show you,' he said. 'I will catch more fish than you with this thing. If I do not, it will prove you are lying!'

He flung open the door and went out.

Marian Kent and the Saint looked at each other without daring to speak.

The door opened again and Netchideff stood there.

'I do not want you to think that you have changed anything for yourselves,' he said. 'I have to pass the time, that is all. It does not suit me to kill you, Templar, until Julius returns and I am ready to leave. So it is good that you have time to think of your mistakes. As for this pretty and foolish girl' – his yellowish cat's eyes shifted to her with the naked directness of an animal – 'I am not in a hurry for her because I do not need to be. I am going to take her back to my submarine where I can enjoy her better, and when I have enough my comrades will be glad to have their turn, until we get home and give her to other comrades who will ask her questions about the Canadian Police.'

6

'If I live to be a hundred,' Marian said at last, and giggled a little hysterically, 'I don't suppose I'll ever listen to a more fantastic argument.'

'It worked, though, didn't it?' Simon grinned tightly.

'I still can't believe it. I can't think why.'

'I gambled on a psychological gimmick. Haven't you noticed the formula in all the Communist purges, how they can't be satisfied with just erasing the opposition, as every other dictatorship has been? Their heretics have got to confess, and acknowledge how wrong they've been and how richly they deserve their punishment. I don't know how a psychiatrist would explain it, I just know how it works. So I figured Igor mightn't be able to resist the chance to make me eat crow before he kills me.'

'How long will he try?'

'An hour – maybe more if he's stubborn.'

'But as he kindly told us, it won't make any difference to what we've got coming,' she said. 'When Pavan gets back with that part, the liquidation will proceed as scheduled.'

'We're still ahead. Any time we can keep him arguing, fishing, or playing charades, is time where he won't be developing his nastier ideas. And time for the cavalry to come galloping over the hill.'

'We didn't kid him when he was listening,' she said quietly. 'Why kid ourselves? There ain't goin' to be no cavalry.'

He met her eyes steadily.

'Are you sure of that?'

'Have you arranged for them?'

'No,' he said. 'I'm on my own. But I hoped you might have.'

'Pavan didn't spring this invitation on me till the last moment, and from then on he didn't let me any farther away from him than a rest-room – where there was no phone. I was afraid to try too hard to get word out, because part of the time I was wondering if the invitation itself was a trap, to see if I'd try to communicate with anyone and how I did it. And at the same time, if I was really getting a break, I didn't want to risk fumbling it.'

'You must have some regular schedule of contacts. When will the other Mounties miss you?'

'Not before Monday. I only work for Pavan Monday through Friday, and I'd already reported everything okay yesterday afternoon just before Pavan asked me to come up here. My boss will think I'm just spending a nice restful week-end – which I should have been.'

Simon smiled fractionally.

'This could be quite a problem for us, if we can't find a way to get loose.'

'Doesn't the Saint always have something up his sleeve?'

'Sometimes I have had a knife. But not today. In any case, it wouldn't have done any good. That's one of the various advantages of handcuffs. You can't cut them off without special tools.' He stared at his wrists. 'Of course, you could cut your hands off. They say some animals caught in a trap will do that.'

She shuddered almost imperceptibly.

'I don't know whether I could do it.'

'Frankly, neither do I. But fortunately we don't have the gruesome decision to make. No knife.'

'How did Houdini do it?'

'If the handcuffs weren't fixed in advance, he had a key stashed away somewhere. But I wasn't told there were going to be handcuffs. No key.'

'And you can't take them apart, can you? No screwdriver. No hacksaw. No file.'

'I'll never be able to look a boy scout in the eye again,' he said, 'but I'm not wearing one of those things.'

'Could you pick the lock?'

'Maybe, if you were wearing a bobby pin, or even a hair-pin.' He glanced over her short-cut dark hair. 'But you aren't, of course.'

'I haven't even a safety pin – or any kind of pin.'

He looked down at his waist.

'And out of all the ordinary belts I've got,' he said, 'I had to pick one with a new-fangled plastic catch instead of a buckle. If I ever get out of here, it goes straight in the ash-can.'

'A bed spring!' she gasped.

It was a forlorn idea, but they went through some strained contortions to explore its far-fetched possibility. This did not take long.

'The hell with Progress,' said the Saint. 'And especially foam rubber.'

They sat on their shared corner of the bunk again, linked together around the corner post.

'There's nothing we could reach, is there?' she said. 'I mean with our feet, as far as they could stretch.'

'No,' he said briefly. 'If I could get at my tackle box, it might be a different story. But Julius and Igor aren't dopes, and they knew I couldn't make my legs twelve feet long.'

He studied the post that their arms were linked around. It was a smooth pole fully five inches in diameter, with the bunk frames fastened solidly to it at their outside corner. Two other corners of the frames were fastened to the log walls, and their fourth corners were in the corner of the cabin itself. The pole went down to some attachment through a snug-fitting hole in the floor planking, and its upper end was notched into a tie beam overhead. It looked and felt as solid as a growing tree, but it was the only possible weak point left to try.

'Let's see if we can shake this loose,' Simon said grimly.

For several minutes he heaved, pulled, jolted, pushed, and twisted against the pole from a number of carefully selected angles. Because of the way their arms were intertwined, he knew that some of his savage onslaughts must have hurt her cruelly, but she never uttered a sound of protest and added all that she could of her strength to his efforts.

Presently they were both bruised and spent; and the pole had not budged or given any sign of budging.

'We could start a fire and hope the pole would burn faster than it burned us,' Simon said between deep breaths. 'But he took my matches and left them over there on the table, and even a boy scout would need another stick to rub against this one.'

'We could start gnawing it like beavers,' she said, 'but I think it would last longer than our teeth.'

Then she suddenly sobbed once, and hid her face in his shoulder.

Simon cursed at not having even a cigarette to bolster an illusion of nonchalance.

So this was what it was like, he thought, when your luck finally ran out. He had been within a hair's breadth of this identical situation a dozen times before; but always there had been some forgotten trump in his hand, some unappreciated weapon up his sleeve, some ultimate implausible contingency that might yet bring rescuing cavalry over the hill. Now every scant possibility had been checked off in remorseless rotation, every prospective mirage had been methodically eliminated.

As a matter of concrete and incontrovertible fact, unless

some fairy-tale trout popped its head out of the water and with a few exceptionally well-chosen words converted Igor Netchideff to Buddhism, they had – as the cliché succinctly says – had it.

It was a curiously hollow and undramatic realisation, in the same way that the sombre machinery of an execution is an anti-climax to the pageantry and excitement of a murder trial.

'I guess it had to come to this some time,' said the Saint. 'But I never really believed it.'

Presently Marian said: 'I wonder why women always have to get raped. And why it seems to matter so much.'

'They should specially avoid tangling with Russians,' he said.

'Do you think you could manage to strangle me?' she asked in a small expressionless voice.

He looked at her, and her eyes were unforgettably serious.

'Shut up,' he said roughly. 'Igor may still drop dead first.'

There was a crunch of heavy feeet outside, and Igor Netchideff stomped back in, very much alive.

He flung the Saint's rod down with a resounding crash.

'You try to make me a fool,' he thundered. 'First, that absurd fly cannot be cast. It is too light, it has no weight, you cannot throw it anywhere. But second, even when I put it out a little way with the rod, in the water, no fish came for it. No fish would be so stupid, even the fish of a capitalist country. Therefore you only pretend you can do things which you cannot, to deceive and frighten other people with nothing, as your leaders would try to do to the Soviets.'

'You're too easily discouraged,' said the Saint. 'I probably wouldn't do any better the first time I tried fishing in the Volga, until I learned how to handle a Party line.'

7

The pilot's face was congested with the frustration of a man who senses that he is being mocked and yet cannot confidently isolate and specify the taunt. After a long moment during which it seemed to be a toss-up whether he would try to rip the Saint to pieces or settle for rupturing one of his own blood-vessels, he turned abruptly and marched himself heavily to the stove.

He chunked fat from a can into the skillet and began to fry the trout which he had cleaned earlier.

The simple activity of watching and turning them, perhaps combined with the savoury aromas that began to permeate the air, seemed to alleviate his temper. After a while he began crooning musically to himself as he had done while he was cleaning the fish. But for the baritone register of his voice, it would have been exactly reminiscent of an easily distracted infant burbling obliviously over a newly invented pastime.

Simon and Marian began to experience a sharpening ache of hunger added to their weariness and cramping limbs and other discomforts. But not for anything would they have spoken of it – or, for that matter, said anything at all that might have regained Netchideff's attention. Any intriguing new line of conversation or argument that might have occurred to them was to be treasured for the moment when Netchideff might need another distraction: for the present he was completely occupied, and that was all that mattered. It was like keeping motionless in the same room with an escaped tiger, hoping in that immobility not to be noticed. But as Simon had said, every minute of precarious survival was still a minute stolen from eternity.

But Netchideff hadn't forgotten them. He was only letting them wait while he attended to something else. When the trout were done to his satisfaction, he brought the pan to the table and sat down and started to eat the fish from it, holding the head in one hand and the tail in the other and taking bites from the fish until it broke apart and he had one piece in each hand to finish in alternate mouthfuls. But in between bites he looked at Simon and Marian with the thoughtfulness of a tiger that is content to deal with one bone at a time.

When he had finished, he licked his fingers, belched resonantly, and continued to sit there looking at them inscrutably, like a conquering Mongol khan considering what to do with his captives. And as he sat, the lids drooped over his eyes, his head nodded, and his breathing became more audible.

He fell asleep.

Simon and Marian sat in still more incredulous stillness as the sound of breathing thickened into an unmistakable snore.

They let it go on for several minutes before they ventured even to whisper.

'We're still getting reprieves,' Simon said.

'Yes, but for what?'

'Time to think of something, maybe.'

'We're not outsmarting him. He's just playing cat and mouse. I know it now. This is his way of trying to break us down.'

'So long as we don't break down, we can use the time.'

'I know. I'll be quiet. I know you're trying to think.'

But for the first time he heard weariness in her voice, the kind of weariness which is the foreshadow of despair.

And he was trying to think, too. He had never stopped.

But no thought led to a way out. And only instinctive obstinacy refused to admit that that might very simply be because there was none.

But he went on trying.

They talked very little more. It was easier not to. But whenever one of them moved to revive a numbed muscle, the other could feel it, and it was like an intimate reassurance in the strange closeness which had been forced on them.

Time, which seemed so precious for the miracles it might have to find room for, nevertheless seemed to crawl in slow motion through the revelation of the miracles it was not going to produce . . .

Until, creeping imperceptibly into dominance against the reverberating counterpoint of the pilot's snores, the puttering approach of an identifiable motor-boat forced itself into the Saint's ears, and he looked down at his wrist watch and was stunned to discover how treacherously three hours had melted away.

A moment later the rhythm of Netchideff's snoring ended in a single grunt. His eyes opened, without any other movement of his body, and he also listened.

He looked out of the window, for a minute or two, while the chugging drew closer. Then he stood up without haste, yawned and stretched mightily, and went to the door. With a brief glance at his prisoners to satisfy himself that they were still helpless, he went out, and they heard his footsteps clumping down towards the lake.

'Well,' she said. 'Have you thought of anything?'

He shook his head.

'No.' It was too late for any more pretending. 'I'm sorry, Marian.'

'I'm sorry too,' she said with a little sigh. 'I always knew I'd meet you some day, but I imagined it very differently from this.'

'You did?' Any conversation would have seemed trivial now, but any triviality was good if it kept worse things out of her mind for a few moments longer. 'How?'

'Didn't my name mean anything to you?'

'I'm afraid not. Should it?'

'Do you remember anyone else named Kent?'

'Oh. Yes.' Two little lines notched in between his brows. 'One of my very best friends, a long long time ago, was named Kent.'

'Norman Kent.'

His eyes were frozen on her face.

'How did you know?'

'He was an uncle of mine. I hardly remembered him at all as a person, of course – I was still in kindergarten when he died. But I heard about it later, what little anybody ever knew. He was killed doing something with you, wasn't he?'

'He gave his life,' said the Saint. 'For me, and a few others – or perhaps millions. He did one of the bravest things a man ever did for his friends, and maybe for the world too. But I never knew—'

'Why should you? He wouldn't be likely to talk about a brat like me.'

He was still staring at her half unbelievingly. And through his memory flooded the faces and the voices and the movements of the band of reckless young men that he had led back in those crusading days that were sometimes almost forgotten, the days that Major Vernon Ascony had uncomfortably reminded him of in Singapore to spark the train that had led halfway around the world to this moment. And most vividly of all he recalled a cottage in England, by the Thames, with the shadows of a peaceful summer evening lengthening over the garden, and the dark serious face of Norman Kent as he signed his own death-warrant and managed to hide from all of them what he had done.*

'Why didn't you tell me before?' he asked.

'Would it have made any difference? There were other things that seemed a bit more urgent. Anyway, I was hoping for a better occasion, when I could ask you to tell me the whole story.'

'And now there's no time,' he said bitterly. 'But I will tell you, you should be prouder than a princess to have Norman Kent for an uncle.'

'If I were the least bit superstitious,' she said, 'I'd have to believe there was some thread of Fate binding the Kent wagon to your star.'

His face had hardened into planes and grooves of bronze.

'It's a coincidence,' he said flatly. 'But I wish to hell you'd kept it to yourself.'

Hurt flicked her face like an invisible whip.

'I'm sorry,' she said. 'I didn't mean to make it worse.'

'I didn't mean that,' he said. 'But in any good corny story, this would be where I repaid a debt and gave you the life that Norman gave me. But I don't even see a chance of that. I think that's what's hardest to take.'

Her arm moved and pressed against his.

'If either of us gets the chance to do the ungodly any damage, right up to the last moment, we'll do it,' she said. 'And, please, I'd like to be kissed just once more by a man who wouldn't have to force me.'

He turned to her and their lips met, firmly and tenderly, yet without passion, in a kiss such as few men can have known.

But not for an instant had the Saint slipped out of his awareness altogether.

*See *The Saint Closes the Case.*

Almost unconsciously, between their speeches and their silences, he had heard the motor-boat throttle down as it reached the dock. Then, after a short pause, he had heard it start up again, and recede again for a certain distance, and stop again: he realised quickly that Netchideff must have jumped in and told Pavan to take him out at once to the seaplane, to make the repair with the part that Pavan had brought. Then for a long time there had been silence, which was broken at last by the sudden shocking roar of the seaplane's engine. The seaplane's engine boomed up in a smooth, vibrant, prolonged crescendo of power, and died no less smoothly down until a switch cut if off. Then, after a much shorter interval, the stutter of the motor-boat replaced it, plodding stolidly back towards the dock.

The repair had been made and tested: it worked, and the pilot was ready to go.

Pavan entered the cabin first, with Netchideff close behind him. Pavan looked sullen, but the pilot seemed to radiate elemental good spirits. He took the Saint's automatic from his hip pocket and released the safety.

'Go on, Julius,' he said. 'Separate the girl, and handcuff her again.'

'Damn it, you're a stubborn bastard, Igor,' grumbled Pavan. 'Why can't I make you see how much more complicated this is? You could have given me the stuff you brought while we were out at the plane. Instead of which, I'll have to go back again with you and—'

'Please,' Netchideff said, grinning – and perhaps only a nervous man would have thought that the gun he held was not too careful about where it pointed. 'Do what I ask.'

Pavan took a small key from his pocket and approached the bunk warily. He held one of Marian's wrists firmly in one hand, staying on the opposite side of her from the Saint, while he unlocked her handcuffs with the other. The instant the hand he was not holding was free, she jerked it around the corner pole and clawed at him like a wildcat; but he was ready for her with strength and leverage. He was extremely skilful, and in only a moment she was handcuffed again, this time behind her back. To escape the still undaunted menace of her wildly kicking feet he flung her bodily at Netchideff. The pilot caught her arm near the shoulder with his left hand alone, holding her at arm's length and chuckling as she sobbed impotently in his gorilla grasp.

'Now, please, the same for Templar,' Netchideff said.

'What's the matter with you?' Pavan argued. 'Why—'

'Please,' Netchideff said.

Pavan approached Simon even more warily, although with the same technique. But instead of pulling away the instant it was released, as Pavan was reasonably anticipating, the Saint's free hand shot forward. It grasped Pavan by the slack front of his plaid shirt and then recoiled again with incredible violence, jerking Pavan forward to hit the pole crunchingly with his face.

In another blurring whirlwind of movement it was Pavan whose arms were pinioned behind him; and Simon was holding him up like a shield.

'How about it, Igor?' Simon asked grittily. 'Shall we talk a trade?'

'I will show you,' Netchideff said genially.

The gun barked in his hand, and Pavan screamed once and then was only a dead weight in more than a mere figure of speech.

Simon let him fall, and waited for the next shot.

'You only shortened his life by a few seconds,' Netchideff said. 'I had decided to kill him in any case. Since he had already been noticed by the Canadian police, and was stupid enough to let both of you find this place, he could be no more use to us.'

'A nice way to reward an old comrade,' Simon remarked.

'He was not a comrade. It was only a business arrangement.'

Without a change of expression or any other warning, Netchideff jerked the girl towards him and hit her on the head with the butt of the gun in his clubbed fist. As her knees buckled, he kept hold of her and hoisted her over his left shoulder with a twist of his powerful left arm, exactly as he might have slung a heavy sack. And through all those movements the automatic made adaptations so that it did not lose its aim on the Saint for more than a decimal part of a second.

It was all done in a fragment of the time it takes to recite, and Simon still looked down the barrel of the gun and wondered what blind hope would keep him obedient until the irrevocable bullet crashed into his brain.

'Pick up your rod,' Netchideff ordered. 'Before I kill you, you will prove that you have lied.'

8

The Saint stood on the floating dock in the bright afternoon sun, the fly rod in his hand. Netchideff had dropped the girl from his shoulder into the bottom of the motor-boat, where she lay still mercifully unconscious, and had cast off the mooring lines. He had not started the motor, but the breeze was carrying the boat steadily away over a widening slick of water. The pilot stood up squarely in the boat with his legs spread like a foreshortened Colossus, the gun which he never forgot to control no matter what else he had to do still levelled at the Saint from his lumpy fist.

'Now, show me if you can cast that thing,' Netchideff said.

'Why should I?' Simon snarled.

Yet in a sort of nightmare automatism he was making the motions of stripping line from the reel, gathering it in loose even coils in his left hand.

'Are you afraid to look foolish?' Netchideff jeered. 'Or are you afraid I shall steal your secret?'

'You're damn right you can't make me this foolish,' said the Saint. 'You can go right ahead and shoot me, but you can't make me give you a lesson in fly casting.'

'It is, perhaps, an American secret weapon?'

'Yes,' Simon said, and the truth wakened in him like a light. 'It is. In a way you'll never understand.'

'Pah!' Netchideff spat. 'You are too stupid to know how stupid you are, like any democratic bourgeois. We are symbols, you and I. I with the gun which I have taken from you, which will kill you – you with nothing but your stupid toy, and your talk of what you call sport.'

The boat was drifting away with surprising speed. The Saint had to raise his voice to be sure that he would be heard.

'And we'll still lick you,' he said, 'because you don't know what that means.'

'You think I do not understand a sporting chance?'

How symptomatic, Simon thought, of the psychosis that is Communism to insist on pounding ideological dialectic even at that impossible moment. And yet his own compulsion forced him to fling defiance back. You went down with your colours flying, or some such traditional gesture.

'Who could interpret it for you?' he retorted. 'Karl Marx, or Groucho?'

'I will give you a sporting chance,' Netchideff shouted. 'Cast your feathers, catch a fish – at once – and I will not shoot you!'

The boat by then was about fifty-five feet away – little more than the minimum range for any class of pistol marksman. But the fly on the Saint's line travelled half that distance as he raised and lowered his rod and set the fly floating lazily back and forth.

'And your Uncle Joe Stalin's moustache,' said the Saint, with the most passionate sincerity he could put into it.

And his rod swept forward once more like a long graceful extension of his arm, and as the line reached forward ahead of it he released the reserve coils in his left hand and let them shoot out through the guides in pursuit of the sailing leader, and the whole line stretched out and straightened like a long living tongue until at the exact extremity of the cast the fly flicked Netchideff's face.

It did not hit the pilot squarely in the left eye, the improbably minuscule target that Simon Templar had extravagantly chosen to aim for. But less than an inch below it, in the soft skin under the lower lid, the little hook struck and pricked and then as Netchideff involuntarily flinched dug its barb deep and firm into the tender flesh.

Exquisite agony needled the pilot's face as the hook set, and lanced blindingly through his vision as the Saint put pressure on the rod. A reflex spasm contracted Netchideff's forefinger on the trigger of the automatic, but he had already lost sight of its mark in the sharp bright flash of pain, and even as the shot exploded another reflex was jerking both his hands up to clutch at the focal centre of his anguish.

There was a remorseless pulling in the pain, a thin pitiless traction that redoubled his torture at the least resistance and offered surcease only from yielding to the pull and leaning in its direction so as to reduce the agonising tension. He leaned into the pull until his feet had to follow his tottering balance and he stumbled against something with his shins and the boat rocked and he was suddenly weightless and then the water struck him and closed over him. Somewhere in that flurry he let go the gun.

But even when he came up again, choking and spluttering, the pain was still under his eye, drawing him steadily towards itself. His clawing hands touched a thread too frail to grasp, yet their own pressure on it only increased the agonising drag on the embedded hook. But the line would not break: the limberness of the rod was a spring that refused to allow a solid resistance against which the line could have been snapped. There was still no relief except in following that fragile but inexorable pull, half swimming and half floundering in the direction it dictated.

With a heart-stopping delicacy that no angler has probably been called upon to match before or since, the Saint played him like a fish, until he was close enough to the dock to be knocked cold with an oar.

9

In Johnny Kan's restaurant in San Francisco, Simon Templar said: 'You'll meet her. She should be here in a few minutes. But the Mounties still wanted her for a lot of dull routine work, digging out the roots of Pavan's distributing organisation as far as possible, and that kind of mopping-up bores me. Is everything ready? The *gai yung yee chee*—'

'Yes, we have your shark's fin soup. And *gum buoy ngun jon*, and the chicken with *wing nien* sauce. What about the Russian pilot?'

'I think they're still trying to decide what sort of protocol to apply to him. When the politicians and diplomats get into the act, I'd rather be included out. So we made a date to celebrate here as soon as she could get away.'

'That was nice of you.'

'Besides, I had to find out how much you really knew when you let out a hint about fishing that was what finally put me on the track – when I got the point.'

'You can hear a lot of things through the Chinese grapevine,' Johnny Kan said. 'For God's sake don't tell anyone, or I'll never be left alone. It was just a rumour that I hoped might do you some good. When I was a kid there were so many lousy stories written about opium dens run by sinister Orientals that it gives me a special kick to think I did something personally to help smash a dope racket.'

'Well, we dented it, anyhow,' Simon said. 'Although I don't suppose it'll be long before the ungodly are trying again.'

'If they ever gave up, what would you do for excitement? Go fishing?'

The Saint grinned, and lighted a cigarette.

'I've been wondering if I could claim some sort of record. He must have been damn nearly the biggest thing ever landed with a fly rod. He was about seventy inches long and would have weighed easily two hundred and twenty pounds. I was using HCH line with a four-pound-test leader; and by the happiest coincidence I hooked him with a fly called a Red Ant.'

Watch for the sign of the Saint!

If you have enjoyed this Saintly adventure, look out for the other Simon Templar novels by Leslie Charteris – all available in print and ebook from Mulholland Books